Excess All Areas

By

Mandy Baggot

Published in 2008 by YouWriteOn.com

First Edition

Published by YouWriteOn.com

To my two beautiful daughters Amber and Ruby –
because I want to make you proud!

Chapter One

'Auburn Blush' it had said on the packet. A multi-tonal hair colour to compliment light brown to medium brown hair. Freya looked at her reflection in the mirror of the ladies' lavatories. 'Auburn Blush' looked more like 'Red Revenge', her head was practically glowing. She didn't care, it didn't really matter, the important thing was it was different. And different was almost cleansing.

She washed the dye off her hands, all the time still gazing into the mirror at what stared back at her. Cilla Black hair circa 'Blind Date' 1990s. She put her glasses back on, added a touch of powder to her nose, a sheen of clear lip gloss to her mouth and she felt instantly better. Well, perhaps not completely better, but improved.

"Passengers for the 16.40 Monarch Airlines flight MON634 to Corfu please make your way to Gate 17 where boarding has commenced"

MON634 was Freya's flight. The tickets were still warm in her hands as they had only been printed a little over an hour ago. There had been no time for thinking logically, she was here and she had to get away. She picked up her handbag and turned to the door. Before she pushed it open she caught sight of her reflection, this time in a full length mirror. Her jeans were too tight, her top could have done with being longer to cover her stomach, her chest was definitely in need of greater support and now she had bright red hair. She was seeing what Russell had seen. What Russell had obviously seen for at least the last six months but neglected to mention it. Or perhaps he had mentioned it. Freya took a deep breath and tried to suck in her stomach. She held her breath and turned to the side, smoothing the bumps down. Perhaps she should invest in a corset.

The door to the ladies was pushed open and Freya let out her breath and coughed, hurriedly pretending to fix her hair. A super slim, super tanned blonde haired twenty-something entered the toilets. Life always had a way of bringing you right back down to Earth. She was never going to be a size 10. Who was she trying to kid? She was never going to be a size 16.

She made her way out of the toilets and headed towards Gate 17. People around her were racing towards the boarding gates, hurrying along the moving walkways, excitedly, frantically. Freya in comparison followed the directions calmly, outwardly appearing almost serene. However on the inside she was far from serene, she was still angry and hurt. And what was worse was she was angry at herself more than anyone else. She had just wasted a year and a half with someone who thought nothing of her.

Gate 17 was indeed boarding and Freya handed over her passport and boarding card to yet another super slim blonde haired twenty something on the desk.

"Thank you Miss Johnson, Seat 3a is at the front of the plane, by the window" the woman told her with a whiter than white smile.

Freya nodded, took back her passport and headed down the tunnel towards the plane. She reached into her handbag as she walked and took out her mobile phone. There were 35 missed calls. As soon as she had left the restaurant she had switched it to 'silent'. She knew he would call her, well it was only natural you would call someone if you were supposed to be meeting them for lunch and you thought they hadn't turned up.

But Freya had turned up, she had even been early. She had then decided to go to the ladies before indicating her arrival to the maitre d'. She had wanted to look her best on her birthday, her 30th birthday. She hadn't wanted a party or anything extravagant, as was her way, but she had wanted to mark the occasion. She had decided on a nice lunch with her boyfriend at her favourite restaurant.

Thinking back, if she had just taken ten seconds longer putting on her lipstick or if she hadn't washed her hands or if she had just skipped going to the loo and sat down at the table, she wouldn't be getting on a plane right now.

She had come out of the ladies and seen that Russell was stood at the bar. The idea had been to surprise him, creep up on him, put her hands over his eyes and make him laugh. So she had crept quietly up towards him and it was as she crept that she listened and heard him say:-

"I wonder if you have seen my girlfriend, I'm supposed to be meeting her here. She's a large girl, you know, with brown hair and glasses, sort of ordinary looking, probably wearing jeans"

When he had said 'large girl, you know' he had used hand gestures to indicate the largeness. Freya had been rooted to the spot for a split second until a voice inside her had said 'run' and she had moved quickly towards the door and out of the restaurant before Russell had even had a chance to notice her.

It had been like having her eyes opened. It had only been thirty seconds or less but it had been enough time for her mind to conjure up all the memories and images of her relationship with Russell as she watched him gesticulating over her size with a barman. A barman called Milo.

Over the past six months Freya had begun to feel the first stirrings of 'The Stutter'. 'The Stutter' was something that was quite familiar to her. It was a feeling, a little voice in her head that nudged her into the realisation that perhaps a relationship had run its course. 'The Stutter' had put paid to every relationship she had had, except one. But this time it had taken longer to happen than usual. Russell had started working longer, later hours, they had barely gone out together, apart from a couple of disastrous evenings at the All You Can Eat Chinese restaurant where they had spent all night sparring with each other. And as for sex, well when Russell had been at home he was preoccupied with the fillies on The Racing Channel instead of giving the maiden he had at home any attention. It was the classic first signs of 'The Stutter', or so Freya had thought, until six weeks ago when there had been a sudden change. Russell had come home from work one evening and looked at her like he had when they had first got together. He had had a large bouquet of flowers in one hand and a bag full of food from the 'Indian Palace' in the other. He had stood in the doorway of Freya's flat, seemingly admiring her, a smile stretched right across his face. That evening, before Freya had even learnt that he had purchased all her favourite dishes from the takeaway, they had made love just like the first time. All thoughts of 'The Stutter' had all but evaporated and she had spent the next month living in a dream, feeling happy and content and almost loved. Almost loved. It sounded a stupid thing to feel but it was as close as she had ever been able to get and closer than she had been with most of the people whose relationships 'The Stutter' had put paid to.

But although Russell was doing and saying all the right things, something just wasn't right. Freya couldn't put her finger on it, perhaps she didn't really want to, afraid to burst the bubble, but the feeling was unsettling. Which was why, when she had stood in the restaurant and listened to Russell describing her to the barman called Milo, along with the immediate pain and shame, Freya had also felt some sense of relief. Now she had a reason to run, she had been right to feel cautious over his change in behaviour, which for what ever reason had been an act.

8

The relationship wasn't just stuttering, this was a permanent, end of the line termination, everybody disembark, or in Freya's case, board the next available plane.

Freya sat down in her seat on the plane and let out a breath. This now felt like the right thing to do. It had seemed somewhat mad when she had hailed a taxi to the airport, bought a ticket to Corfu and then bought a hair dye, in that order. But now she felt more relaxed about it all.

A large girl, yes she was a large girl, there was no point in denying it. But she had been a large girl when Russell had wooed her. He had told her she was beautiful and pestered her for a date until she had no choice but to give in. And, as time went on, she had thought that he had loved her. She thought he might have been the man that she told everything to. As she sat on the plane, on her birthday, her partner having been revealed as a prize shit, the sense of relief was rapidly turning into hurt and disappointment. She hadn't cried yet but she knew the tears would come, probably as soon as she saw Emma.

Freya turned off her mobile phone. She would call Emma from Corfu. The last thing she needed was someone to try and rationalise things right now. She had never been the rational type which was probably why she carried her passport around in her handbag.

Freya fastened her seatbelt and shut her eyes. Suddenly she felt very tired, tired of everything. If she could just get a few hours sleep while the plane completed its three and a half hour flight it would be a start.

She was however woken abruptly, shortly after the plane had finished making its assent and had settled at its cruising altitude. Her head was being thumped against the back of her seat. At first, on waking from her snooze she considered it might be turbulence, however it soon became rhythmic – boom, boom, boom over and over again. Someone was kicking her seat.

Freya had never been good humoured on waking, but today had not been the best day and she felt particularly intolerant. She took off her seatbelt and knelt up to peer over the headrest at whoever was occupying the seat directly behind her. An angelic looking girl of about 6 years old, with plaits, was kicking the back of Freya's seat as hard as she could manage with pink patent shoes on.

"Could you stop doing that please?" Freya said firmly, glaring at the girl.

The little girl gave Freya a well practiced 'butter wouldn't melt' smile and then landed another kick onto the seat, even more forceful than before.

"I said could you stop that please?" Freya barked. This was no time for beating around the bush when she needed sleep.

"You're not my mum Fatty!" the girl replied and she stuck her tongue out at Freya and kicked the seat again.

"Where is your mother you little brat?" Freya questioned as the rhythmic thumping started up all over again.

The seat next to the girl was empty and the middle aged man in the aisle seat of that row was pretending as hard as he could to be asleep.

"If you don't stop kicking right now I am going to tell the air stewardess" Freya said seriously and she gave the girl another glare.

"And what's she going to do about it?" the girl replied, leaning forward in her seat and glaring back at Freya.

"She is going to tell you off"

"Big deal. Why is your hair so red? It looks really stupid" the child answered back.

"Look you little beast, I have had a horrible day and I just want to get some sleep so would you please stop kicking my seat"

Threats hadn't worked, perhaps begging would or perhaps bribery was better, offer her a few Euros. Except she didn't have any Euros. Where was this kid's mother?

"No! I'm bored and this is fun" the child spoke and she started kicking harder and faster.

Freya could feel what little patience she had crumbling. This was all she needed. She snapped.

"For God's sake, who does this child belong to? Apart from Satan! Come on, own up! Who is the mother or father of this child? If she is flying alone I swear I will remove her!"

Freya hardly recognised the sound of her own voice as the words flew out. She sounded almost unhinged. She was yelling at a flight full of people, all because a bored child was kicking her seat. Hadn't she been a bored child once? Yes she had but she had not even been allowed to remove her seatbelt let alone achieve enough leg swing to wallop the seat in front. Now she felt hot, she was perspiring. She felt out of control and sick, she needed to sit down. Everyone was staring at her. People had put down their crosswords to look at her, one woman across the aisle had dropped two stitches in the scarf she was knitting. She needed to calm down but what she wanted to do most of all was cry.

11

"Are you alright?" the woman with the knitting asked Freya who was now bent over, her head in her hands. Freya didn't reply, she was trying hard not to throw up. She had known that eating a family sized bar of Dairy Milk in the departure lounge was wrong and now she was paying for it.

Boom boom boom – the girl's kicking was incessant. What was she doing on a plane to Corfu with no Euros, no luggage and no guarantee that Emma would have somewhere for her to stay? Was she crazy?

And then it stopped. Her seat was no longer being kicked out of its fixings and the banging in her head had lessened. Had the Devil Child found something else to entertain her Freya wondered. Tying people's shoelaces together? Activating the emergency lifejackets? Creating an elaborate bomb using nothing but the survival leaflet, a can of cola and some Kirby grips? Freya dared to turn her head and peek through the gap between the seats. The girl's mother had returned and the girl was still looking angelic but this time she was asleep, her head on her mother's lap.

"Is everything OK madam? Can I get you a drink?"

Freya had not noticed the air hostess arrive, but she did now and she also noticed she was pushing the drinks trolley which contained a large selection of alcoholic beverages. All of them looked appealing at the present time, even the sherry.

"Can I have a brandy and coke please? A large one" Freya asked her, trying to compose herself.

"Of course Madam, with ice?" came the reply.

"Please" Freya answered.

"That will be £5.60 please" the air hostess informed her as she placed the drink and a napkin on Freya's stowaway tray.

Oh my God, money! Did she have any cash? She had bought the plane ticket with her VISA card and now she didn't know whether she had enough cash on her to pay for a drink. A drink she badly needed.

She picked up her handbag from the floor of the plane and began searching through it to try and find her purse. On opening her purse she discovered she had precisely £2.26, a supermarket trolley token and a French franc.

"Um do you take credit card?" Freya inquired with a hopeful look at the stewardess who also happened to be a super slim blonde twenty something.

"We do take VISA madam, but only for purchases of more than £10. We take Euros however, if you want to use your holiday money" the hostess replied with a helpful smile.

'If only I had some' thought Freya. There was only one solution.

"I'd better have two then. When do we land?" Freya asked as she handed over her credit card.

"Just over an hour now, not too long. There you go, if you would just enter your PIN number......thank you" she spoke, completing the transaction.

Freya took a large mouthful of one of her drinks and tried to relax herself. It wasn't long now until she would be in Corfu.

"I see the little terror behind you is asleep now so I'd make the most of the peace and quiet. Lets hope she isn't staying at your hotel" the stewardess spoke in a hushed voice as she moved her trolley past Freya and along the aisle.

Freya nodded and smiled. That would be too cruel to imagine and Fate could not be that cruel on your birthday.

It was an hour and five minutes before the plane touched down. It was 10.30pm local time and dark. Freya was glad to arrive. She had never been a lover of flying and three and a half hours was about her limit. She had done a long haul trip to Canada once to photograph the Rockies for a client, these days she stuck to scenery nearer to home.

As she stepped out of the plane and on to the steps Freya took a deep breath of the night air and filled her lungs with it. It was warm, it was sweet and it filled her whole head up with its comforting scent. There was absolutely nothing on Earth as wonderful as Corfiot air and it made Freya feel welcome every time she visited.

"Excuse me, we're in a bit of a hurry"

One of her fellow passengers nudged Freya's shoulder and she was brought back to the reality of having just landed with Britain's fraught and impatient holidaymakers desperate to start queuing for their suitcases. There was nothing like a bit of argy bargy for your bags to really get you into the holiday spirit.

And thinking of spirit, the brandies in Freya's stomach were swimming around nicely with the chocolate but her insides were suggesting from the groans and rumblings that she should think about getting them some company pretty soon.

After a short bus ride, which Freya never thought was really necessary, she arrived at the terminal and she was at last stood in Corfu International Airport waiting to have her passport scrutinised. While she was stood in line she scrutinised the photograph herself. She had been just twenty when it was taken, ten years ago. Her hair was long and brown and she wore huge spectacles which made her look like a cross between an owl and a headmistress. She was almost unrecognisable now, apart from the weight. The weight hadn't changed in ten years.

The queue for passport checking was unmoving and Freya decided that now was as good a time as any to call Emma. She just hoped that she answered, as she hadn't considered what she would do if she didn't answer.

Freya turned on her mobile. There were now 54 missed calls and a low battery. She scanned down the phone to Emma's mobile number in the phone book and pressed 'call'. Nothing happened. Freya checked the screen which revealed she had no network coverage. This could not be happening! She knew she was able to make international calls, she had always been able to make international calls, from anywhere to anywhere, so why wasn't it working? What was she going to do? She had no money to make a call from the public phone. She was stuck in Corfu Airport with no means to get out.

Just as she was about to go into full blown panic mode the words 'Vodafone Greece' appeared on her phone's display, together with a full signal. Freya took a long slow breath and mentally thanked the Greek Gods, or at least those representing communication.

The phone rang several times in that infuriating continental way until at last..........

"Freya!! Happy Birthday!"

Emma's voice answered and Freya smiled, feeling comforted by the sound of her friend's voice.

15

"Thanks and thanks for the card and the earrings, they are lovely, very me" Freya responded.

The queue in front of her began to move at last.

"So what are you up to? Russell taken you out somewhere nice?" Emma inquired.

"Not exactly" Freya answered moving towards the booth ahead of her.

"What time is it there? I still get confused, what with clocks there going forward and back" Emma continued.

"It's ten to eleven" Freya replied and she braced herself for her friend's reply.

"No it can't be, that's what time it is here silly" Emma spoke.

It was at that moment that the airport announcer decided to tell the terminal, in Greek and English, that the flight going to Stansted was about to leave from Gate 3.

"Freya you're at Corfu Airport aren't you?" Emma stated matter of factly.

"Oh Em, act a little surprised please!" Freya begged.

"Nothing surprises me with you, I can't remember the last time you made a planned visit, I'm getting used to it" Emma admitted.

"I'm sorry, I didn't know where else to go. I'm stupid aren't I? I shouldn't keep doing this when I hit a low, running away from everything, I should have called...." Freya began.

The tears were welling up in her eyes already and she was now fourth in the queue. She was feeling weak and that in itself made her angry, how dare Russell make her feel like this.

"Don't be silly Freya its fine, get a taxi here. Infact don't get a taxi, go to arrivals, find the 'Sun n Sea' rep, should be the only one dressed entirely in mint green, it will be Madeline or Tracey. Tell them you're my friend and hitch a ride to Kassiopi" Emma ordered.

"Are you sure there will be room on their coach? I don't want to be a pain" Freya spoke.

"Trust me they will have room. So just get off the coach at The C Bar, I'll meet you there and we'll have a big drink and a chat OK?" Emma told her.

Freya felt a surge of relief that Emma had taken control of the situation. She needed someone to lean on right now and she had been right to count on Emma, as always.

"Ok, thanks, look I've got to go, I'm next in the passport queue and I'm running out of battery, I'll see you......"

At that moment the battery died and Freya was called forward to have her passport checked. She did the best she could to look like a school teacher and an owl and was let through into the arrivals hall.

Once there it wasn't difficult to find the 'Sun n Sea' representative. Tracey was head to toe in mint green, including her shoes, which Freya decided was very scary indeed. She hadn't remembered Emma ever having to wear green and could only assume it was a recent change made by the company. Whoever sanctioned that needed serious style coaching.

Tracey pointed Freya in the direction of the 'Sun n Sea' coach no.51 and she was soon sat amongst the holidaymakers waiting for the vehicle to depart.

It was the sixth time she had been to Corfu. She had first visited the island with Emma when they were both 20. It had been a package trip, the cheapest one they could find which was very significant at the time. It had been so much fun and had given Emma the taste for travel. She embarked on a career as a travel representative with 'Sun n Sea' and on her third posting was sent to Kassiopi, a pretty village with a beautiful harbour in Northern Corfu. Emma had fallen in love with Kassiopi and, having also fallen in love with local boy Yiannis Petroholis, she had never wanted to leave. She now worked for a small travel company in Kassiopi booking trips for holidaymakers by coach and boat around the island. She also guided some of the trips herself.

Freya could understand her friend's love for Corfu and for the village of Kassiopi itself, as it was simply beautiful. Although tourism had given the place numerous restaurants, bars and even a nightclub or two, somehow it still managed to retain its traditional charm.

Her thoughts were interrupted by Tracey boarding the coach and picking up the microphone, which did, as all microphones do, and let out a loud screech of feedback which had everyone reaching for their ears.

"Good evening everyone, or should that be 'kalispera'. On behalf of 'Sun n Sea Holidays' I would like to welcome you all to Corfu. My name is Tracey and your driver today is Spiros. Now before we get underway could I ask you not to eat or drink on the coach and, as the roads around Corfu are very winding in places, please use the seatbelts provided. Now as we go along I will be telling you a little bit about Corfu and passing out some leaflets, but, before I start, I expect you will have heard by now that we have a famous Hollywood actor staying in Corfu at the moment. Yes Nicholas Kaden is filming on the island and staying in Kassiopi, so for those of you heading to that resort you are in for more of a visual treat than you might have expected. I hear from a reliable source that he has been spotted at several of the restaurants and bars, so perhaps you will be lucky enough to get some photos or an autograph"

Tracey had the most monotone of voices Freya had ever heard which would have been dreadful had she needed to listen to the information, but as it was it was pretty much perfect to fall asleep to. Freya rested her head against the window and shut her eyes.

It was Tracey's monotone voice that woke her up some time later, but on this occasion it was unaided by a microphone and Freya felt her shoulder being gently shaken.

"Freya, we're about five minutes away from the harbour. I thought I'd better wake you" Tracey spoke.

"Oh thanks, thank you. God I've slept through the whole journey? That's usually my favourite part, you know going through Sidari and Roda and entering the Municipality of Kassiopi" Freya answered, sitting herself up and rubbing her eyes.

"You looked like you could use the sleep. Is Emma meeting you?" Tracey queried.

"Yes at The C Bar" Freya responded.

"Oo well don't be surprised if you bump into Nicholas Kaden, I hear that is one of his favourite haunts for a late night drink" Tracey informed her.

"Oh right, well perhaps he will buy us one" Freya answered and she picked her bag up from the floor of the coach.

The coach stopped right outside The C Bar, as 'Sun n Sea's' Arcadia Apartments were just a few yards up a steep incline to the left of the building.

Freya followed two couples off of the coach and then she saw Emma waiting for her, looking amazing as ever.

"Freya! Oh my God, your hair!" Emma exclaimed and she threw her arms around her friend and hugged her tightly.

If felt nice to have a cuddle after a rotten day and there was not a person in this world that Freya felt more for than Emma. She was the only constant in her life.

"Never mind me! Let me look at you! You look fantastic" Freya said, holding her friend's hands and taking in everything about her appearance.

In complete contrast to Freya, Emma was a tall, super slim, blonde twenty something. She was the type of woman that turned men's heads, although the majority of the time she was completely oblivious to it. She was the sweetest, most generous person Freya had ever known and she felt lucky to have her as a friend and unfailing confidante.

"Yiannis says I've lost weight and need feeding up, although Mr P is doing his best with those meatballs of his" Emma replied, talking of Mr Petroholis Senior.

"I don't expect he will say I need feeding up but the meatballs will go down well nevertheless" Freya told her.

"Right, well, let's get your bags and we can have a drink" Emma spoke and she headed towards the boot of the coach where Spiros was getting cases out.

"I don't have any bags" Freya called out to her.

Emma stopped in her tracks and turned back to face her friend.

"No bags this time! Freya, you are getting worse! What did you bring?" Emma queried.

"Just myself, to be honest there wasn't anything else worth bringing" she answered.

"I think we have a lot to talk about, particularly that hair colour, I'll just thank Tracey for getting you here in one piece" Emma said and she went over to the woman in mint green.

Freya took a deep breath and couldn't quite believe she was back in Kassiopi. She looked around, taking in her surroundings. The harbour, the boats bobbing about, the street lamps giving everything a warm glow, the bars with people sat down outside enjoying the warm night air. A shiver ran up her spine, it felt wonderful to be here standing in a place she adored. She didn't regret getting on the plane now. This moment now, when she could feel the Corfiot air on her skin, smell that fantastic sweet aroma in the breeze and see the vast expanse of sea in front of her were the best minutes of her birthday so far. She only wished she had her cameras to capture it. She did have one small Nikon in her handbag but it really deserved something better.

"Come on you, let's get some drinks and have a chat. Fancy 'Sex on the Beach'?" Emma asked as she linked arms with Freya.

"A cocktail first I think" Freya answered with a smile.

Emma laughed and led the way to the bar.

Before long, the two women were sat at a table outside The C Bar, under a cream parasol, with two large drinks in front of them. The C Bar was located on one side of the picturesque harbour and from the seats outside there was a wonderful view of both the water and the crumbled ruins of the fort which overlooked the bay.

"I hope I didn't mess up any plans you had for tonight" Freya said, sucking on her straw and enjoying her first taste of Greek alcohol.

"Its quarter to one now, the only plan I had was going to sleep. I've got a shopping trip to Corfu Town tomorrow which leaves at 8.00am and it's nearly fully booked" Emma informed her.

"Sorry, I always was good at timing wasn't I?" Freya replied and called to mind one of her unplanned visits when she had burst into Emma's apartment yelling 'surprise' only to be confronted with the sight of Yiannis and Emma minus their clothes.

"Don't be silly, it's your birthday for God's sake and something must have happened for Russell not to be with you" Emma said.

"Mmm so tell me what you've been doing since we last spoke, all the details, leave nothing out" Freya ordered, trying to avoid Emma's question.

"Freya you can't travel all this way and not tell me what happened. Come on, tell me, you can tell me anything remember, and you know I won't stop asking until I know, so better to get it out of the way now" Emma continued.

"It was stupid, thinking back on it, I probably overreacted" Freya began.

"Go on" Emma urged.

Freya recounted the tale of what Russell had said about her at the restaurant. However she didn't stop there. The floodgates opened and Freya told Emma all the details of the past six months of their relationship. Details that somehow hadn't seemed important enough to mention in any of their phone conversations.

"Well you know, I've been put down by everyone for most of my life and in that restaurant, when I heard him describe me like that, I just knew I couldn't and shouldn't take anymore" Freya finished, having regaled her friend with the tales of the nights at the All You Can Eat Chinese, Russell's preoccupation with racehorses and their sporadic sex life.

"Oh Freya" Emma spoke, reaching out to pat her friend's arm consolingly.

"But before today, I thought things had turned a corner, which is why I haven't told you any of this before. Just lately he was back to being the Russell I fell for, all romance and impromptu acts, I thought things were going to work out, I....." Freya started, her voice tailing off as she felt a surge of upset in her chest.

It was now that the tears really came. Freya could do nothing but let the emotion go and big fat tears came rolling down her cheeks. She sobbed, bent over in her chair, her face on her knees.

Emma hurried to the chair next to Freya and enveloped her friend in a hug, holding her tightly as she cried.

"It's OK, you cry and let it all out. You're here now, in beautiful Kassiopi, with me and a large cocktail, what could be better than that?" Emma asked her.

"Two large cocktails?" Freya replied feeling able to lift her head up from her lap. She took off her glasses and wiped at her eyes with her fingers.

"I'm pathetic aren't I? God I'm 30 years old I ought to be able to cope with a few insults. I should have stayed and faced him and told him what an arse he was. I just didn't know what to do and I panicked" Freya spoke, picking up her handbag and looking inside for a tissue.

"You shouldn't have to hear what he said from anyone, let alone your own boyfriend. And that, on top of all the other stuff you've just told me about, I think you did exactly the right thing. It sounds like he's turned into a complete pig and I'm surprised you put up with that for so long" Emma responded and she passed Freya a serviette from the holder on the table.

"I know the answer to that one" Freya spoke, blowing her nose.

You didn't put up with snide remarks and knock backs because it was fun, you put up with them for one reason and one reason only.

"Because who else is going to look twice at me?" Freya answered plainly.

"Freya, now you are being silly" Emma exclaimed.

"I'm not, come on Em, look at me! I'm a size 20, there I've said it, no point denying it to myself anymore. A size 20 with double d boobs and thighs any rugby player would kill for. My waist is non-existent, it seems to blend into my bust more every day and I have bingo wings, which might be mildly amusing if I actually played bingo" Freya said and she snatched up her drink and sucked furiously on its straw.

"Freya..." Emma began, trying to protest against her friend's words.

"I'm surprised Russell stayed with me as long as he did. My God he must have been so ashamed. People probably thought someone like me was all he could get, how embarrassing" Freya continued.

"Freya please stop this" Emma begged her.

"The reason hearing what he said upset me so much was a) because I could see the venison steak I had envisaged eating disappearing from the agenda and b) because what he said was true. I am large, I am ordinary. In fact why am I angry with him for telling me how it is? I should have just shrugged it off and ordered a salad" Freya carried on as she thought back.

"Freya! Stop it! If he can't see you are beautiful then he isn't worth a second thought, let alone tears in your cocktail! You have the most amazing eyes, you have a fantastic smile and more importantly a brilliant sense of humour. And if we are being really honest with each other here, I always wished I had half the confidence you have because you always know what to say in every situation, I'm just not like that" Emma said to her friend.

"Now I know why you're my best friend and that was exactly the right thing to say in this situation. Oh I don't know, I just never seem to be able to get it right, or should that be I never seem to be able to get Mr Right. Before today, before finding out how Russell really sees me do you know what I did? I looked at one of those 'Weight Watchers' adverts in the newspaper, I picked up the phone and I almost dialled the number" Freya spoke.

25

"Freya, you hate diets and not only that, you are the absolute worse dieter I know" Emma remarked.

"And doesn't it show?" Freya commented.

"I didn't mean that like it sounded" Emma added hastily.

"No, it's OK, you're right. I am a great eater and lousy on nutrition. I still can't walk past a bakery without sampling a sausage roll just to see if is tastes as good as it should, in fact often they call to me" Freya told Emma.

"So why even think of 'Weight Watchers'?" Emma queried.

"Because perhaps trying to find someone who takes me as I am isn't going to work, maybe I need to change things, perhaps I need to face up to who and what I really am and take control of that" Freya suggested.

"Absolutely not! There is nothing that needs to be changed apart from your attached status and the offloading of that creep! Freya, after all you have been through I am not going to let someone as superficial as Russell make you feel bad about yourself. And while we are on this subject, why haven't you mentioned any of this in our phone conversations?" Emma demanded to know.

"I told you, it didn't seem important, and there always seemed to be other stuff going on and, like I said, over the past month or so he has been so attentive it made me reconsider whether the relationship had really got 'The Stutter'" Freya spoke.

"Do you think there was someone else?" Emma asked bluntly.

"Female or equine?" Freya inquired.

"He isn't still betting is he? I thought you said he had stopped that"

"Do gamblers ever stop betting? I think it is a permanent disorder rather than a learned habit and all I know is he would rather sit and watch Frankie Dettori pushing out an outsider at Newmarket than spend time with me, up until very recently. Unless you are right and it was just me, perhaps a different, thinner female was distracting him" Freya spoke, pondering on the thought.

"I don't really think we need to waste another minute talking or thinking about Russell. In fact I forbid the mention of his name for the rest of the night, or should that be morning? Now are you going to order us both another drink? I'll just have an orange juice because I've got that early start" Emma said passing Freya her glass.

"Making me drink alone? I'm not sure I can allow that" Freya said, standing up and preparing to go to the bar.

"Hang on! Hang on, wait, look look" Emma exclaimed as she became animated in her seat.

"What? What exactly am I looking at?" Freya questioned as she looked across the harbour to where Emma was pointing.

"Nicholas Kaden! There! With Bob Crosby and Gene Bates, just leaving the nightclub, you can't tell me you can't see them, there are about fifty people taking photographs" Emma said leaning over as far as she could to get a better look.

"Hmm cool, I'll go and get the drinks" Freya said and went towards the bar.

"Freya! You don't have to go to the bar, they will bring the drinks over if you call them. Oh how many times has she been here?" Emma said as Freya disappeared from view.

After the women's second drink they began walking away from the harbour towards the village square. Having had nothing to eat Freya was feeling woozy and also desperate for sleep.

"Look Em, I am sorry about turning up unannounced, I should have called from London. I mean will 'The Calypso' have a room free?" Freya asked, hoping they did as she needed a bed now more than ever before.

"Yes they have, well they did at half past eleven tonight, that's where I was when you called me, I've got myself another little job doing the weekly quiz" Emma admitted with a snort of laughter.

"But you hate quizzes" Freya reminded her.

"Taking part in them yes, setting them is a bit of fun and Yiannis helps me out with the round about all things local" Emma told her.

"I don't believe you're a quiz master, you even hated 'Blockbusters'" Freya remarked with a shake of her head.

"Don't take the Mickey or I will make you set the questions next week, if you're going to be here next week that is. How long did you plan to stay?" Emma asked as they reached the entrance to 'The Calypso Apartments'.

"I don't know, I haven't really thought too far ahead, I have no money or clothes remember" Freya stated.

"Then I have a great idea, why don't you join me on the Corfu Town shopping trip in the morning. We can have a look at the clothes, get you some hot new outfits and have a nice lunch, a proper girlie outing" Emma suggested as they headed for reception.

"I don't think so" Freya replied.

"Why not?" Emma questioned, disappointment in her voice.

"Because I'm sure you said it left at 8.00 in the morning"

"It does but come on, it's 2.30am now, four and a half hours sleep and a quick shower you will feel like a new woman" Emma cajoled.

"I will feel like a wreck, probably worse than I feel now, but I haven't the energy to argue with you so where do we meet?" Freya asked with a tired smile.

"At the square" Emma answered excitedly.

Ten minutes later, after Emma had booked Freya in with the manager, Stephanos, and obtained a key, Freya was standing in her apartment.

It was a standard apartment with no plush fixtures and fittings but it had all the essentials. There was a small kitchen area with a hob, kettle, toaster and sink, a bathroom with toilet, basin and shower but most importantly there was a large double bed taking up the majority of the room which had been made up with crisp white sheets. Nothing had looked so appealing to Freya before.

Her eyes were heavy and sore and she had been constantly yawning for the last hour. She wanted a cup of tea and she could see that there were some complimentary tea bags by the kettle, together with some small pots of milk. But boiling a kettle seemed such hard work. She didn't have the energy.

She took off her shoes and lay down on the bed to reflect on the day. How much had changed in a few hours. She should have been lying in bed with Russell thinking about the great birthday she had just had. Instead she was lying alone in an apartment in Corfu, Greece, having been insulted by her boyfriend, bullied by a psychotic kid on the plane and, perhaps worst of all, had ended up with hair the colour of a tube of Pringles Original. It had been some 30th birthday. Sleep came quickly, she was completely exhausted.

Chapter Two

Freya's stomach contracted for the umpteenth time since she had woken. At 6.00am the people in the room above had decided to have sex. And not ordinary, run of the mill, 'five minutes and its all over' sex, loud noisy Discovery Channel sex which went on and on and on. Freya was left with no choice but to get out of bed, make a complimentary cup of tea and sit out on her balcony.

Her balcony, she discovered, had a fantastic view of the mountains and Freya took the opportunity to take some photographs with the early morning mist that was enveloping the peaks.

Now it was a quarter past seven and she was making her way to the bakery in search of some fresh, warm rolls, two for her and two for the fish in the harbour. She always fed the fish when she visited and they leapt out of the water sometimes in a bid to be the first to swallow the food. It was a relaxing way to pass half an hour or so and the fish made good subjects if you happened to have the right photography equipment with you, which she didn't.

Freya entered the bakery and breathed in the delicious yeasty smell that hit her. It made her stomach contract all the more vigorously. She was aware of someone entering behind her so she held the door open for them and a middle aged woman in a tweed suit came into the shop after her. Freya thought the tweed suit was a little inappropriate for the climate, seeing as the sun was already up and making its presence felt.

"*Kalimera*, could I have 4 large white rolls please?" Freya ordered from the elderly Greek woman behind the counter.

Freya was very nearly licking her lips in anticipation of eating the rolls, perhaps she would have three, seeing as she was so hungry. Freya watched as the woman bagged up the rolls and tried to stop herself from drooling.

"75 cents" the woman asked.

Freya handed over a ten Euro note she had borrowed from Emma the night before and muttered an apology about having nothing smaller.

The woman handed her her change and the bag of rolls and Freya left the shop hardly able to wait to sink her teeth into one. She did decide to wait however, until she was sat at the harbour looking out towards Albania.

"Excuse me" a voice called from behind her.

The American accent surprised Freya, as did the volume of the address. Freya stopped walking and turned around to see the woman in the tweed suit from the bakery, hurrying down the road to catch up with her.

"I'm sorry, you seem to have the only remaining white rolls from the first batch this morning" the woman spoke and dazzled Freya with her whiter than white smile.

"Oh do I? That's bad luck for you, I can highly recommend them" Freya replied.

"No no, you misunderstand me, I want those rolls" the woman stated plainly and she pointed at the paper bag Freya was holding.

Freya looked at the woman in her stern suit with her perfectly coiffured hair and beautifully manicured nails. No one had looked more out of place in the increasing heat of a Kassiopi morning than her. She actually reminded Freya of her mother. Was she having a hallucination brought on by lack of sleep? She couldn't help herself, she burst out laughing, putting a hand to her mouth and clutching the bag of rolls to her chest.

"I'm sorry for laughing but did you say you wanted my bread rolls? There's a whole shop full of bread back there" Freya managed to say through her laughter.

"I am well aware of that but they are not white and they are not as fresh. Do you know that those rolls come out of the oven at exactly three minutes past seven?" the woman continued.

"I don't care when they came out of the oven, they're mine and I'm going to enjoy them" Freya spoke with a smile and turned to leave.

Suddenly her arm was being pulled back and she could feel the manicured nails digging into her skin.

"I don't think I've made myself clear, I want those rolls, I need those rolls and I am willing to pay for them" the woman hissed.

"Get off me! You're insane! This is my breakfast, I haven't eaten in 24 hours and it isn't helping my humour" Freya spoke loudly.

"I'll give you 10 Euros for them" the woman continued and she took a wallet out of the leather bag she was carrying over one arm and proceeded to produce a note and hold it out towards Freya.

"The rolls are not for sale" Freya replied firmly.

"20 Euros and that's my final offer" the woman said as she produced another note.

"Now I am intrigued. What makes you want my rolls so much? Are they hollowed out? All crust and no filling with a stash of jewels inside? Or is it cocaine? Have I stumbled upon a drugs ring? Are you some kind of Mrs Big?" Freya questioned as she looked the woman up and down.

"Not in the way you mean honey. Listen, 30 Euros and that really is my limit" the woman told her.

"This is madness, you could offer me 100 Euros and I still wouldn't be interested" Freya exclaimed loudly.

"200" the woman responded.

"Goodbye" Freya answered and she turned away from the woman and began walking towards the harbour once again.

"Give me the rolls!" the woman ordered as she began to chase Freya along the road.

"No! Piss off will you!" Freya yelled, trying her best to ignore the woman's presence.

"What can I give you in exchange for the rolls? Name your price" the woman continued, matching Freya stride for stride.

"OK" Freya said and she stopped in her tracks and faced the woman again.

"How much?" the woman questioned.

"Not money. You tell me the reason you want these rolls so badly and, if the reason is good enough, you can have them" Freya told her.

"Without charge?" the woman checked.

"Yes, I mean you must have a really good reason to want them if it means you have to chase me down the road" Freya said.

"Fine. My boss has been eating these rolls every morning for the last two weeks. He likes them with olive oil spread and honey, garnished with mint and followed by two large glasses of blueberry juice. My boss, is Nicholas Kaden" the woman announced with a smirk of satisfaction.

That was about the fourth time Freya had heard the actor's name since arriving on the island. Had he completely taken over? Now he wanted her rolls! Should she perhaps feel honoured? Freya looked at the woman who was now smiling widely, certain that her name dropping had won the day.

But Freya's stomach was contracting all the more now and, sneaking a quick look at her watch, she saw she only had twenty minutes before she had to meet Emma.

"Sorry! Not good enough. Number one, my need for these rolls is far greater than Nicholas Kaden's and two, anyone who sends someone else to buy their breakfast, rather than getting it themselves, deserves to lose out to the early bird who did bother to get out of bed despite only having had a few hours sleep. Now you can go back and tell Mr Kaden that if he wants these particular rolls in future he had better set his alarm early and not rely on his mother to get them for him" Freya snapped.

With her point made she dug into the paper bag, took out a roll and sunk her teeth into it.

The woman looked furious. Her lips were tight, her face had reddened and she looked like she might explode out of the tweed suit altogether. But she didn't speak, she just turned on her heel and headed back towards the bakery.

Freya shook her head and took another bite of the roll. What was the matter with some people? Why did they think they mattered above anyone else? It was that sort of mentality that angered Freya more than anything.

Ultimately it was the fish that lost out, due to the fact that Freya had less time to feed them and that she had been so ravenous she had eaten three of the rolls herself.

Emma was ticking names off a list on the clipboard she was holding when Freya arrived at the square. There was quite a crowd of people waiting and as she approached she saw the coach appearing at the top of the road.

It was only five to eight in the morning yet the sun was already radiating an extraordinary amount of heat which meant an even hotter day to come. If Freya was honest she could hardly wait to get some new clothes. Her jeans weren't ideal wear for daytime in a hot country and her t-shirt was starting to smell.

"Morning, sleep well?" Freya spoke, having crept up on Emma.

"Freya, there you are. I was beginning to think you weren't going to make it" Emma said.

"It's a strange story, an argument in the street over my choice of breakfast" Freya told her.

"What?............yes this is the Corfu Town shopping trip. What are your names please? Mr and Mrs Michaels, yes that's fine, oh here's the coach now........sorry Freya, just let me make sure everyone's here" Emma spoke as she flew into organiser mode.

By just after eight o clock everyone was on board the coach and they had set off on their way to Corfu Town.

36

The journey would take about an hour and a quarter and the route was picturesque so Freya hoped to see the bits of the island she had missed while travelling from the airport the night before.

Freya was sat at the front of the coach with Emma who was announcing to the passengers the safety guidelines and informing them that she would be pointing out items of interest en route.

"Sorry about that, go on, I have about fifteen minutes before I have to speak again" Emma said, sinking into her seat and turning to her friend.

"Well I thought I would have some of those gorgeous rolls from the bakery for breakfast and just as I was leaving, this forty something Miss Moneypenny, only American not English, starts offering me money for them. I think she got up to 200 Euros at one point" Freya started to explain.

"What? For some rolls? What happened?" Emma asked, intrigued.

"Turns out she is something to do with Nicholas Kaden. They were 'his' rolls" Freya continued.

"Oh my God! Nicholas Kaden's secretary or something and you spoke to her!" Emma exclaimed in awe.

"I didn't just speak to her, I gave her a piece of my mind" Freya told her.

"You mean you didn't sell the rolls! Not even for 200 Euros?" Emma said in disbelief.

"No I didn't. It was the principle of the thing. They were mine and I bought them, end of. I'm not having someone with a super sized ego dictating to me. I had enough of

37

that with my father" Freya announced, screwing up her face as she cast her mind back.

"Well good for you but I think I would have been tempted to exchange them for an autograph or something" Emma told her.

"Oh please! You're as bad as those people taking photos of him last night" Freya replied.

"Now that is something you could have bargained with. You could have suggested a session to photograph him" Emma said.

"I can think of 101 people I'd rather photograph, at least. What is the hype with this guy? A couple of his films are OK-ish but he's nothing special, easy on the eye I admit but hardly Bruce Willis" Freya spoke.

"Well I think it's the fact that Kassiopi doesn't get Hollywood actors visiting very often and the film he is shooting is set predominately on mainland Greece so he's only here for a month or so. As for people going crazy over him, you have to admit he is totty" Emma said with a giggle.

"I'll tell Yiannis you said that, if I ever get to see him that is" Freya remarked.

"You are going to see him tonight because its his night off and he is booking us a table at 'Banas', the table you like best where you get the best view of the sunset. I have decided that tonight is going to be your 30th birthday all over again and hopefully it will be a lot more successful than yesterday's" Emma announced excitedly.

"That sounds fantastic" Freya admitted with a smile.

"So all we need to do now is fix you up with some outfits" Emma told her.

"Mmm, can't see Corfu Town having an 'Evans' but we'll give it a go" Freya responded as enthusiastically as possible.

When they arrived in Corfu Town it was already busy and the temperature had risen dramatically during their journey southward. Freya decided that a sun hat was another essential item she should purchase, together with some sunscreen of at least factor 15. She had quite fair skin and although she loved being in the sun it didn't always love her.

Emma had already given her instructions for her coach party to be back on board no later than two o clock which gave everyone four and a half hours in the island's capital.

As Emma helped some of her party with directions Freya looked across at the Paleo Linmani (the old fort) and remembered her first visit to Corfu Town. She had been impressed by the architecture, the buzz in the town and the way the whole place was magnificent without appearing boastful. She had taken lots of black and white shots that holiday, of the two forts, the Venetian style buildings and Emma larking about in front of all of them. She still had the picture of the view from the top of the old fort hanging in her hallway at home.

"Come on daydreamer, we've got shopping to do" Emma said, breaking Freya's thoughts and linking arms with her.

The two women strolled through the streets laughing and recapturing their youth, remembering the times they had spent drinking too much and making fools of themselves.

"Remember that awful waiter who kept being rude to us because we couldn't stop laughing?" Emma asked Freya as they walked.

"Because he thought we were laughing at his stupid moustache, which of course we were" Freya answered.

"But we were his customers and he should have remembered that and we might have left him a tip" Emma said.

"I did leave him a tip, I told him if he treated any other customers the way he treated us, he could expect a sparse summer" Freya reminded her.

"I wonder where he is now" Emma said.

"Selling pitta gyros probably" Freya remarked.

"Right, here we are, our first stop for clothes" Emma told her and she indicated the boutique in front of them.

Freya looked into the window and saw lots of, what looked like, designer outfits. All of them appeared only big enough to fit on one of her arms.

"Are you sure they are going to have something that fits me? I hate being trussed up in things that don't even meet where they're supposed to, let alone do up" Freya said with a sigh.

"Don't be silly, of course they will have things to fit you. Come in and meet Agatha. She's nearly sixty years old but has the greatest fashion sense" Emma said and she pulled Freya towards the entrance.

As they entered the shop, Freya was taken aback by how much bigger it was inside than it appeared from the outside. It was like a cavernous labyrinth with winding aisles all packed with rails of clothes for as far as the eye could see. Emma looked at Freya's surprised expression and smiled.

A short Greek lady with greying hair appeared. She immediately let out a scream and greeted Emma excitedly in the native tongue while kissing her on both cheeks.

"Please! A very rusty and limited Greek speaker here, could we converse in English?" Freya asked as Emma and the lady continued to talk in Greek.

"Sorry Freya. Agatha, this is my best friend Freya, remember I told you about her?" Emma introduced.

"Nice to meet you" Freya replied.

"And you my darling, Emma has told me much about you" Agatha replied and she embraced Freya, kissing her on both cheeks.

"I'm sure she has, all bad I expect" Freya answered.

"Not all, most, but not all" the woman joked and winked at Emma.

"Agatha, Freya has come to stay with me for a while, a few weeks, possibly more I hope, but she travelled light and we need outfits, lots of them. Daywear, nightwear, beachwear, club wear, you name it she needs it" Emma explained.

"Well hang on, my VISA might melt if you overload it" Freya exclaimed.

"Fantastic! A challenge I love, lots of choices, come come, this way" Agatha ordered and she led the way down one aisle of the shop.

"I'm not sure I like being called a challenge" Freya replied as she followed Emma and Agatha.

"Agatha sees everyone has a challenge, until she has dressed somebody they have never truly known style" Emma recited.

"Blimey, you have certainly swallowed her mantra" Freya said.

Agatha was rifling through the rails, pulling garments out, hanging some of them over her arm and rejecting others.

"I know she has red hair now Agatha, but by the end of the day it will be blonde so I don't want you to let that put you off" Emma informed as she began looking through the clothes as well.

"Blonde? Since when?"

"Since I bought a hair colour at the pharmacy this morning on the way to the square. Don't worry, you'll have help to do it" Emma told her.

Freya watched the two women parting outfits and discussing which colours would best suit her skin tone. She hated shopping for clothes back in England because she always had to try things on and inevitably they were too small. Lately she had bought a lot of things on the internet. No embarrassing changing rooms and you could send it back if it didn't fit, no going red at the counter when you exchanged it for a larger size.

"Here are the first outfits, go try and let us see each. Then we see how things look yes?" Agatha spoke handing Freya a pile of clothes.

Parading around in front of them like she was a plus size catwalk model suddenly filled Freya with dread. But she looked at Emma's eager face and Agatha, with her stylish floaty clothes, waving her arm towards the dressing room and could see they were going to get a lot of pleasure out of it. Who was she to deprive them of it?

Freya pulled the curtain of the dressing room and disappeared behind it.

"I want no looking until I am dressed. I have two day old underwear on and it isn't pretty" Freya called to them.

"She left England in a bit of a hurry" Emma explained to Agatha.

The first item was a pair of black trousers. Freya pulled them up her legs and was surprised to find that they were indeed a good fit. The button and the zip both did up with ease, which was a novelty with most of her current wardrobe, and the cut of the material even made her thighs look less rugby. She put the emerald green top that went with the trousers over her head and tied up the halter neck. She observed herself in the mirror. She looked almost slim, well perhaps not slim, but definitely better and with a more defined shape. She looked feminine. Seeing herself look so different she couldn't help but let out a shriek of pleasure and she drew aside the curtain.

"Will you look at me?! I have a waist! A waist! And my boobs don't look like they are going to take over the rest of my body" Freya announced, hardly able to contain her excitement.

"You look amazing!" Agatha said, clapping her hands together in delight as Emma hugged her friend.

"I do look amazing don't I? So which outfit is next?" Freya asked eagerly.

She dived back into the changing room now ready to parade around like a plus size catwalk model in front of anyone.

An hour later Freya had purchased no less than seven outfits, plus three pairs of shoes, two handbags, two sarongs, three swimming costumes, five tops, four pairs of trousers and two cardigans. Emma had even managed to persuade her to purchase a bikini which Freya knew she would only wear with a suitable t-shirt over the top, but it had made Emma happy.

"I am going to need to speak to the bank about my overdraft after buying this lot" Freya announced as Agatha put everything in bags for her.

"You deserve it, a birthday treat. Besides, you work hard enough, why shouldn't you spend some of your hard earned cash?" Emma pointed out.

"Don't speak about work! I am supposed to be doing school photos next week, I'll have to ring Simon and get him to rearrange. He's probably wondering where I am" Freya spoke, suddenly being reminded of her responsibilities of running a small business.

"He'll cope. I mean it isn't like you haven't disappeared before" Emma reminded her.

"That's true enough. She knows me too well Agatha, we've been friends for too long now and she knows all my secrets" Freya told the Greek lady.

"That is not a bad thing. Everyone need someone to tell everything to" Agatha replied.

"Yes they do" Freya agreed, looking at Emma.

"Now Freya, you listen to an old lady yes? These clothes, they make you look wonderful but that is only half the mountain we climb. You must learn to feel wonderful. I sense this is something you no find easy, yes?" Agatha began, looking seriously at Freya.

"There isn't much about me that's wonderful, well apart from the apparently sexy eyes and of course the sparkling wit" Freya responded.

"I know from Emma and I feel you are a very special person, I warm to you the minute I meet you. You have a spark, a light inside, no everyone has a light inside of them but you do. Now, you take these wonderful clothes that make you look so pretty and promise Agatha that when you wear them you let the light out and make it fill the room" Agatha ordered and as she said 'fill the room' she waved her arms about as if filling the room herself.

"I promise I'll try and thank you for all your help Agatha, you and your clothes are amazing" Freya told her. Agatha leant across the counter and kissed both of Freya's cheeks.

"You meet special man soon I think, one who sees the light inside" Agatha told her in a serious voice.

"I'm kind of off men at the moment but if he is tall, dark and devilishly handsome I might be persuaded" Freya joked with a smile.

The women finished their goodbyes, packed themselves up with Freya's bags and headed out of the boutique.

"Well I really didn't think we would have finished our search for outfits by quarter to eleven" Freya admitted as they started to walk down the pavement away from the shop.

"I had every faith in Agatha, she's promised me a wedding dress one day" Emma admitted with a smile.

"Does that mean that you and Yiannis have talked about it?" Freya inquired.

"We've spoken about it but it's difficult. We don't have that much money and we would really like a place of our own. Mr and Mrs P are great but living with your boyfriend's parents isn't ideal" Emma said.

"Living with my own parents was never ideal, let alone living with someone else's. Come to think of it living with someone else's would have been a whole lot better" Freya responded.

"We're saving up for a place but it takes time. The restaurant is doing really well but the money is all tied up" Emma continued.

"You'll get there" Freya assured her.

"I know but I'm almost 30 now and I don't want to leave it too late, I did want to be married before we had children" Emma spoke.

"Marriage, children and here I am single again" Freya commented with a sigh.

"Freya, I'm sorry, God how insensitive am I? I shouldn't be thinking about me, I should be thinking about you" Emma exclaimed.

"Don't be stupid, all you've done since I've arrived is think about me. It was a good job I didn't marry and have kids with Russell wasn't it? If he thought I was large now he would have had a shock if I'd got pregnant" Freya told her.

Emma couldn't help but laugh out loud.

"Have you spoken to him yet?" Emma asked.

"No, no battery left. Can I borrow your phone charger later?" Freya asked.

"Of course"

"Thanks. I may as well hear what the idiot has to say for himself in all those messages he's left. So, seeing as I'm all kitted out now and it's only eleven, what are we going to do now? It's a bit early for lunch isn't it?" Freya asked, checking her watch.

"Oh yes, far too early and we've got other stuff to do yet, like dying your hair and having it cut and sorting out those nails of yours" Emma told her.

"What? Well hang on, where are we going? I hope it's not too far because these bags aren't conducive to long distances and it's nearly the midday sun, I'm in jeans and you know I perspire like a weight lifter" Freya called as she tried to hurry along and catch her friend up.

Emma introduced Freya to Helena, who cut and dyed her hair, and Sophia who manicured her nails and gave them a French polish.

Freya looked almost unrecognizable from the pale, jaded and dejected red-haired individual who had arrived at Corfu airport the night before. Firstly, she was smiling and secondly it felt great to be able to pamper herself and do it all with her best friend.

After the hairdressers the two women settled themselves at a café in The Liston and ordered lunch.

The Liston was an arcaded street which had been designed during the French occupation of the island back in the nineteenth century. The restaurants were expensive but it was worth the extra cost to sit amongst the beautiful surroundings and watch the world pass by.

"So how do you feel now? Better than when you arrived?" Emma questioned.

"Do I feel better? Hmm, I'm sat in Corfu Town at a nice café, about to eat a tasty chicken *souvlaki* with my best friend, having spent the morning being pampered in every way. Yes, I think I am feeling better. So, does blonde suit me?" Freya asked her, looking down over her glasses.

"Very much so and I'm so glad you're having a good time" Emma replied.

"Well that's why I run away here when I lose the plot and not somewhere like Grimsby" Freya spoke.

"I'm glad you came, I do miss you you know" Emma admitted a little emotionally.

"Hey is everything OK? Is there something you have been leaving out of our phone conversations that you want to share now?" Freya asked her.

"No, no I just miss seeing you like we used to before I moved out here. I don't have that many friends here, I mean there are a few girls at the office but we're always so busy, there's hardly any time to socialise" Emma continued with a deep breath.

"But you've got Yiannis, that has got to be better than having me around" Freya reminded her.

"I know but there are some things you can only tell your best friend, as you know" Emma said.

"Well I'm here now and I'm going to stay a while, have a proper holiday" Freya decided.

Chapter Three

That evening the dilemma was which one of her new outfits to wear out to the restaurant.

Freya had arrived back at 'The Calypso Apartments' at just before four o clock and had felt completely shattered. She had still felt like she was suffering from a lack of sleep but the pool had looked so inviting she had raced back to her room, changed into a swimming costume and got into the water. It had felt even better than it looked, cool, fresh and rejuvenating. A few lengths dodging the ten or so extremely loud children playing water polo had been just what she needed to get her ready for a siesta, a siesta that had lasted for three hours.

Now she was panicking, because she was due to meet Emma and Yiannis in half an hour at 'Banas Restaurant'. And now with so many wardrobe choices, it was difficult to decide what to wear.

She had borrowed Emma's phone charger when they had arrived back in Kassiopi. Her mobile now had a full battery and was ready to go. She had called her assistant Simon and told him to take care of things while she was away and she had listened to the messages from Russell. Surprisingly, despite the number of missed calls, there were only three:-

"Hi babe, I'm here at the restaurant. It's nearly half past one now, so give me a ring as soon as you can, you've obviously been held up I guess"

"Hi Hon, its seven o clock now, I've been trying your phone and the office since this afternoon. I'm worried about you, could you give me a ring as soon as you get this, let me know you're OK. Love you Babe"

"Hi Freya, I don't know whether you got my other messages or the missed calls but ....have I done something to upset you? If I've done or said something or you want to shout at me for some reason just give me a call and we can talk about it. I love you"

He sounded almost genuinely concerned in the first two messages but the third sounded guilt ridden.

Freya had phoned him just ten minutes ago and had reached his voicemail.

"Russell, this is your large girlfriend, you know, the plain one you've wasted a year and a half of your life with. Just to let you know that I'm fine, I'm with someone who cares about me and is loyal and faithful to me, something which I don't think you have been. Don't ring me again, don't ring Simon at the office and get your things out of my flat. I never want to see you again"

Freya smiled as she remembered the satisfaction she had felt when she had hung up. Talking things over with Emma had definitely helped her to clarify her feelings. Now for a clothes decision. The black trousers and green halter neck top, without a doubt.

She wore high heeled black sandals with sequins on and picked up the matching handbag. Looking at herself in the full length mirror she could see a change in herself, now all she had to do was feel that change. She had done it before, she could do it again.

'Banas Restaurant' was only a few minutes walk from 'The Calypso Apartments' and it was just after 8.30pm when Freya arrived there to find Emma already waiting for her.

"Styled by Agatha! Now get ready to fill the room with your light" Emma spoke as Freya joined her.

"Don't joke, Agatha was completely serious about my light! Where's Yiannis?" Freya questioned, noticing immediately that Emma's boyfriend was absent.

"He had to work. One of the waiters is sick and he couldn't get cover. He's really sorry, he was really looking forward to seeing you" Emma told her.

"You are still going out with him aren't you? Its just I haven't seen him since I landed" Freya commented.

"I know I know but I thought we could maybe go back to Petroholis restaurant for late night drinks" Emma suggested.

"That sounds like a great idea" Freya agreed.

"Good, well, let's go and have a birthday meal" Emma said excitedly, taking Freya's arm.

"Have I got a balloon on my chair? Tell me I have a balloon on my chair" Freya spoke as they entered the restaurant.

'Banas' was an extremely popular restaurant in Kassiopi due to its location on the edge of Kalamionas beach. It served high quality international cuisine and was also famed for being in the perfect position to watch the sun set over Albania. It was always a spectacle.

The restaurant was busy and the women had to wait for one of the dozen or so waiters to come and attend to them.

Emma spoke to the waiter in Greek explaining that they had booked Freya's favourite table. The waiter immediately began to look flustered and started to shuffle from foot to foot looking uncomfortable. Although Freya's

Greek was pretty limited, she could sense that something wasn't quite right.

"What's going on? Why is he looking like that?" Freya asked Emma.

"There's a problem with the table, he's going to get the manager" Emma told Freya.

"What sort of problem? A wobbly leg? Someone still sat there from the first sitting? We can wait a bit, have some complimentary drinks for the inconvenience" Freya said, looking forward to the evening.

"It sounded slightly more terminal than that but we'll see what the manager has to say" Emma said with a sigh.

"Terminal? You mean...........hang on, I can just see our table and there is someone on it! There's a whole party taking up three tables, including ours" Freya announced as she looked through into the restaurant.

"Mmm he mumbled something about that, but don't worry, the manager will be here in a minute and I'm sure he will sort something out" Emma said calmly.

"Hang on a minute, I don't believe it! Do you know who is sat at our table? Bloody Nicholas Kaden and there is his minion who tried to buy my rolls! That man has completely taken over the village" Freya exclaimed in anger.

She stared over at the table and could just see Nicholas Kaden, dressed in a white shirt, open at the neck, looking older than she had remembered him looking in the last DVD she had rented. He looked slim, yet muscular and there was no denying that he was handsome. However, as Freya looked at him, all she felt was irritation. Who did he think he was? She had been in Corfu less than 24 hours and already he had made a nuisance of himself and inconvenienced her in many ways. Now him and his film buddies had taken her table, the sunset table, the table she loved, the table Emma had booked especially for her birthday. Freya's temper was rising rapidly. If there was one thing she could not stand it was people with inflated egos thinking they were better than anyone else. She had spent her life running away from people like that! Just because he was an actor who happened to get his face on the front of magazines he did not have the right to stamp all over her and pinch a table they had reserved.

Emma was now talking to the manager of 'Banas' and Freya demanded to know what was being said.

"Are they going to be finished soon? On their desserts are they?" Freya questioned the manager.

"Freya he says he's sorry. Apparently they booked for six people originally and then turned up with more" Emma attempted to explain.

"Well that isn't our fault. So what's he going to do about it?" Freya asked, becoming more riled by the second.

"As I have said to your friend, I can only apologise and offer you a table tomorrow night with some free drinks" the manager told her.

"I know it's not the same but I could make tomorrow night if Yiannis can manage without me at the restaurant" Emma told her, trying to make the best of the situation.

"No I'm sorry, that won't do. Excuse me" Freya said and before anyone could stop her she headed off into the restaurant, walking swiftly past other tables in the direction of Nicholas Kaden.

He was oblivious to Freya's approach. He was sat next to a super slim, super blonde woman, who wasn't wearing very much, and Freya could see that they had just started their main course. He was laughing at something that had been said to him by one of the men sat opposite him. It was only when he had finished laughing that he noticed his bodyguard was now standing at the table next to a blonde haired woman in a green top, preparing to escort her away.

"Get off me!" Freya shrieked, flapping her arms so as to relieve herself from the bodyguard's grasp.

"Roger, it's OK, if she wants an autograph I'm quite happy to do it" Nicholas Kaden spoke hurriedly as he watched Freya attempting to rid herself of the tall black man.

"I don't want a pissing autograph! What I want is my table, the one you're sat at. My friend booked this table, she reserved it for us, for my birthday and now you and your cronies are squatting on it" Freya exploded, loud enough for the entire restaurant to hear.

"Squatting on it? What does she mean?" the super blonde bimbo next to Nicholas Kaden asked.

"It means occupying something that isn't yours, it's an English expression" the woman who had tried to buy Freya's rolls commented.

"Look lady, we're trying to have a quiet meal here. How much would it take for you to go away?" Gene Bates, one of Nicholas Kaden's co-stars asked, turning around in his chair to face Freya.

"Oh my God, it's always about money with you people isn't it? You must lead sad shallow lives for money to mean so much to you. I don't want your stinking money, I don't want an autograph or a snap for the album, I want you to realise that you have ruined the night for me and my friend. But I don't expect that means anything to you" Freya carried on, unable to contain her emotions.

She glared at Nicholas Kaden, the bimbo, the Roll Lady and back to Nicholas again. He was just sat still in his chair, looking back at her, offering no comment.

"Go away you stupid girl, you are drawing attention to us which is the last thing we wanted.... Roger, perhaps you could organise someone at the entrance" Roll Lady spoke to the bodyguard.

"Well perhaps you should have thought about unwanted attention before you stole someone else's table, you invited this situation!" Freya yelled back.

"Roger please escort this woman away" Roll Lady ordered.

Freya again avoided being manhandled by the bodyguard. She quickly turned around, grabbed a large basket from the waiter serving a group of four behind her and slammed it down on the table in front of Nicholas, just missing his plate of food.

"Bread rolls Mr Kaden, I hear they are your particular favourites. Well, tomorrow morning, place in a warm oven, wait ten minutes and voila, breakfast. Give her one less thing to fetch for you" Freya finished pointing at Roll Lady.

Her point had been made to her satisfaction and not wanting to be forcefully ejected from the restaurant Freya turned and left the way she had come, oblivious to the fact that the whole restaurant was now looking at her.

Once back with Emma she took her arm and pulled her towards the exit.

"Come on, we're leaving, we'll go and eat at 'Petroholis Restaurant'" Freya told her, still shaking with anger.

"What did you say to him? Did he speak? What was he like?" Emma questioned excitedly as she let herself be dragged along.

"I hardly noticed" Freya replied.

"Who was sat with him? Was it Bob Crosby and Gene Bates?" Emma inquired.

"They were all rude and one of them looked like an anorexic Barbie" Freya answered.

"Hey!"

The loud yell made both women stop and turn around to where the shout had come from. Nicholas Kaden was a few yards away from them, hurrying down the street to catch them up, much to the surprise and delight of the people he passed in the street.

"Oh my God, Hollywood's finest is running down the road chasing us. Freya what have you done? I think I am going to die" Emma muttered, paralysed to the spot.

"I'm surprised he doesn't need someone to help him walk" Freya replied, watching him approach.

"Hi. Look, I'm sorry about your table" Nicholas spoke as he reached them.

"Save it" Freya snapped immediately.

"It's OK, 'Banas' is one of the best restaurants in Kassiopi, it's quite understandable you would want to eat there" Emma said diplomatically.

"Yes, but really not at the expense of your evening" Nicholas insisted.

"So what are you going to do about it? Finish up? Skip dessert and give up the table?" Freya asked him.

"No. But I was hoping you would come back and join us, perhaps we could share the table" Nicholas suggested.

He seemed taller in the flesh and more athletic in build than Freya had thought him to be. His usual dark hair looked like it had been bleached by the Corfiot sun but his eyes were as large and as blue as they appeared on screen. He was now offering an olive branch and that made him appear less arrogant. Perhaps some of what she had said had hit home.

"No thanks" Freya responded immediately.

"Freya!" Emma exclaimed in horror, not believing that her friend was about to pass up the opportunity of having a meal with a film star.

"I wanted to spend the evening with you, not him and his stuck up entourage" Freya spoke, not caring who heard.

"Would you excuse us, just for a second" Emma said to Nicholas and she jerked Freya just out of earshot.

"Freya, that is Nicholas Kaden, NICHOLAS KADEN!! He's won 2 Oscars, he models for a famous aftershave, he is worth millions, he is one of the most famous men on the planet and he's asking us to have dinner with him" Emma told her.

"Emma you know none of that impresses me" Freya reminded her.

She looked again at Nicholas who was stood still in the same spot, looking away from them, trying to avoid drawing attention to himself.

"Well you don't have to be impressed, you can be as unimpressed as you like but I know people who would kill for this opportunity, my mother for one" Emma told her.

"You want to have dinner with him" Freya stated.

"I want us to have dinner with him, at the restaurant we planned to eat at, at the table we booked, just with extra dining companions. We can still do everything we wanted to do and still see the sunset if we hurry up" Emma spoke.

Freya sighed. It wasn't the evening she had been looking forward to, courting rich people, making small talk. She looked at Nicholas again. He looked slightly uncomfortable stood in the road on his own. His hands were still in the pockets of his dark jeans and then he turned and looked at the two women. He caught Freya's eye and she hurriedly looked back to Emma.

"But, it is your birthday so you should decide" Emma told her.

"OK" Freya replied.

"OK? You mean we can go and have dinner with him?" Emma asked.

"Yes, why not, he did run a full fifty yards on his own without a camera rolling" Freya said.

"Great! Great! I can't wait to tell my mum about this! Ooooo it's so exciting!" Emma said as she and Freya walked back over to Nicholas.

"Are we going to eat together?" Nicholas inquired.

"Yes we are, we would be delighted to join you for dinner" Emma told him.

"You're both happy with that decision? Because I have to say that the girl who had red hair this morning looks kinda put out" Nicholas remarked.

"I can tell Roll Lady has been bigging me up" Freya replied with a half smile. She was so doing this for Emma.

They re-entered 'Banas' and Nicholas arranged an additional couple of chairs for the two women to sit on. The waiter took their orders and Nicholas had more champagne brought for the table.

The other people dining with them were hurriedly introduced by Roll Lady, much to her displeasure. The slim blonde seated next to Nicholas was his romantic interest in the film, Hilary Polar. She was not immediately recognisable to Freya or Emma and it transpired that this was her first major movie. Gene Bates and Bob Crosby were well seasoned actors and also at the table were Jack Barnes and Andrew Masters, members of the production team. Roll Lady was in fact Nicholas' personal assistant and was called Martha Wilson.

Freya was seated with Nicholas on one side of her and Emma on the other. Emma had Bob Crosby squeezed in next to her. It was a bit snug and Freya was not in a good position to see the sunset and decided this was a situation she must rectify when the time came.

"So we've done all the introductions but we don't know your names" Bob Crosby spoke, getting as close as he could to Emma.

Freya shook her head at his pathetic attempt at flirtation. He and Gene were both in their forties and these days played mostly character roles. This usually involved them being either gangsters in action movies or father figures in romantic comedies.

"I'm Emma and this is....." Emma began.

"This is Freya" Nicholas interrupted and announced to the table.

Freya looked surprised that he knew her name.

"I overheard Emma use your name when she was persuading you to come back and eat. It's a cool name, unusual" Nicholas whispered to her.

"It suits" Freya responded.

"Well Emma and Freya, its nice to meet you, just please, can we call time on any more baskets of rolls, they kind of mess up the table settings" Gene Bates retorted and laughed out loud.

Freya bit her tongue. She was going through this charade for Emma, kind sweet Emma who had welcomed her back to Kassiopi with open arms and was now being letched over by an aging Hollywood lothario.

"So Freya, are you here on holiday?" Nicholas asked her, taking a sip of his drink.

"Yes, kind of. I sorted out some business at home and then decided to visit a friend" Freya told him.

She picked up a bread roll from the small basket in the middle of the table and bit into it. She was starving and she wished the food would hurry up as smelling Nicholas' plate of kleftico was accelerating her hunger pangs.

"Been to Kassiopi before?" Nicholas continued as he ate.

"Yes, several times. You?" Freya asked politely.

"This is my first time" he admitted with a smile.

"Ooo a Kassiopi virgin" Freya replied.

"Yes that's right. Well, even you must have been a virgin once" Nicholas joked, unable to contain a smirk.

"So what do you think of the village?" Freya asked him, not responding to his comment.

"I think it's terrific. The scenery is spectacular, the people are friendly, well the locals at least, and it has a great feel to it" Nicholas told her.

"Yes, it has" Freya agreed.

"Be careful there, you're agreeing with me on something, you might soon have to admit I'm not the awful person you think I am" Nicholas spoke, looking directly at Freya.

"Pass the water would you?" Freya asked quickly, feeling a touch of embarrassment.

Nicholas smiled and passed her the jug.

"So how is filming going Nicholas?" Emma piped up, sipping her drink and beaming from ear to ear.

"Please, call me Nick, I've never been struck on the full name. It's going well, we had a little trouble today with the heat but we're getting there" he answered.

"It's out on the boat tomorrow isn't it?" Hilary Polar spoke, putting her arm around Nicholas' shoulders and nearly hitting Freya's shoulder as she did so.

"Yes and some work for the stunt double" Nicholas said.

"Goodness, what have you got to do on the boat that you need a stuntman for?" Emma asked him, intrigued.

"Well my character gets knocked overboard and then dragged along by the boat" Nicholas explained.

"He wanted to do the stunt himself but insurance would not allow it" Martha informed everyone.

"Pity" Freya remarked, under her breath.

"Come on, you really don't mean that" Nicholas said, turning in his chair to face her.

"No? Not after you and your entourage have been a thorn in my side since I got here? I would pay good money to see you be dragged along by a boat" Freya told him.

"Look, Freya, I really apologise for any inconvenience I might have caused you, all of it was unintentional I assure you. I really don't set out to wreak havoc wherever I go and I'm sorry if it's appeared I have little consideration for anything other than myself, that really couldn't be further from the truth" Nicholas answered sincerely.

Freya found herself incapable of a response, which was extremely unusual for her, however she was saved from any embarrassment by the arrival of her and Emma's food.

She ate hungrily and devoured the moussaka. She was halfway through the chocolate ice cream when it started to happen. She dropped her spoon in her bowl and leapt up from her seat.

"Excuse me" she said hurriedly and picking up her handbag she rushed towards the patio doors of the restaurant. She tugged them open and stepped out onto the paved area which separated the restaurant from the pebbled beach.

"What is she doing now?" Martha questioned as all the people seated at the table watched Freya.

"Oh it's the sunset. She'll be out there until it goes down now, fifteen/twenty minutes or so, taking photos. That's what she does, she's a photographer" Emma informed the group.

"And here was me thinking she was a professional food taster or something" Gene remarked with a laugh.

Hilary giggled at the comment, Martha covered a smirk with her serviette and Emma hid her face in her glass not knowing what to say.

"Well you have left no one in any doubt that your profession isn't comedy Gene, I would suggest you inform your agent, avoid any inappropriate castings" Nicholas retorted and he turned his attention away from the table.

He looked outside to where Freya was crouched down on the floor, pointing her camera at the horizon.

By the time she had returned to the table her ice cream had melted. She felt little disappointment however as she had eaten most of it anyway and the sunset had been fantastic. There had been few clouds in the sky and she had had a prime position.

"Did you get some good photos?" Emma asked when her friend had sat back down.

"Not bad. I just wish I had my other cameras with me" Freya admitted.

"Emma tells us you are a photographer" Martha said as she took a sip from her wine glass.

"That's right" Freya responded.

"Do you have your own studio?" she continued.

"Yes I do" Freya answered.

"And yet you come away on holiday with nothing but a digital the size of a credit card, amazing" Martha spoke.

"I left in a bit of a hurry. Anyway, sometimes it's good to use something inappropriate, it makes you appreciate quality better" Freya responded. She narrowed her eyes and looked over her glasses at the woman.

"I'll drink to that" Gene said raising his glass into the middle of the table "to all things inappropriate"

Everyone raised their glasses.

The meal had not been as disastrous as it could have been. The food had been really good, the champagne had made Freya slightly light-headed and she hated to admit it but Nicholas had been reasonable company.

"Isn't he gorgeous?" Emma stated excitedly when she and Freya went to the ladies toilets to freshen up.

"Who?" Freya inquired.

"Nick of course and so nice. You were wrong about him you have to admit it" Emma said as she touched up her lipstick.

"I'm not admitting anything, anyway I'm surprised you could get a clear view of him with Bob Crosby virtually sat on your lap. I hope you told him he is nearly old enough to be your father" Freya spoke.

"Hardly, he's forty six. Anyway I told him I was practically married" Emma said as she washed her hands.

"That wouldn't deter him" Freya remarked.

"It's been OK though hasn't it? The meal I mean, in the circumstances of having to share a table with all these famous people"

"It's been OK, in fact I would go as far as to say it has been quite interesting. Martha made it completely plain that we were not welcome, she spent the whole night looking down at me, Hilary Polar is as thick as you would expect a blonde haired anorexic actress to be, which was comforting to establish and as for Bob and Gene, they seemed to behave like hormonal teenagers for most of the meal, definitely midlife crisis material" Freya spoke.

"I didn't understand their fascination with the olive pips" Emma admitted.

"Gene was trying to throw them down your top" Freya told her.

"No!" Emma exclaimed and looked down into her décolletage.

"I don't think his aim was very good. Right, shall we go to 'Yasmine's' for a bit of karaoke?" Freya suggested.

"Yes, it sounds like fun. I wonder what the film lot are up to" Emma said as they left the toilets.

"Something that doesn't involve us, they've done their duty, restored their popularity" Freya told her.

"Oh I know, I was just wondering. At least I can now say I've had dinner with a Hollywood actor, my mum is not going to believe it" she said, still in awe of the scenario.

"Something to tell the grandchildren" Freya commented.

"Something like that" Emma said hurriedly

"Come on then, 'Yasmines' it is" Freya said turning towards the exit.

"Hang on, I've left my jacket at the table, I won't be a second, wait there for me" Emma spoke and she dashed off towards the table.

Freya waited by the bar area and caught sight of herself in the mirrored back plate. Her hair actually looked quite good now, it was still strange to see a blonde staring back but it was definitely better than the red.

Just as she was looking at herself and adjusting the halter neck of her top she heard voices. Gene and Bob's American tones were instantly recognisable.

"Nick is always up for a challenge. Remember the last time, on location in Morocco? Wouldn't fancy it myself, she'd probably crush me" Freya heard Gene speak.

"Or eat you!" Bob answered with a laugh.

"So what shall we say? We foot the bill for a weekend at that boys only club in Miami if he actually survives a date with her, your villa in the Caymans for a week including the masseuse if they make out, urgh God, are you picturing this? And if he beds her I think we should make it two weeks skiing in Aspen, all food and drink and a sleigh ride or two with some local beauties to get over the pain" Gene spoke.

"But we would need photographic evidence" Bob replied.

"God I am not sure that is something I would want to see!" Gene responded.

"And if he doesn't manage any of it?" Bob inquired.

"Come on, this is Nick we are talking about, charm personified, and a prize pig who would probably be grateful to lay anything let alone an acting icon" Gene spoke.

"I think I want his Ferrari, for a month" Bob answered.

"Fine, you have the Ferrari and I will settle for use of his membership to the golf club, in Hawaii" Gene said.

"Nice" Bob responded.

"So do you think you have a chance with Emma? Those two are a class apart aren't they? Little and large" Gene spoke.

"Pretty and pretty ugly" Bob replied as they appeared in the main room.

Freya hurriedly stepped behind the large plant by the bar, her eyes stinging with tears. Twenty four hours, new hair, nails and clothes hadn't changed the way that people saw her. They had bet Nicholas to go out with her. She had only felt this humiliated twice in her life before and once was yesterday having overheard another conversation.

"Hello Fatty! Didn't think you'd see me again did you? Dyed your hair again? It still looks silly" a voice spoke.

Freya looked down to see the devil child from the plane skipping about in front of her. This had to be an illusion, she had upset herself into hallucinating.

"Have you always been fat?" the girl asked, spinning round and round in circles.

"Have you always been rude?" Freya snapped back at her.

"My mum says I came out with attitude" the girl responded proudly.

"And I bet there isn't a day goes by when she doesn't wish she had said 'no not tonight dear I have a headache'" Freya bit back.

"You go red when you shout. Red face, stupid hair, red face, stupid hair" the girl chorused as she danced around.

Emma arrived back with her jacket.

"Who is that little girl?" she questioned.

"A pain in the arse. Can we go? I need a drink" Freya spoke with a sniff.

"Are you OK? Have you been crying?" Emma queried, trying to look into her friend's eyes.

"Yes, crying because I need more alcohol. Come on, let's go before Devil Child gets her mother on to me" Freya begged.

The two women headed for the door of the restaurant but just as they were about to depart Nicholas appeared and called out to them.

"You going already?" he questioned.

"Yes, we don't want to outstay our welcome, you probably have lots to discuss about the film and stuff" Emma spoke.

"But more importantly than that we don't want to miss karaoke at 'Yasmines'" Freya replied.

"I can understand that, so um, Emma, would you mind if I just had a quick word with Freya?" Nicholas asked with a deep breath.

"Oh, OK, sure that's fine I'll just head off to 'Yasmines' and I'll meet you there. It was nice to meet you Nick" Emma told him sincerely.

"You too" he agreed and he took hold of Emma's hand, brought it to his lips, and gave it the faintest of touches.

"Right, well, I'll see you in a minute" Emma said, blushing as she turned to walk down the road towards the bar.

Freya braced herself for what she knew was coming next.

"I was just wondering, if you would come out with me, maybe tomorrow night?" Nicholas asked.

"Like on a date?" Freya inquired, pretending not to know what he was talking about.

"Yes! Exactly like a date. We could have a few drinks, something to eat, anything you want to do" he spoke, relieved she had guessed his intention.

Freya could feel the fury rising in her as she looked at him, his dark hair, his perfect smile, acting like his life depended on it for the sake of a paid holiday and a few perks he could buy himself anyway.

"Why would you want to date me? Particularly when you have so obviously been sleeping with Hilary Polar" Freya stated, giving him a stern look.

Nicholas laughed out loud which took Freya by surprise.

"She'd like to, I think, but she's not for me. I want to date you because I thought it might be fun" he responded.

"Yes us big girls are fun aren't we? A whole big bundle of fun" Freya commented, finding it hard not to show her anger.

"So what do you say? Do you want to come out with me? I have to tell you, as fun as it is sparring with you, I don't usually have to work this hard to make a girl say yes" Nicholas told her.

"No I'm sure you don't but then I'm not your usual kind of date am I?" Freya replied.

"I realised that when I nearly got the bread rolls in my meal. Fine, come out with me, don't come out with me it's your decision, contrary to popular opinion not everyone has to do what I say" Nicholas stated.

Freya didn't respond. He was sticking up for himself, not many people were brave enough to fight their corner when she was on the attack.

"But it would be nice if you could give me a chance to prove I'm not the total jackass you think I am. I do hate bad press" Nicholas informed her and flashed a Hollywood smile.

God he was good! This performance alone was worthy of Oscar number three.

"OK then, yes" Freya found herself saying.

"Sorry? Was that a yes?" he asked her, seeing as Freya had uttered the words so quietly anyone could have missed them.

"Yes it was a yes. Meet me at 8.00 tomorrow night at 'The Calypso Apartments'. And I'm choosing what we do and where we eat" Freya told him.

"Whatever you want. Well then I'll see you tomorrow night" Nicholas spoke.

He leant forward and kissed her cheek before she could back away.

"Yeh, tomorrow" Freya answered and she turned her back on him and hurried down the road towards 'Yasmine's' hoping her sequinned shoes would stay attached to her feet.

If there was one thing she had learnt from their encounter it was that he was a fine actor. If she had been watching the scene on screen she would have believed he was genuine. The hurt was passing now, it was time to think about pay back. Russell had to be paid back properly yet, but in the meantime it would be fun paying back Nicholas 'Mr Hollywood' Kaden for daring to make her a subject of a bet.

'Yasmine's' was packed with people when Freya arrived and she very nearly didn't see Emma who was sat in the conservatory area next to a large Trifidesque plant almost identical to the one she had hidden behind in the restaurant. Freya decided that large plants had a lot to answer for. Emma waved and indicated that she had bought her a drink.

Freya joined her, sat down and immediately took a big swig of her drink.

"Well come on, don't keep me in suspense, what did he say to you that I wasn't allowed to hear?" Emma questioned.

"I don't know what the secrecy was all about, he asked me out" Freya said simply.

Emma coughed and spat out her mouthful of drink onto the table.

"Urgh, that's gross, here have a napkin" Freya said, passing her friend one from the holder on the table.

"Are you being serious? Nicholas Kaden asked you out on a date?" Emma repeated.

"Yes. Just saying it sounds ridiculous doesn't it? Look how surprised you are"

"Well it is a surprise, I mean, wow! Nicholas Kaden asking you out on a date" Emma said for the second time.

"Christ Emma, get a grip, you're making it sound like I've accepted an audience with the Pope" Freya spoke.

"He's more famous than that. He's a devastatingly handsome Hollywood actor that the entire female population would bitch fight for a date with. A man, who owns at least half a dozen houses in enviable locations, has his face on every magazine cover in existence and someone who is probably on first name terms with Bruce Willis. He probably has his number in his mobile" Emma announced, practically hyperventilating.

"But apart from having money and things and connections he is the sort of person who accepts the challenge of dating a fat woman for the grand prize of a weekend at a boys club. And if he gets his tongue down my throat he gets a week in the Caymans being massaged and the pies de résistance, if he gets me into bed it's a whole two weeks skiing and fondling buxom yodelling milkmaids while sleigh riding, which quite honestly sounds like an impossible combination" Freya explained.

"You've lost me now?" Emma stated, the turn in conversation too quick for her.

"Oh come on Em, catch up, you didn't really think someone like him with all his cash and flash and probable Bruce Willis connections would want to actually date someone plain and ordinary like me! Like you said, he could have his pick of women. Gene and Bob, our amiable dining companions, bet him to date me, I overheard them. So when we left the restaurant I knew he was going to come looking for me to ask me out" Freya told Emma as she finished her drink.

"Oh Freya no" Emma said, putting her hands to her mouth in shock.

"Yes, so there you have it. I'm going on a date tomorrow night with someone that thinks so little of the feelings of another human being that he is willing to kick them when they are down already, for the sake of a cheap thrill and a few lousy treats, which of course to him are the equivalent cost of a Marks & Spencer sandwich. Remind you of anyone?" Freya asked.

Emma took hold of both her friend's hands and squeezed them tightly. And then she let go, slowly reacting to what Freya had actually said.

"Sorry? Did I hear you wrong? Did you say you were going on a date with him?" Emma asked, looking at Freya.

"Oh yes, I accepted" Freya replied.

"But why? Normally you would have called him something extremely rude and told him you would rather poke your own eyes out than date him"

"You are so in tune with my vocabulary, even after all our time apart, it's impressive"

"Freya be serious, you're not going to go are you?" Emma asked.

"Yes I am and I'll tell you now, it is going to be a date like he has never had before. I'm going to show him that no one, no matter who they are, no matter how much cash they have in the bank, no one makes a fool out of me. I've done it before and I will do it again" Freya stated seriously.

She took a deep breath and held the thought.

"Freya, don't think back about things, it's all behind you" Emma spoke, as if reading Freya's thoughts.

"I know, it's just events keep stirring things up all the time. Just when I think it's really all gone, something like this reminds me and I get angry like I was before" Freya answered her.

"You've come so far. You were right, they are all arrogant, childish and pathetic and we shouldn't have joined them for dinner" Emma stated.

"Well, it's done now, why don't you get us some more drinks and sign me up for the karaoke" Freya suggested with a smile.

"Are you sure? We don't have to stay if you don't want to, it's your night" Emma reminded her.

"Exactly. It's my night and nothing is going to spoil it. I'll do something by Cher'" Freya told her.

"OK" Emma agreed and she picked up their glasses and went towards the bar.

As soon as she had gone Freya's smile dropped and she took off her glasses to rub her eyes. She felt drained and sad, but most of all disappointed. Disappointed with herself. Why did she let these people get to her? She had worked so hard to become the person she was today yet not only could she not succeed in changing the one thing that seemed to matter to everyone, her appearance, her weight, she still let herself be bothered by it. She desperately wanted to be slim and have the confidence that being slim gave you, not the big girl bravado she had now. But it was hard.

The comfort eating had started when she was sixteen, it was an accessible vice and food had been one of her only friends during a traumatic period of her life. Food had always been there for her, never let her down, always left her feeling satisfied and never asked any questions.

She liked nice tastes, who didn't? But Freya knew she liked a lot of nice tastes a lot of the time. And she did not want to spend her life eating Ryvitas or eating ten trifles and chucking them back up again thirty minutes later. That was what her mother had done, probably still did. Freya had been a disappointment to her in so many ways.

Freya wiped her eyes and put her glasses back on her face. Nicholas Kaden and his fancy friends had chosen the wrong person to mess around with this time. He did not know what she was capable of.

Emma returned with the drinks and Freya hurriedly replaced her smile.

"How many people before me on the karaoke?" Freya asked her.

"Two, including Samos from the kebab shop so you have real competition" Emma told her as she passed Freya her glass.

"Let's have a toast" Freya started, holding her glass aloft.

"What to?" Emma asked.

"To Gene and Bob, may they both retire to daytime television and guest appearances on 'Sue Thomas F B Eye'" Freya spoke.

"I'll drink to that" Emma agreed and knocked her glass against Freya's.

"And as for Mr Kaden, well he's going to get what's coming to him" Freya added and took a swig of her drink.

It was close to one o clock in the morning when the two women arrived at 'Petroholis Restaurant' which was the establishment that Yiannis and his parents owned. It was an outside restaurant with a large canopy covering all of the thirty five tables. It was set a road width away from the edge of the harbour and was in the perfect position to entice in custom because of its good view of the sea.

There were still a few people finishing their meals when they arrived. Freya assumed they were locals, as the Greeks did tend to eat a lot later than holidaymakers, mainly due to siestas in the afternoon and working later into the night.

Slim, dark haired Yiannis was wiping down tables when the women entered the restaurant and Mr and Mrs Petroholis were sat at a table with another couple chatting over what looked like a bottle of retsina.

"I return triumphant!" Freya exclaimed loudly and she held aloft a bottle of sparkling wine. She quickly realised that she needed another hand to steady herself when she fell hard against a chair.

"Freya won the karaoke. It was a sing off between her and Samos but Freya's rendition of 'Come on feel the noise' had the whole bar on their feet and won the day" Emma announced as she approached her boyfriend.

"You sound like you have good time" Yiannis spoke, slipping his arms around Emma's waist and kissing her lightly on the lips.

"We did but we missed you" Emma told him sincerely and held him close to her.

"Oh please! Put him down! Where's my hug?" Freya exclaimed and she man handled Emma out of the way and enveloped Yiannis in a giant embrace.

"Hello Freya, it is great to see you. You look well" Yiannis told her as he kissed her cheek.

"Hmm you mean I haven't lost any weight since you last saw me" Freya translated.

"No, I mean you look different, it is your hair I think, a new style" Yiannis remarked, holding her away from him to get a better look.

"Yes, thanks to my fashion adviser here" Freya announced and threw her arms around Emma, very nearly causing her to topple over.

"Freya? Is that you my darling girl?" Mrs Petroholis called as she made her way over to the group.

Mrs Petroholis was a mountain of a Greek woman, six feet tall and almost as broad. She was a stark contrast to her husband who was barely over five foot and of slim build, but together they were an affectionate couple who went out of their way to make people feel welcome in their company.

"Mrs P! It's wonderful to see you" Freya spoke and she let herself be caught up in the arms of Yiannis' mother.

"You look like you have lost weight! You need meatballs at once, come, I get Spiros to make you some, come come" Mrs Petroholis ordered and she pulled Freya towards Yiannis' father.

"Oh Mrs P I've had quite a lot to eat tonight, I'm not sure I could do justice to your meatballs" Freya spoke, secretly ravenous because of all the alcohol she had consumed.

"Hmm you had a lot to drink huh? Then you need more food, Spiros, some meatballs for Freya" Mrs Petroholis ordered her husband.

"Ah Freya, it is good to see you, come, sit down. This is Nikos and Angelica, come, all of you, sit down, I get some food and more drinks" Mr Petroholis announced, moving chairs hurriedly around to accommodate everyone.

"Oh well, if you insist" Freya replied and joined the couple at the table.

"Yiannis, come help in the kitchen" Mr Petroholis ordered him.

"I won't be long" Yiannis told Emma and he followed his father into the kitchen.

"So girls, you have nice food tonight?" Mrs Petroholis asked as she too sat at the table.

"It was nice, we had the sunset table, in the end" Freya told the group.

"You won't believe it but we ended up having our meal with Nicholas Kaden, Gene Bates, Bob Crosby and their film colleagues" Emma announced.

"Oh these Hollywood people, I no impressed with them. They come into village and stir everything up" Mrs Petroholis said waving her hands about.

"That is exactly what I said Mrs P, nearly to the word" Freya told her.

"It can only lead to one thing and that is trouble" Mrs Petroholis concluded.

Freya caught Emma's eye and smiled. Yes it did mean trouble, trouble for Nicholas Kaden the following night.

Chapter Four

Another day, another hangover and another session of rampant lovemaking from the couple in the room above. This time Freya was forced out of her apartment completely, due to the fact that the couple had left open their verandah door and the noise was just as loud, if not louder, when Freya was sat on the balcony.

Freya had a headache and no painkillers so she headed out of 'The Calypso Apartments' to visit the pharmacy. It was nearly nine o clock and Kassiopi was already bustling with delivery lorries for the bars and shops and visitors wanting breakfasts.

The sun was already shining viciously and Freya soon began to wish that she had worn her hat. Sunscreen she had put on early in case she had actually got to sit on her balcony.

As she neared the harbour she saw that the jewellery shop was just opening its doors for business. That fact excited her and she stepped up her pace a little. She was soon at the entrance and walking up the stone steps to enter the shop. At once Freya was surrounded by all manner of rings, bracelets, necklaces and watches. It was a lovely little shop filled with bright, shiny things and Freya just loved being in it.

"Hello there, on holiday again" the dark haired woman who worked in the shop spoke as she entered from the rear.

"Yes, I'm staying with a friend" Freya said, still looking around the shop in awe.

"Then I expect you would like me to get something out for you to look at" the woman said with a smile.

"Oh! It's still here?! I didn't expect for a minute it would still be here" Freya exclaimed in pure excitement.

"Yes, it is still here..........here we are" the woman said and she brought out a tray of rings and placed it on the glass counter.

"It looks even more beautiful than I remember it" Freya remarked as she looked at one particular ring on the tray.

It was a platinum band with a cross shape in diamonds and aquamarine attached to it. It was the most gorgeous item of jewellery that Freya had ever seen.

She had been going to the shop and gazing lovingly at it since she was twenty five. Every time she visited Emma she went to the shop always expecting it to have been sold. It was a one off, an original, hand crafted. And here it still was, five years on.

"You can try it on" the woman reminded her, as she always did.

"No, I don't want to try it on" Freya said quickly.

She never tried it on. It wouldn't be right. She looked at its lustre, watching the light reflecting off its many facets. It was the perfect ring.

"Is it still the same price?" Freya inquired.

"Yes, is the same" the woman answered.

"It's beautiful" Freya said again.

"I can put it by for you" the woman spoke.

"No, don't do that, its fine. Thanks for letting me look again" Freya spoke with a sigh.

The woman returned the tray to the display cabinet and Freya walked towards the door.

"One day a man will come to me and ask for a ring for you and I will tell him with delight which one" the woman called to her.

"Maybe, but not today" Freya answered with a smile and she left the shop.

She doubted anyone would ever buy her that ring because, apart from Emma, she had told no one of her habitual visits to the jewellery shop. It was pathetic to covet something so much, especially when coveting was against all you believed in, but it wasn't about the value of the ring, it represented much more than that. It reminded her of a ring she had had once, a much cheaper, less shiny, but equally cherished ring. No other rings had graced her fingers since. So Freya had decided that she would only have this ring when she thought she was ready for it. And she wasn't ready, not yet.

She walked to the pharmacy, bought some headache pills and a bottle of water and then made her way across the harbour. As she walked she could see, at the side nearest the lace shop, a lot of commotion going on involving a motor cruiser, scores of people and several cameras, some of which were on rails. There was a crowd of people gathered around watching from behind a security cordon.

As Freya got closer she could see Nicholas Kaden and Hilary Polar aboard the boat, dressed in swimming attire and lifejackets.

Freya stopped where she was, at the edge of the ever increasing crowd, and watched the action on the boat. Hilary was having her make up touched up by someone, including having some powder put on her non-existent cleavage which was covered by a red bikini. There was nothing of her in any department, except hair.

Freya took two headache tablets out of the packet and swallowed them down with some of the water as she continued to watch.

Nicholas got up from his sitting position and prepared to do something, although Freya wasn't quite sure what, as she was too far away to hear what was being said. But then a loud hailer announced 'action!'. Gene and Bob plus two men that Freya didn't recognise appeared from inside the boat, there was dialogue (Freya could see their lips moving) and then Gene started grappling with Hilary while Nicholas tried to pull him back. Bob and the two men with him then restrained Nicholas, holding him down on the deck of the boat.

"Cut!"

The people watching all began to clap and Freya wanted to laugh. There was absolutely nothing to be impressed about from what she had seen.

"FREYA! HEY! FREYA!"

Freya looked up at the sound of her name being bellowed from the direction of the boat. People in the crowd began to turn around and look to see who was being called to. It was Nicholas who was hollering at her and Freya's cheeks reddened as all eyes turned to her.

"Hey Roger, can you let her through please?" Nicholas called to the black moustachioed bodyguard from the restaurant the night before.

Freya didn't move, what was he expecting her to do? Rush towards him?

"Freya! Come on, just a few seconds" Nicholas called.

Freya so wished she had worn her hat now a) because her bright blonde hair wouldn't have stood out so much and he might not have seen her and b) because she could have put it over her face right now.

"Freya! Come on! Don't make me come into the crowd with just these Speedos on" Nicholas yelled, removing his sunglasses as he spoke. There was a whoop of excitement from the crowd.

How embarrassing was this? Roger the bodyguard was nearly upon her. People were oo-ing and ah-ing at her, a few had even got their cameras out and were taking photos of her. Reluctantly she took hold of Roger's arm and let him guide her through the crowd as people jostled them to get a better look at her.

"Hey, come up on the boat for a second" Nicholas called as her and Roger arrived at the cordon.

"I'm not coming up on anything! You come down here if you want to speak to me" Freya shouted back to him.

"OK. Do you want a soda?" he asked.

"No! Just stop shouting will you? You're causing a scene" Freya said.

She took a look behind her to see that the crowd had almost doubled in size and there seemed to be twice as many cameras whirring into action.

Nicholas took off his lifejacket and hurried down the ramp of the boat towards her. Freya didn't know where to look, he was wearing nothing but Speedos.

"Hi, did you come down hoping to see me fall in the water?" Nicholas asked, putting his hands on his hips and smiling at her.

"No, I came to the pharmacy and suddenly realised I couldn't actually cross the harbour to get to the bakery. It looks like a cinematic war zone" Freya told him.

She couldn't help but look at him and be a little impressed by his physique. He had well defined muscle all over and a fine covering of hair on his broad chest. He was also very tanned.

"The bakery? You are a bit late for rolls aren't you? Martha got there at 6.00 this morning, just to make sure" Nicholas replied.

"Very amusing. Now did you actually want to say something to me or are you just up for humiliating me again?" Freya wanted to know.

"Yes I did want to say something about tonight" Nicholas told her.

"You've had second thoughts? A better offer?" Freya asked him.

"No, I just wondered if we could make it nine o clock instead of eight? We're going out on the boat in a minute and it's likely to be an all day all evening thing and by the time I get back to my villa.....well nine would be better for me" Nicholas told her.

"Oh right" Freya replied.

How clever of him to cut an hour off the date, he would have to carry out the act for less time now. He was good and was obviously skilled at this kind of thing. Freya had no doubt that he had done this before.

"So is that OK with you?" he questioned.

"Yeh that's OK. Makes no difference to me. I was just wondering if you would have kept me waiting for an hour if we hadn't 'bumped' into each other now" Freya remarked.

"What do you think I would have done?" Nicholas asked her, looking at her seriously.

His eyes were indescribably blue and he had very long dark eyelashes Freya hated herself for noticing.

"I have no idea" Freya replied.

"I'd have left a message at the apartments" he told her.

"You mean Martha would have" Freya responded.

"There are some areas of my life I like to manage myself" Nicholas said.

"You surprise me........look I've got a busy day ahead so I'm going to go" Freya told him.

"OK, but before you do, let's swap cell numbers and then if you get a better offer for tonight or, if I'm running late, no one will be left waiting around like a clown" Nicholas suggested.

"Is that really necessary do you think?" Freya inquired.

"Not going to change your mind about tonight?" Nicholas asked her.

"I'll be there, I'm looking forward to it" Freya responded with a smile.

"Good. Well let's exchange numbers anyway and then, if tonight goes well, we won't have to break up the goodnight kiss to do it" Nicholas told her with a wink.

So he had already decided he was going for at least the Cayman Island masseuse! He had pre-warned her to expect a kiss at the end of the night, the man was a genius.

"Now you have to be kidding me, you never have a mobile phone in those trunks" Freya remarked, her eyes dropping to his crutch.

"Wanna see?" he teased, twanging the elastic.

Freya felt herself going red again. Why did he always seem to get the last word? There were few men who had ever got the last word with her. Sensing her embarrassment Nicholas whistled to someone on the boat.

"Bob, is my cell up there?" he called to Bob Crosby.

Bob Crosby, one of the evil duo who had devalued her, appeared at the side of the boat, the sun gleaming off his balding head.

"Yeh, want me to pass it down?" he called back.

"If you could…………..thanks" Nicholas shouted back as Bob threw down the phone and he caught it.

"OK, shoot" Nicholas said, opening the phone up and getting ready to type.

Freya recited her mobile number and he typed it in.

"Now I've saved you under 'Freya' for now, but you never know, by tomorrow you could be 'Hot Babe'" Nicholas told her in jest.

"Do you know I'm never quite sure whether you're joking or serious" Freya spoke with a shake of her head.

"But it keeps it fresh doesn't it? So, do you want my number?" he asked her.

"If I must" Freya answered and she fished about in her handbag for her phone.

He recited his number and Freya typed it in.

"Now I've saved you under 'Jackass' for now but play your cards right tonight and you could be saved under 'Mr Kaden' tomorrow" Freya told him with a satisfied smile.

"You're good" he admitted with a nod.

"I know, right, is our business concluded?" Freya asked of him.

"All done, so I'll see you tonight, at nine, 'The Calypso Apartments'"

"Yes, meet me at the bar, I'll be the one with the jug of sangria and two straws" Freya said as she headed back towards the cordon.

"Drinking challenges I like" Nicholas told her.

'Not by the end of the night you won't' Freya thought to herself as she waved at him and flashed a smile.

Then she stopped herself in her tracks and turned around to face the boat again.

"Wait! One last thing" she called.

Nicholas turned to face her from halfway up the ramp of the boat.

"Do you have Bruce Willis in your cell phone?" Freya questioned.

"Bruce Willis? In my cell? Come on Freya, they are making cells the size of matchboxes now and Bruce has got to be at least six feet" Nicholas told her with a grin.

"Yippee Kai Ay" Freya responded and she turned to go.

"If I did have his number in my cell would you maybe like me a bit more?" Nicholas called to her.

"If you did I'd ask if I could date him tonight instead" Freya replied as she ducked underneath the cordon.

"You don't mean that, you haven't been able to keep your eyes off me since we met" Nicholas shouted, not caring who heard him.

"Dream on" Freya retorted and she began to walk back through the crowd, which seemed to be even more difficult now that she had spoken to Nicholas as people were grabbing hold of bits of her.

"Are you dating him?" one woman questioned, tugging at Freya's arm.

"No" Freya responded immediately, taking back her arm and trying to manoeuvre her way through the people.

"But you're going out with him tonight?" another person asked, this time a teenaged girl.

"Sadly yes" Freya answered.

"You don't look like a film star's girlfriend" a boy of about ten commented as he stared up at her.

"That's because I'm not, excuse me" Freya spoke, now resorting to pushing people out of her way.

She was feeling slightly claustrophobic with the amount of people around her, penning her in, and the sun beating down on her uncovered head.

"Hi there, I'm Sandra McNeill from 'Shooting Stars' magazine in America, could I have a few minutes of your time Miss.....?" an American voice spoke while two large flashes went off in Freya's eyes.

"God, will you leave me alone?" Freya begged.

"How long have you and Nick been dating?" she continued, getting a pen and pad out of her bag and beginning to jot on it.

"We aren't dating. Look, I'm a nobody, I'm just here on holiday, I have nothing to say to anyone about anything, I just want to get back to my apartment" Freya stated angrily.

"Nobodies don't get invited up onto Nicholas Kaden's motor cruiser" Sandra McNeill commented.

"It's just a prop" Freya responded with a smile.

"It was a prop, but he liked it so much he bought it. He did the same with the villa, he loves this village, but I'm sure you already knew that Miss.....?" Sandra continued.

"No I didn't know that which goes to show that you know far more about him than I do. I really have nothing to tell you unless.........."

Freya's mind was working overtime. This time tomorrow she might have a great deal to tell 'Shooting Stars' magazine, about Nicholas Kaden dating her for a bet organised by Gene Bates and Bob Crosby. How all three Hollywood stars had tried to make her a laughing stock. That should give the film some unwanted publicity and make the millions set to watch it think twice about the morals of its stars.

"Could I take your number?" Freya asked her, getting her mobile phone out.

With Sandra McNeill's number saved into her phone Freya managed to get away from the masses and head up the road towards the travel agency where Emma worked. It was a small office with a glass frontage and outside there were picture boards advertising the various trips the company provided. Inside there was a desk, three chairs, a sofa and a coffee machine.

Freya entered the office quietly and was surprised to see Emma with her head down on the desk seemingly asleep.

"Em? Are you OK?" Freya asked as she approached the desk.

"Oh God, oh sorry, hi, I must have dropped off for five minutes" Emma said, jumping up and trying to wake herself quickly.

"You look awful, do you want some tablets?" Freya asked, offering her the box in her hand.

"No I'm OK" Emma insisted.

"So is it a hangover because I am sure I drank way more than you last night" Freya remarked as she sat down in the chair opposite Emma's desk.

"You definitely did, it's not a hangover, I'm just tired" Emma answered.

"And I don't suppose having me here, with all my issues, is helping" Freya commented.

"No it is helping, it takes my mind off things" Emma insisted, taking a sip from the glass of water on her desk.

"Em, I asked you yesterday if everything was OK and you told me about money being tied up in the business and wanting your own place etc. but is there something else?" Freya asked her seriously.

"I'm pregnant" Emma stated simply.

Freya's jaw dropped and she took a sharp breath inward.

"Oh my God" Freya said before she could stop herself.

"Yes, oh my God" Emma echoed.

"No I meant 'oh my God' as in the 'oh my God' you would say if you were happy about something, surprised but happy. It's great news! A baby! You're going to have a baby!" Freya exclaimed and she jumped up, went around the desk and took Emma by the hands. She pulled her out of her chair and they began jumping up and down like two excited schoolgirls, much to the amusement of passers by.

"Oh Em, this is exciting news! I am going to be an aunty, well kind of, the nearest I will ever get to being one. What does Yiannis say?" Freya asked, smiling at her friend.

"That's one of the problems, I haven't been able to tell him yet. It's just not how I planned things Freya. You know me, I am a planner, I've always been a planner. I have lists of things with tick boxes for everything and I had a list for this which read 'buy house', 'get married', 'have baby'. I know it's probably an agenda everyone has, but, being a planner, my plan should have been foolproof" Emma spoke with a sigh.

"So what are you saying? You haven't told Yiannis because baby has made an appearance at position number 1 instead of position number 3?" Freya questioned.

"Yes. No. Well partly. He is working so hard to save money so we can get a place and get married and now this is going to change everything. We will be even more tied to his parents than we are now" Emma explained.

"But Em you will have a beautiful son or daughter who will probably have Yiannis' dark hair and your blue eyes and you are going to be a completely amazing mother" Freya told her.

"Do you think so?" Emma asked.

"Well put it this way, you've been mothering me since we met and look how I've turned out. OK, maybe a bad example" Freya replied.

"I just wanted to do things properly, traditionally, it was so important to me" Emma spoke.

"What's important is that you are having a baby with a wonderful man who you love and who adores you" Freya said matter of factly.

"I will tell Yiannis, it's just I wish we could get married before the baby comes, I think that is more important to me than having a place of our own. Maybe it's my mother's voice telling me it's immoral to have a baby before you are married or perhaps it's just the traditionalist in me" Emma said in deep thought.

"Then why don't you get married before the baby comes? You must have some months to go"

"Seven" Emma told her.

"Seven months, well there you go, who can't organise a wedding in seven months?" Freya queried.

"It isn't the organisation, it's the money. I don't want to get married at the town hall, I want a church wedding with a blessing on the beach, a white dress with bridesmaids and fancy cars and a big party with a giant cake" Emma explained.

"My parents should have swapped me for you because they would have loved all that" Freya replied.

"But it's all a dream, I can forget about that now" Emma said with a sigh.

"Maybe not. How much do you think 'Shooting Stars' magazine would pay for a really juicy story about Nicholas Kaden?" Freya asked her.

"What sort of story?" Emma asked.

"How he and his co-stars got involved in 'Betting for Bedding'" Freya told her with a smirk.

"You wouldn't?! Sell the story to a magazine? That would seriously tarnish his image" Emma told her.

"But it would also buy some serious wedding cake. How do you fancy four tiers? Chocolate? Coffee? Something fruity?" Freya asked her.

"I think you are the best friend a girl could wish for" Emma concluded and she put her arms around Freya and hugged her.

"Right back at you" Freya replied, holding Emma tight.

Chapter Five

"I don't know what to wear" Freya spoke into her mobile phone that night.

She was sat on her bed in her room at 'The Calypso Apartments' with her entire selection of clothes from Agatha's boutique strewn around her. She had been trying to decide what to wear for almost an hour.

"Does it matter? I mean the guy is a loser remember, he is dating you as some stupid game with his stupid friends" Emma's voice answered.

"Yeh I know. I just, I'm a bit worried, about the photographers, you know, having my picture taken. There were people taking photos at the harbour today and I have to bury my face in my sunhat" Freya spoke nervously.

"Oh God, yes, I hadn't even thought, well your hair is very different and in that case I think you should wear the red outfit, the one with the bandeau top and wide leg trousers" Emma stated.

"Because then everyone will be focussing on my bust rather than my face or trying to work out why Kellogg's have chosen a size 20 to advertise Special K. Good idea!" Freya replied.

"And the black shoes and bag, not the gold" Emma added.

"Got you. OK, thanks, well I have twenty minutes to finish getting ready so I'd better go. I'm bloody starving" Freya admitted.

"Good, that means you will be able to eat him out of pocket. Have two starters or better than that, have a meze all to yourself" Emma suggested.

"You are full of good ideas tonight. So did you brief Zorba and Lorraine?" Freya checked.

"All briefed and ready to go and I had a word with Samos too because I presumed you would be dropping into the kebab shop for a gyros to end the evening" Emma replied.

"If he manages to hold out that long" Freya responded.

"Well good luck and I want a full run down of events first thing tomorrow" Emma told her.

"It goes without saying and don't you go working too hard at that restaurant tonight, rest is important you know" Freya told her.

"I know, stop worrying, you're the one who is mothering me now" Emma declared.

"Perhaps I should have done it earlier, we could have had a contraception talk" Freya joked.

"You're not funny, go on, get dressed and get on with the date" Emma ordered.

"OK, I'll call you tomorrow, bye" Freya spoke and ended the call.

Red top and trousers it was. Freya put the outfit on, brushed her hair, added a hairclip and cleaned her glasses. She looked fine. She still looked size 20 but she looked a well groomed size 20.

It was nearly nine o clock and she had never been one for turning up late so Freya made her way downstairs and out into the pool complex where the bar was situated. Or should that have been where the bar was usually situated. The bar had disappeared. The reason that Freya could no longer see it was because a crowd of people, four or five deep, were stood around it. Freya knew that it was not a queue to be served and could only assume that Nicholas was in the middle of the crowd.

Before she could move any further towards the bar Roger the bodyguard appeared, took her arm and guided her in the opposite direction, towards the back gate of the apartments.

"What's happening?" Freya demanded to know when Roger had finally stopped shepherding her and they were outside the grounds.

"Nick apologises. It got kind of crazy while he was waiting for you, so he's just going to sign these autographs and then meet you in the car" Roger explained.

"Car? What car?" Freya inquired.

"This car M'am" Roger answered.

Freya looked up the road to see a black Mercedes with privacy glass heading towards them.

"What is going on?" Freya demanded to know as the car pulled up in front of them.

"If you could just wait inside M'am, to avoid any unwanted attention" Roger spoke as he opened the back door for her.

"I'm not getting in there. For all I know it could drive off and I'd end up in the bottom of the Aegean with a plastic sack over my head. This was not the arrangement, I was supposed to be organising the night" Freya exclaimed and she slammed the door shut.

"Nick said you might be a little reluctant, I'll just call him on his cell" Roger spoke and he reached in his pocket for his mobile phone.

"Let me speak to him the minute he answers" Freya ordered, getting madder by the second.

She didn't know what to do now. How was she going to make him have a hellish evening if he was calling all the shots? She had been planning this all day, how dare he take over!

"Nick, we're having a bit of trouble with the car thing, like you said, what would you like me to do?" Roger politely spoke into the phone.

"Give me that.............now you listen here, what the Hell is going on?! You only saw me this morning, you didn't mention a car then, what is happening?" Freya yelled into the phone.

"I hadn't organised the car then, it was an idea I had on the boat today when I was thinking about surprising you with something" Nicholas' voice replied.

"I don't like surprises"

"Oh come on, all women love surprises" Nicholas answered.

"Not this one. Look I am not getting in this car until you tell me where we are going" Freya ordered.

"OK, so if I tell you where we are going you'll get in the car?" Nicholas asked.

"Seeing as I am now being hounded by photographers and the bar of my apartments has become a meeting place for your groupies, I don't think I have much choice" Freya replied.

"I love it when you're feisty" he said.

"Where are we going?" Freya repeated.

"Two minutes out of the village, 'Harry's Place', do you know it?"

"'Harry's Place'? Do I know it? I used to work there" Freya told him with satisfaction.

"I know, I was just kidding with you. Harry told me you helped him out there, nice guy, did you know there is still a photo of you on the wall, great specs" Nicholas continued.

"Fine, we'll go to 'Harry's Place', I'll get in the damn car but you'd better not be long because I am a whisker away from changing my mind" Freya replied.

"I just love all your English expressions, 'a whisker away', I really must try and sneak that into a script" he responded.

Freya ignored his comment and handed the mobile phone back to Roger. She folded her arms across her chest in annoyance. What was she going to do? All her plans had gone to waste, gyros was the only thing she might still be able to accomplish. It was a disaster.

"Yes, uh huh, yes I will make sure she gets in the damn car" Roger spoke into the phone, much to Freya's irritation.

He ended the call and opened the back door of the car for the second time.

"M'am" he spoke, inviting her to get in.

"No offence to your perfect manners Roger, but call me Freya, M'am makes me sound like the First Lady" Freya spoke and she got into the car.

"I will try to remember that" Roger replied and shut the door behind her.

Leather seats, an in car DVD system, drinks cabinet and multicoloured mood lights made the car more of a house on wheels. It didn't impress Freya, but that didn't stop her wanting to press all the buttons. She chose the button in the centre of the cherry veneer panel and suddenly the speakers vibrated loudly and the whole car was filled with the sound of Barry White crooning 'I love you just the way you are'.

Freya panicked, she couldn't get it to stop no matter which button she tried. It was so loud it was hurting her ears. She had no choice but to bang on the dividing screen in the hope of assistance.

Roger's face appeared and before she had a chance to say anything he shouted:-

"Square button on the door to stop and the dial for volume control"

Freya hurriedly turned down the music to a more subtle level.

"And if I've had enough of Barry White?" Freya inquired.

"Can you ever have too much of the Walrus of Love?" Roger asked her.

"I've lasted a minute or so and believe me I'm all Barryed out" Freya replied.

"Flip open the panel in front of you and there is a list of CDs to select from" Roger informed her.

"Got any 50 Cent?" Freya asked him with a grin.

"Most probably" he responded and the dividing screen slid back into position again.

Freya, feeling rebellious, selected 'Guns n Roses' and opened the drinks cabinet. There was a wide selection of wines, beers and spirits and Freya chose a brandy. She unscrewed the bottle and took a swig.

The back door opened suddenly and Nicholas slipped into the seat beside her. He was wearing khaki coloured linen trousers and a beige linen shirt with brown leather sandals. It was a smart, yet casual outfit and Freya noted that he was wearing a rather fragrant aftershave which her nose did not disapprove of.

"Starting without me? Pass me a Jack Daniels" Nicholas said to her, noticing the small bottle of brandy in her hand.

"Here. The measures are too small by the way, you should complain" Freya responded, finishing up her drink and passing him one.

"You're right but I usually have two........OK Mikey, let's go" Nicholas spoke, pressing the intercom which connected to the front of the car.

"I'm still mad by the way" Freya stated as the car set off.

"I expected nothing less. Guns n Roses, good choice" Nicholas commented with a nod.

It took no more than five minutes to arrive at 'Harry's Place' as it was only a mile out of the village. The car pulled up outside and Freya went to get out. Nicholas touched her arm to stop her.

"Hang on, let a guy do things properly" he spoke, opening his door.

"You aren't going to hold the door open for me are you?" Freya exclaimed with a laugh.

"And what if I am?"

"This is the 21st century, you don't need to do that anymore, the world is so over Charles Dickens or didn't you know?" Freya continued.

"Well Dickensian or not I like to treat a lady properly so you will sit there and let me do this" Nicholas insisted.

Freya didn't reply. She knew he was trying to charm her and she couldn't help but wonder whether he treated all the women he dated to this performance, or just the ones he took bets on.

Nicholas opened the door and took her hand to help her out of the car.

"Now, wasn't that nice?" he remarked, smiling at her.

"Yes I feel so much more of a lady now, if only I had remembered my silk gloves and dance card" Freya responded.

"Shall we?" Nicholas asked and he offered her his arm.

Freya took it and they headed towards the door of the restaurant.

"Roger is coming in with us but he won't sit with us and he's very discreet, you'll hardly notice him" Nicholas told her as he opened the door for her.

"He can sit with us if he likes, he's quite amusing" Freya replied.

"So now you want to date Roger as well as Bruce Willis?" Nicholas asked her.

"Not at the same time obviously, because that would be rude and very unladylike" Freya answered.

Before Nicholas could make further comment Harry came out to greet them in the foyer. He was a short, rotund man with grey hair and glasses and a smile as wide as the River Tyne, which was the river of his town of origin.

"Freya! Hello pet, don't you look well?" he greeted in his broad Geordie accent which was still present despite him having lived in Corfu for many years.

"You look well too Harry. Is Margot here?" Freya inquired, speaking of Harry's wife.

"No not tonight pet, she's sorry to be missing you, but she's gone to Corfu Town with some of her girl pals for a meal and a show" Harry informed her.

"Well maybe I will pop up and see her later in the week" Freya spoke.

"She would like that. Hello Nick, nice to see you again" Harry said and shook Nicholas by the hand.

"Hi Harry, so is everything arranged?" Nicholas asked him.

"Yes, just like you asked for, I'll show you to your table" Harry said.

Harry led the way through the main restaurant where several people were dining. There were plenty of whispers and nudges the moment Nicholas, Freya and Roger walked amongst them.

Harry led them to the courtyard outside where all the tables had been cleared away, except for half a dozen which had been put together to form one larger table. It was set with a white tablecloth, candles and a dozen white roses. It was the most beautiful table setting that Freya had ever seen. There was also a cooler housing champagne, stood next to the table.

Nicholas smiled as he saw Freya's face light up.

"Right, you're all set. I'll start bringing out the food in about fifteen minutes" Harry spoke.

"That will be perfect" Nicholas replied.

Harry left them and Nicholas turned to Roger.

"I'll be just inside, sampling some of the stew, just call me if you need anything" Roger said to him.

"Thanks Roger" Nicholas replied.

Freya walked up to the table and inhaled deeply as she smelt the roses. They were gorgeous and smelt velvety, soft and sweet. She had always loved the outside eating area at Harry's. It had a pergola style roof with flowering vines making a leafy canopy and there were lantern style lights suspended from it. At the height of the summer season Harry had live music in this area and when Freya had worked there the events had been extremely popular.

"You like the table?" Nicholas asked her as he stood beside her.

"It's very nice. So did you actually do any work today or did you spend the whole time thinking of ways to impress me?" Freya wanted to know.

"Am I impressing you?" he asked her.

"Is there more to come?"

"You'll have to wait and see"

"Then I will let you know at the end of the night" Freya answered.

She sat down at the table and let Nicholas pour her some champagne. He sat opposite her and raised her glass.

"To our first date" Nicholas toasted.

"May it end without bloodshed" Freya added as she raised her glass and knocked it against his.

"Right, so where shall we start? A first date is usually about getting to know one another so do you want to begin? Ladies first after all" Nicholas suggested.

"You want to know about me" Freya spoke, taking a sip of champagne.

"Yes, of course" he replied.

"I'm pretty much what you see is what you get, where would you like me to start?" Freya asked.

"I don't know, start where you feel comfortable. Put it this way I was going to skip mentioning my alcohol and prostitute addiction and my bit part in 'Katie does Kansas'" Nicholas told her.

"Again not sure if you are joking or being serious" Freya replied.

"I'll keep you guessing. So tell me about your job, you're a photographer right?" Nicholas spoke.

"Yes, I suppose I gave it away rushing out to snap the sunset last night" Freya answered.

"Well there was that and the fact that Emma told us. So what is your speciality?" Nicholas asked her.

"Weddings and schools, that's what pays the bills. Occasionally I get referred to more illustrious clients and get to travel" Freya told him.

"But what's your favourite subject? What are you passionate about? I presume there must have been something that sparked your interest in photography" Nicholas asked her.

"It's the only thing I've ever been any good at. I prefer to take photos of scenes rather than people if I'm honest. Seascapes, coastlines, grassland, the sky, sunsets are a big thing of mine" Freya answered.

Why was she telling him this? He wasn't really interested, it was just small talk, but something was driving her to answer his questions.

"So why not concentrate on the things you enjoy? Why the weddings and schoolchildren?" Nicholas wanted to know.

"Like I said, it pays the bills and you have to be really talented to make a living out of the other stuff and I don't think I am quite that good" Freya told him.

"Well perhaps you just haven't been discovered by the right person yet" Nicholas suggested.

"Maybe. So what about you? Why an actor? Did you put on performances for the local neighbourhood at the age of 3 and dress yourself up as Robin Hood or something?" Freya asked.

"I could tell you that but it wouldn't be true. I had no interest in acting at 3 or any other age, I was too interested in playing ice hockey, that was my big thing" Nicholas told her.

"So why aren't you an ice hockey player?" Freya inquired.

"I gave it up. After my parents died I pretty much gave up everything. I was at Harvard, studying law and I was doing well, but when my parents died I dropped out. But, when I think back on it now, it really wasn't me anyhow. I might have made a good lawyer but it would have bored me stupid" Nicholas spoke.

"I'm sorry, about your parents, was it an accident or something?" Freya wanted to know, genuinely interested.

"Yeh, a truck ran a red light, they didn't stand a chance, my little brother was in the car too and he thankfully came out of it without a scratch" Nicholas replied.

"Well thank God for that" Freya responded.

"Yeh, he was very lucky. Anyway, although there was life insurance it wasn't enough to put us both through school so I dropped out and got a job. I did anything just to get food on the table and make sure Matt had everything he needed just like my Mom and Dad would have done. First I was a cab driver, then I was a barman, then I was a chef but they found out I couldn't really cook so then I was a waiter. One day, this guy comes into the restaurant and hands me a business card and tells me that he is auditioning people for an advertisement for 'Cheesy Twangers'" Nicholas spoke.

"Cheesy what?" Freya queried with a laugh.

"Cheesy Twangers. They are this disgusting tasting potato chip, in production for about a year and I've never seen a packet since. Anyway, I got the job and believe me the commercial was far more cheesy than the chips. After that I got a phone call and was invited to audition for a small part in a movie called 'The Devil's Curse'. And that was my first movie and my big break" Nicholas explained.

"I don't remember seeing that film" Freya admitted.

"Don't watch it! It's terrible and I have a freaky hairstyle. God knows what anyone saw in my performance to offer me other roles but they did and the rest, as they say, is history" Nicholas concluded.

It was just as he finished that Harry and two of his waiters brought out huge platters of food.

"I wasn't sure what you liked so I ordered everything" Nicholas told her.

"You're kidding! I know I like my food but there are over fifty dishes on Harry's menu" Freya exclaimed.

"Sixty six, if you are counting sides" Nicholas answered.

It was at least five minutes before Harry and his team had finished putting the food on the table.

"This is a feast isn't it?" Nicholas remarked as he surveyed the table.

"I can't believe you ordered the whole menu. Why?" Freya exclaimed.

"Why not? Shall we start I'm kind of hungry" Nicholas remarked and he began helping himself to the food.

"Yeh me too" Freya agreed.

They filled their plates up with a variety of dishes and began to eat. All the food was delicious and the champagne was also slipping down nicely. Freya had almost forgotten that this date was fake. Almost, but not quite.

"Do you enjoy what you do or is there something inside you that really wishes you were still driving a cab?" Freya asked him as she ate some bread and tzatziki.

"The acting I love, like you I've found something I'm good at and I've stuck with it. That wasn't supposed to sound conceited by the way, but there are a lot of people in this industry who can't act at all and are making a fortune out of it. I consider myself lucky to be able to do it well and not feel like a fraud" Nicholas told her.

"What about the having a bodyguard around you and photographers hassling you all the time? Do you enjoy that?" Freya asked.

"Would anyone? No, I loathe it, it's a major downside to what I do. Would you want your face in a magazine when you'd been caught on camera at 7.00am going to the store in your jogging pants with a three day growth of stubble?" Nicholas inquired.

"Oh God, anything more than a two day growth of stubble and I would be beside myself" Freya replied with a smile.

"But you got the jogging pants connection" Nicholas stated.

"I might have. So what about the money? It must be nice being able to spend what you like and not have to worry, like ordering an entire menu from a restaurant" Freya remarked.

"I enjoy having the money, I would be lying if I said I didn't, but I could live without it. I mean you are talking to someone who raised his teenaged brother on restaurant leftovers and went to the sales at Wal-Mart to clothe us both. I wouldn't want to live like that again but I could" Nicholas answered.

Freya nodded and helped herself to some Greek sausages.

"But I really don't want to be the only one talking tonight, over to you" Nicholas told her.

"Oh I really don't know what to say. I'm not used to talking about myself. I tried once, on the tube, this little old lady started up a conversation like I was her long lost niece or something and I had had a bad day so I started talking, telling her all sorts and by the time we got to Embankment she was asleep. We'd only travelled from Waterloo, it's like one stop" Freya admitted, taking a sip of her drink.

"Well I promise not to fall asleep. Why don't you tell me about your family?" Nicholas suggested.

"Well, um, I'd really rather not talk about them, it's a bit of a sore subject" Freya told him.

"Oh?" he questioned.

"I don't see them that's all. I believe in America kids can divorce their parents, well I would do that with mine if I could, but instead we just don't communicate anymore, which equates to the same thing anyway" Freya answered.

"OK, well, subject closed then. So how about hobbies, that should be safe ground" Nicholas said.

"I don't really have any. If I'm not working I'm sleeping, or trying to sleep, or watching TV" Freya told him.

"Sounds to me like you work too hard. Now you know what they say about all work and no play Freya" Nicholas spoke.

"So I'm dull now am I?"

"Not yet but you really need to play more. Perhaps it's something we can work on" he responded with a smile.

"And remind me, your hobbies are?" she asked.

"Hobbies are overrated" he responded with a grin.

"See! You don't have any either" Freya said with a laugh.

"I do have them, I just don't get time for them. If I'm not filming I'm learning scripts and if I'm not doing that I'm doing interviews or if I'm not doing that I'm in the gym" Nicholas told her.

"Ah ha! The gym is a hobby" Freya exclaimed.

"It's only a hobby if you enjoy it. I hate it, I'd much rather be reading a good book or going out on my motorbike or something" he admitted.

"You have a motorbike? I have a motorbike, what have you got?" Freya asked excitedly.

"A Harley" he responded.

"I should have guessed"

"They're fun though aren't they? When I'm out on the bike it's like there's nothing else, just me, the bike and the air around me" Nicholas told her.

"It's a great place to think and it's relaxing in a noisy, exhilarating kind of way" Freya spoke.

"Yeh, you're right" he agreed.

"So have you hired a bike over here yet?" Freya questioned.

"No, to be honest I haven't had a lot of time to myself. We are only here for two more weeks and then we go to mainland Greece again" Nicholas informed her.

"The mainland is nice but it's not as picturesque as the islands" Freya spoke.

"No, I agree, and this village, Kassiopi, is like the jewel in the crown of this island as far as I'm concerned"

"Is that why you bought a villa here?" Freya inquired.

"News travels fast. Who told you that?" Nicholas asked.

"It's the word on the street" Freya said, not wanting to make any reference to 'Shooting Stars' magazine.

"Well your source is correct. I've bought Villa Kamia" Nicholas told her.

"I know it. It's beautiful, right on the headland, you must have fantastic views" Freya spoke, knowing where the villa was located, with unrivalled views of the ocean.

"Photo worthy definitely. You should come up and take some pictures" Nicholas offered.

Freya didn't respond. Who was he trying to kid? After tonight she would never see him again.

"Is the food OK?" Nicholas asked her.

"It's lovely" Freya answered.

"You've gone quiet on me Freya"

"No I haven't, me and quiet, never been heard in the same sentence"

"Perhaps you are feeling some disappointment because I didn't come dressed in my Speedos" Nicholas joked.

"I'm devastated, can't you tell?" she answered.

"Then perhaps you need something to compensate for the loss" Nicholas suggested.

He put his fingers to his lips and whistled. At the sound of that command two men, one with a mandolin and one with a *bouzouki,* entered from the restaurant and moved into the courtyard. Both bowed politely to the table and began to play.

"You are crazy! What is this all about?" Freya exclaimed as the music filled the air.

"I decided that you were the type of woman to appreciate Greek culture so I thought I would bring some of it to our evening" Nicholas told her, smiling at her excitement.

"I do love traditional Greek music" Freya admitted.

"I confess, Harry told me. He also said that when you worked here you very nearly ran off with the mandolin player. He quoted you as saying 'who cares what he looks like, have you seen what he can do with his fingers'" Nicholas spoke.

"How long did you spend talking to Harry? Has he divulged all the confidential things I ever told him during that period of my life? There must be employment laws about that kind of thing" Freya questioned.

"I don't think he told me everything, I got the feeling he was still holding out on me on some things, it was the twinkle in his eye that got me suspicious" Nicholas said.

"There was no need for you to go to all this trouble" Freya stated with a heavy sigh.

"It wasn't any trouble, besides I had fun arranging it all" Nicholas told her.

Why was he doing this? Did he think the more surprises he provided her with the more chance he had of getting her into bed? It was sick. Money was of no significance to him, he had said so, and he had devalued it even more by forking out a fortune on a date for the sake of winning a few favours from his co-stars.

"Dance with me?" Nicholas asked her, as the music being played turned into a slow lament.

This was all wrong, she shouldn't be here. She should be back in the village watching him eat a meal infused with chilli powder.

"Come on, I know you're one for dancing" Nicholas said, getting up from his chair and standing in front of her.

"Harry tell you that too?" Freya snapped.

"Hey, come on, dance with me, it'll be fun" Nicholas insisted and he took her hand and pulled her gently from her seat.

"Looks like I don't have a choice" Freya remarked as Nicholas put one arm around Freya's waist and held her other hand in his.

"So, am I going some way to making you change your opinion of me? Can you now see I'm just a regular guy?" Nicholas asked her.

"I thought we were dancing not talking" Freya replied.

"Can't we do both?" Nicholas suggested.

"Look, the dinner was really nice, the music is great, it's just...." Freya started.

He smelt so nice, of musk and spice and his hand was warm in hers. She could feel his breath on her neck and the firmness of his body close to hers. It was then that it struck her exactly what was wrong with this date. She wanted it to be real. And that realisation scared her to death.

What was the matter with her? She had formed her opinion of him before she had met him. He was a stuck up, arrogant arse who had too much money and too little concern for anyone else. Except he didn't seem like that, tonight he had been interesting and funny and he was easy to talk to. But it was all a big charade and that made the fact that he had been fun and interesting even worse because it had all been a performance. He was good at what he did, he had said so, he was a professional. He was using her and that made him even worse than Russell.

"What is it? I can hear your mind working overtime" Nicholas spoke, fixing her with his perfect blue eyes.

"Why are you doing this?" Freya questioned, giving him an opportunity to come clean.

"Doing what?" Nicholas asked as they continued to dance.

"The table, the food, the music, making sure everything is perfect" Freya explained.

"Because I want everything to be perfect" Nicholas replied.

"Why?" Freya inquired.

"Well who wouldn't want a first date to be perfect?" Nicholas responded.

"What is this first date business? We both know there isn't going to be a second date" Freya announced and she let go of him.

"Let a guy down gently won't you? I thought it was going well. You know, all I really wanted from tonight was for you to give me a clean slate to start from, see how we got on" Nicholas told her.

They were stood opposite each other, in the middle of the courtyard while the musicians continued to play their instruments, trying desperately not to be distracted by what was going on in front of them.

"All you wanted from tonight was to get me into bed and collect your prize from Gene and Bob" Freya screamed at the top of her voice, just as the players came to the end of a song.

It was so quiet you could have heard a pin drop.

Chapter Six

Nicholas looked at her and shook his head. He put one hand to his mouth as if in thought and then he turned to the musicians.

"Can you just give us five minutes guys?" he asked them.

"It will take more than five minutes for me to tell you exactly what I think of you" Freya spoke, her body shaking with anger.

"Oh Freya" Nicholas said with a sigh when the musicians had gone. He put his hands to his head and took a deep breath as if wondering what he was going to do next.

"I know about the bet, I overheard Bob and Gene laughing about it. They had bet you to date 'the prize pig', they were practically wetting themselves they found it so funny. I was hurt and upset and humiliated. I'm surprised you didn't ask them to raise the stakes, I mean Demi Moore gets offered a million to sleep with Robert Redford and you get offered a couple of tacky holidays and the services of some Canadian call girls, didn't you find that insulting? Particularly as I am no Demi Moore" Freya continued, tears forming in her eyes even though she was trying hard to fight it.

"I should have told you, I'm sorry" Nicholas spoke.

"What? Cut me in on the deal? Well it would have been something I suppose, but slightly too close to prostitution for my liking and for too little, I mean I really would get them to revise their idea of the going rate for fat girls these days" Freya answered.

"Can we sit down? Have another drink? Come on, have some more champagne and let me explain" Nicholas said and he picked up Freya's glass and the bottle of champagne and began filling it up.

"I don't want any more pissing champagne, it makes me feel sick, this whole fake date makes me feel sick. I mean I can't believe a thing you have told me tonight, I highly suspect your parents are alive and well and have retired to the Florida Keys" Freya shouted.

"Believe me, they aren't living it up in a retirement complex" Nicholas replied.

"Aren't you going to try and defend yourself? Tell me it was all a joke and you didn't mean any harm?" Freya questioned, staring at him.

"I don't have to defend myself because I haven't done anything wrong. I should have come clean about the bet first thing, when I got into the car tonight" Nicholas said, taking a swig of his drink.

"You should have thought more of me and told them to piss off with their pathetic bets" Freya said loudly.

"I did. What do you think I am trying to tell you? I told them it was pathetic, that they were acting like two kids in kindergarten and I wanted no part in it. I did a bet with Gene, once, a long time ago on the last film we worked together on. It was stupid and I was very, very drunk" Nicholas informed her.

"Do you know how sad you sound?" Freya asked him.

"I told them tonight that I wouldn't be involved in any bet because it was stupid and they ought to know better and also because by the end of the evening I had already decided that I wanted to ask you out" Nicholas told her.

"I'm not following this now" Freya replied.

"Freya this isn't anything to do with Gene and Bob or any bet, I asked you out because I wanted to go out with you. I was going to tell you about the bet because I didn't want something like this to happen, but I decided not to mention it because I didn't want you to know what they had said about you, because it's all crap" Nicholas spoke, sounding sincere.

"This is stupid, la, la, la, la, not listening" Freya stated, unable to take in what he was saying and covering her ears with her hands.

"What's stupid? I like you, why is that so hard to believe? When you burst into the restaurant last night and tore a strip off me I couldn't take my eyes off you. I didn't know what to say to you. You were like this big ball of energy, full of opinions, and I just knew that I wanted to get to know you a bit better" Nicholas attempted to explain.

"This is all part of the act isn't it?" Freya spoke.

"Freya there is no act. This is me, this is it, I'm just a normal guy, trying to spend an evening getting to know you" Nicholas insisted.

Freya shook her head. This was crazy, Nicholas Kaden, the Hollywood actor, looking and smelling so good, having organised a romantic dinner with flowers, candles and music was telling her he really liked her. She couldn't believe it, this had to be a sure fire way for him to win the bet. He was trying to convince her he was genuine so he was one step closer to moving in for the kill, and the glory.

"I think you're terrific" Nicholas told her.

"Stop it, I've heard enough" Freya answered.

"You're mad at me?" Nicholas questioned.

"Yes"

"Why? I'm trying to be honest with you" Nicholas insisted.

"I don't know what to think, it's too confusing" Freya stated with a deep breath.

What had supposed to happen was for her to get him to drink too much ouzo, make him eat the doctored dinner and dance at Zorba's Greek Dancing bar. She was supposed to be teaching him a lesson for taking liberties with her.

"What's confusing?" Nicholas questioned.

"This, all of this, you, the meal, the organisation this must have taken" Freya spoke, sitting down on the wall at the side of the courtyard.

"Look, what do I have to gain by lying to you?" Nicholas asked her.

"Hmmm, what was the top prize again? Ah yes, the fortnight skiing and indulging yourself with the local milkmaids" Freya answered.

"I hate skiing and anyway, I don't think there's much chance of winning the top prize now do you?" Nicholas spoke.

"No" Freya agreed.

Nicholas came and sat next to her on the wall, his drink in his hands.

"So you heard them say I had accepted the bet did you?" Nicholas asked her.

"Well no, but they said...."Freya started.

"And you had such a low opinion of me it seemed natural that I would do something like that. Well, I suppose I can't blame you, I mean as I said, I did do it once, when I was drunk, in Morocco, when they tried to set me up with a man in drag" Nicholas said.

Freya couldn't help but burst out laughing. Nicholas joined in her laughter and smiled at her as she looked back at him.

"I don't know what to say, I don't know what I believe, it isn't every day I get people laying bets on me, I have no previous experience to draw on" Freya told him, her tone turning serious.

"Do you know, I think you want this date to have been fiction. I think that if you let yourself believe that it was real it would freak you out so much you wouldn't be able to deal with it" Nicholas spoke.

"Don't flatter yourself" Freya retorted.

"I think you and I have a connection" Nicholas continued.

"I think you are deluded" Freya replied.

"Well I know that I felt something the minute you walked up to my table at the restaurant. I don't know what it was but it was something I wanted to pursue. I think you felt something too but you are too frightened to admit it" Nicholas carried on.

His words made her skin prickle. He was looking at her as he spoke and he was sat just inches away, making her stiffen with what could only be described as excitement. She didn't know what to do.

"So what are we going to do? We have all this food, we have two musicians waiting in the wings and we have Roger halfway through a bowl of stew, you can't really want to break up the party" Nicholas spoke, his words cutting through the tension.

"I'm having trouble dealing with this, I wasn't prepared for having a date, I was prepared for revenge" Freya told him.

"God I am so glad I organised this, I could be in hospital right now" Nicholas remarked.

"So you asked me out on a proper date, because you liked me, because you found me attractive?" Freya asked him.

"Yes. The attitude I wasn't quite sure about, but I decided to run with it" Nicholas replied.

"God, do you know, I really think you're telling the truth, either that or you're a really good actor" Freya responded.

"Can't it be both? Give a guy a break" Nicholas begged her.

"Get me another drink, I'm too sober to even consider this" Freya ordered him.

"Come sit back at the table, have some more to eat, I'll get the duo back, you know you want to" Nicholas told her, standing up and taking hold of her hands.

Freya stood up and let him walk her back to the table. She sat down, unable to take it what was happening, this hadn't been on her agenda at all.

"Just so you know, Gene and Bob are not friends of mine, they're just colleagues who I have to get along with. It's the same as working in an office, there are people you like and people you don't much care for" Nicholas told her as he handed her another full glass of champagne.

"Well I don't much care for them" Freya stated.

"I can understand that and I agree, they definitely think too much of themselves" Nicholas agreed.

"But you're different?" Freya questioned.

"I keep telling you, I'm just a guy in a strange larger than life world. To be really honest with you, this is the first date I've been on in over three years" Nicholas spoke.

"Now that I don't believe" Freya answered.

"It's true, I don't get a chance to date and again, being honest, I'm not too in to dating. I find it difficult" Nicholas said.

"What?! You, the famous celebrity who could charm the birds from the trees, finds dating difficult!" Freya exclaimed.

"That's right, mock me, I have confidence issues too you know" Nicholas responded.

"You have confidence issues! This is too much, how can someone who looks like you have any sort of confidence issue?" Freya wanted to know.

"Underneath this tough exterior I'm a shy guy trying to break out" Nicholas said with half a smile.

"I am the one who has confidence issues, about a million of them" Freya stated.

"And I have no idea why" Nicholas responded, taking a sip of his drink.

"No?" Freya asked, thinking it was completely obvious.

"No, I mean I see you Freya. All of you. And I really like what I see" Nicholas told her looking straight at her.

Freya swallowed. It was by far the nicest thing anyone had ever said to her and it had sounded like he meant it.

"Shall I get the musicians back?" Nicholas asked her.

"That would be nice" Freya agreed.

The musicians came back and after about another half an hour Harry brought them dessert which was one of each choice on the menu. Freya didn't know what to choose.

"You didn't say earlier how you are with the whole dating thing? Have you dated much recently?" Nicholas asked her, taking a mouthful of ice cream.

"No. Actually, I was in a relationship up until recently" Freya told him.

"What happened? If that isn't too personal a question for a first date" Nicholas asked her.

"I think he realised that the sort of person he was involved with wasn't really what he wanted" Freya responded.

"Had you been going out long?" Nicholas questioned.

"18 months" Freya stated.

"Then it was serious" Nicholas remarked.

"No, actually I don't think it was serious, I think we were both just marking time" Freya spoke.

"So who ended it?" Nicholas asked.

"Does it matter?" Freya replied.

"No, sorry I was just being inquisitive, sometimes I can't help myself" Nicholas told her.

"I finished it" Freya answered.

"And it's over" Nicholas stated.

"Yes" Freya said.

"Good, I mean I wouldn't want to be stepping on anyone's toes" Nicholas told her.

"And how about you? Would I be stepping on anyone's toes?" Freya wanted to know.

"About half the world's female population if you believe what you read in the news. No, I told you, I haven't dated for over three years" Nicholas spoke.

"So was your last relationship serious?" Freya asked him.

"My last proper relationship was my marriage, so I guess you could say it was serious" Nicholas replied.

"What happened?"

"Well the story she tells is that I was having an affair, the truth is we didn't want the same things. She wanted the fame and the money and I wanted children and a ranch full of horses away from everything" Nicholas informed her.

"I think people should complete a questionnaire before they get married, so a third party can check their compatibility. It would save a lot of heartache in the long run" Freya spoke.

"That is a great idea, you should patent that" Nicholas said with a laugh.

"Perhaps I will" Freya responded.

Before either of them were aware it was nearly midnight and Harry was due to close up.

"We should go, we're the only ones left and Harry's not as young as he used to be" Freya remarked as she watched the proprietor carry their dishes away.

"Sure, let's go" Nicholas agreed, rising from his seat.

Freya stood up and Nicholas took hold of her hand. Slowly and gently he ran his fingers up and down the back of it and then he held it in his, squeezing it gently.

"I just want you to know that I am having the best time" Nicholas spoke.

"It got off to a weird start but I think it is ending up OK" Freya replied, enjoying the feel of his hand in hers.

"Good" Nicholas answered and still holding her hand he led the way back towards the restaurant.

Harry and Roger were talking as Nicholas and Freya emerged from the courtyard.

"How was your meal? Everything to sir and madam's satisfaction?" Harry asked them.

"Harry you surpassed yourself, it was sensational" Freya answered and she kissed Harry on the cheek.

"I second that and I was floored by the homemade apple tart, man that was so good" Nicholas told him.

"Well no one makes an apple tart quite like Margot" Harry responded.

"Give her my compliments and if she ever wants to sell the recipe she could probably make a fortune in the States" Nicholas spoke.

"Give her my love Harry, I'll try and pop in and say hello before I go back to England" Freya told him.

"That would be nice pet, take care" Harry ended and he watched as Nicholas, Freya and Roger headed for the door.

"There are photographers hanging around, do you want me to send the car around the back?" Roger asked Nicholas.

"No, we'll just get straight in the car and go, it will be OK. As long as you're OK with that Freya" Nicholas said, looking to her.

"I'm OK with getting in a car, I've done it several times before, and I can't imagine why anyone would want to take a picture of me doing it" Freya responded.

"You'll be fine. Just hold on to me and head for the car" Nicholas told her.

With that said, he pushed open the door and stepped outside the restaurant.

Freya immediately had to put one hand to her face as she was almost blinded by flashbulbs going off. People were shouting and there seemed to be dozens of them, shadowy figures making lights go off in her eyes at close range. Freya felt herself being jostled and then before she could react, Roger was holding the arm that Nicholas didn't have hold of, and he was almost frogmarching her towards the car. She felt like she was desperately trying to get away from an assailant but then, as abruptly as it began, the noise had gone, the door of the car was closed behind her and she was alone with Nicholas on the back seat.

"OK?" he asked her.

"I don't know" Freya replied truthfully.

"You look flustered, do you want a drink?" Nicholas offered.

"No, I don't think so, maybe. I'm camera shy, much better on the other side of the lens" Freya replied, trying to think straight.

"Here" Nicholas said hurriedly pouring a brandy into a glass and handing it to her.

Freya took the glass and drank some of the warming liquid.

"Is it like that for you all the time?" Freya wanted to know as the car pulled away from the restaurant.

"No, usually it's a lot worse" Nicholas admitted.

"How can you live like that?" Freya wanted to know.

"You get used to dealing with it" Nicholas told her.

Freya finished her drink.

"Listen, I've got a rest day on Friday, would you like to do something?" Nicholas asked her.

"Like what?" Freya questioned.

"Well I don't know. Why don't you have a think about it and decide, seeing as I hijacked tonight" Nicholas suggested.

"So you did, completely ruined all my plans. Right now you should be sat on the toilet with chronic stomach-ache" Freya told him.

"God I've heard enough, I can imagine you're quite creative when it comes to revenge" Nicholas replied.

"Mmm, you'd better believe it"

"Then I will do my best not to upset you" Nicholas answered.

The car pulled up outside 'The Calypso Apartments'.

"This is my stop" Freya told him.

"It is" he responded.

"I would invite you up to my room for coffee but the couple above me will probably start having sex" Freya told him.

"Just for our benefit? How flattering" Nicholas joked.

"It's a bit like having a novelty alarm clock waking you up in the morning" Freya explained.

Nicholas was looking at her and he took hold of one of her hands.

"I'm not going to kiss you" he stated simply.

"No? Oh, OK, that's fine, unusual end to a date, but fine" Freya told him.

"I'm not going to kiss you because I think at the back of your mind you still think I'm not serious" Nicholas explained.

"It's OK, honestly" Freya said, trying hard to hide her disappointment.

"I do want to kiss you. Believe me I would like nothing better than to kiss you right now" he admitted with a deep breath.

Freya just looked at him, watching the rise and fall of his chest, looking at his lips, wanting them to kiss her. She inched forward, unable to stop herself, she wanted to feel his mouth on hers.

"No. I can be strong, I can do this and I am not going to kiss you" he said with a satisfied nod as he straightened himself and moved slightly away from her.

"That's OK, you don't have to kiss me because I was going to kiss you" Freya said.

Nicholas took hold of her other hand and held them in his.

"If we kiss now I don't think I'd be able to stop there and I don't think it's right, not yet" Nicholas spoke seriously.

"And here was me thinking all the gentlemen were extinct" Freya replied.

Nicholas smiled.

"So I guess I'll be going back to my lonely room, to my single bed, alone" Freya commented, picking her handbag up from the floor of the car.

"And I guess I'll be going for a cold shower. Listen, you've got my cell number, call me tomorrow" Nicholas told her.

"You mean today" Freya said, looking at her watch.

"Yes I do" Nicholas whispered.

He kissed her hands.

"Make sure you call me" he repeated.

"I'll see you" Freya responded.

She opened the car door, took one last look at him, taking in just how good he looked and then shut the door behind her.

The car pulled away leaving her stood outside 'The Calypso Apartments' and Freya watched it head off up the road in the direction of Villa Kamia. She took a deep breath, feeling slightly giddy. What had just happened to her life?

Chapter Seven

Beep. Beep.

Freya opened one eye as her mobile phone started to vibrate on the bedside cabinet. God she felt awful. Who was texting her? What time was it? She sat up and looked at her watch. It was 9.50am. It couldn't be! Surely she couldn't have slept through the bonking bunnies upstairs.

'R U OK? CALL ME'

It was a text from Emma. Freya had promised to call her first thing and tell her about last night. She was probably worried she hadn't heard from her as Freya had never been one for lying in.

Freya called Emma's number.

"Hello" Emma answered.

"It's me. Are you at the office?" Freya inquired.

"Yes I am"

"Are you busy?"

"Not yet. In fact this morning I've had time to read the newspapers, did you know that Greece now gets the daily English papers almost before they get them in England? And today they are quite a good read" Emma told her.

"Oh?" Freya inquired.

"Yes, there's a good photo too, of Nicholas Kaden" Emma said.

"Right, well shall I come round? I'll just get showered and dressed and I'll be there in twenty minutes"

"It's a photo of Nicholas Kaden and you outside 'Harry's Place' and you're holding hands" Emma exclaimed.

"Mmm OK, shall I make it fifteen minutes?" Freya suggested, getting out of bed and holding the phone to her ear with her shoulder.

"What happened? Why is he holding your hand? The amount of chilli and laxatives Lorraine was going to put in his food should have had him doubled up. What were you doing at 'Harry's Place'" Emma continued.

"It's a long story, look just give me ten minutes or so and I'll be there" Freya said.

"They are asking people to contact the newspaper to name you, they are describing you as his new love interest" Emma carried on.

"God no, I've heard enough, ten minutes OK and I'll tell you everything" Freya insisted.

"I'll put the coffee machine on" Emma replied.

Freya showered and dressed as quickly as she could while still trying to figure out in her head exactly what had happened the night before. She had dated Nicholas Kaden, it had been good and he had held her hand. Had she imagined it? The inside pages of English tabloid "The Daily News" told her not.

"I look awful" Freya announced as she stared at the photograph in Emma's paper.

She had arrived at Emma's office a few minutes before and now had the English paper in front of her, together with a hot cup of coffee.

"I agree it isn't the best photo of you but you're sort of smiling" Emma remarked, looking at the paper over Freya's shoulder.

"Grimacing more like, it was horrendous, it felt like there were a thousand cameras" Freya announced.

"So what happened? When I spoke to you last night everything was arranged, you were going to give him the date from Hell and teach him a lesson for taking up a bet to go out with you" Emma reminded her.

"I know, but it all went wrong right from the start. He got besieged by fans at the apartments and then he'd organised a car to take us to 'Harry's Place' for dinner. It was fantastic, there was a big table set up in the courtyard with candles and flowers and he'd ordered every dish from the menu and there was a mandolin player" Freya explained as she recalled the previous night.

"Very flash, so that made you forgive him for taking bets on you did it?" Emma questioned.

"No of course it didn't but he was being really nice to me and being interested in me and he was telling me about his life and then we almost had a fight. I told him I knew about the bet" Freya spoke.

"Go on, I can't wait to hear what he had to say for himself" Emma urged.

"Well, the upshot of it all is that it wasn't a fake date, there was no bet, well there was but he didn't accept it.

137

He asked me out for real because he actually likes me" Freya informed her excitedly.

"Let me get this straight in my pregnant head, it was a real date and he likes you. Well what about what Gene and Bob said?" Emma asked her.

"He said they had made the bet, but he had told them he wasn't interested because he had already decided he wanted to ask me out" Freya concluded with a smile.

"And you believe him?" Emma queried.

"I know what you're thinking, that he has charmed me and taken me for a mug, that is what I would be thinking if you were telling me all this, but you weren't there. He was genuine, he was nervous about things, he wanted everything to be perfect like you would on a first date and he's asked me out again tomorrow" Freya told her.

"You didn't sleep with him did you?" Emma questioned.

"No! Em, are you OK? Did you get out of bed the wrong side or are those hormones causing problems again?" Freya asked her.

"I'm sorry, I'm tired that's all" Emma answered with a sigh.

"Can you not take some time off work? I really don't think you should be working night and day in your condition" Freya told her.

"I don't have a choice, we need cover at the restaurant, I'm working again tonight" Emma informed her.

"You can't! Look at yourself, you're washed out. I'll do a shift tonight instead" Freya told her.

"Don't be silly, you're on holiday" Emma replied.

"So? You need a break. I can remember how to waitress. It is just waitressing isn't it? I mean I wouldn't have to cook would I?" Freya checked.

"No just waitress and clear tables but it's OK, I can manage" Emma insisted.

"I'm not going to take no for an answer, clear it with Mr and Mrs P and I will be there whatever time they want me. God knows what I am going to wear though, nothing of yours will fit me" Freya told her.

"I am sure Mrs P will have something" Emma assured her.

"It's going to be a traditional costume isn't it?" Freya remarked.

"I don't think she has those anymore, staff kept complaining. Look are you sure you don't mind" Emma spoke.

"I'm sure I don't mind, it might be fun" Freya said and she took a swig of her coffee.

"Do you think your parents might call you, you know, if they see you in the paper" Emma asked her.

"If they do it will be because they are unhappy about it. Thank God they didn't name me" Freya announced.

"But what if they find out who you are? I mean they're bound to find out, that's what newspapers do" Emma reminded her.

"Who is going to tell them? No one knows, only you, and I have changed my appearance quite considerably since I was eighteen. I have to admit, stupid as it may sound, having all those photographers outside the restaurant shocked me. I didn't think it would be like that, I was like a rabbit caught in the headlights" Freya told her.

"What do you think Russell will think of the picture?" Emma asked.

"I think he will wonder what Nicholas Kaden is doing with someone so large and plain" Freya responded.

"So how was it left with you and Nick?" Emma questioned.

"He told me to call him today. Do you know, he wasn't at all like I thought he would be, what I assumed he would be. He was funny and interesting and down to earth" Freya spoke.

"And what happened at the end of the night?" Emma asked her.

"Nothing. He dropped me off at the apartments and we said goodnight" Freya stated.

"With tongues?" Emma asked.

"No. He didn't kiss me" Freya told her.

"What?"

"He said he thought I still believed the bet thing so he said he wouldn't kiss me to prove he was genuine. Either that or I ate too much garlic sauce and he was just being polite" Freya remarked.

"God that sounds really romantic in a restrained kind of way" Emma said.

"It feels strange though, I mean yesterday I hated him and today...." Freya began.

"Go on" Emma urged.

"Today I just can't wait to hear his voice again" Freya admitted with a swallow.

Emma looked at her and Freya returned her gaze. Then, as if reading each other's minds they screamed at the top of their voices and Freya jumped up from her chair and grabbed hold of her friend. They jumped up and down madly until Freya suddenly stopped and looked at Emma.

"Oh bugger!" she announced.

"What?" Emma asked.

"I've got no story to sell 'Shooting Stars' magazine for your wedding fund, I mean I could tell them about Bob and Gene but they aren't high profile enough for anyone to be really interested" Freya stated.

"It doesn't matter. It would never have worked out, Yiannis and I can get married after the baby is born. I just have to come to the terms with the fact that some things don't happen as you would prefer them to" Emma told her.

"No, maybe not, but you deserve your plans to work out. I am going to think of something, leave it to me" Freya said with a nod.

"So what do you have planned for the rest of the day?" Emma inquired.

"I am going to stare at my mobile and hold myself back from calling him" Freya spoke.

"Good plan, you don't want to appear too keen" Emma agreed.

"No, so I thought I would give it ten minutes or so and then I'll call him" Freya announced with a grin.

Emma laughed and then, just as quickly, her expression changed as she caught sight of something outside the office.

"Freya, there are people with cameras, large cameras with zoom lenses and everything, outside the office" Emma stated.

"Yeh I know, they followed me here from 'The Calypso'. See the short guy with the beard and the blue t-shirt, he's from Channel 290 in America" Freya told her.

"Oh my God, you're kidding me" Emma exclaimed, peeking outside.

"Can I go out the back way?" Freya asked her.

Freya left by the back entrance that led up an alleyway and ended up coming out near 'Banas Restaurant'. She went in, ordered a coffee and sat at her favourite table.

It was now nearly half past eleven and Freya wondered if it was too early to call Nicholas. They had nearly been apart for twelve hours. Perhaps she should wait and see if he called her. She took a sip of her coffee and it nearly burnt her mouth. She picked up her phone, found Nicholas' entry in the contacts book and taking a deep breath she pressed 'call'.

It rang several times and then:-

"Hello"

Freya was momentarily taken aback at the sound of a woman's voice on the end of the phone.

"Oh hello, is, er, Nick there please?" Freya asked.

"Who is calling?"

Freya then recognised the voice as that of Martha Wilson aka Roll Lady.

"This is Freya Johnson, perhaps you could help me, I'm thinking of selling my breakfast tomorrow and I thought I would give Nick first refusal. Do you think that would be something he would be interested in?" Freya began sarcastically.

There was no reply from Martha but Freya could hear rustling and hushed voices and then:-

"Hello"

At the sound of his voice Freya's stomach contracted, which served to remind her that a) she really did feel an attraction towards him and b) she hadn't actually had any breakfast yet.

"Hi Nick, it's Freya" she managed to say.

"I was hoping it would be you. Guess where I am" Nicholas asked her.

"Um, let me think, you're on top of a tall building dressed in nothing but dark trousers and a dirty white vest, covered in sweat, a machine gun around your neck, oh and you've got bare feet" Freya spoke.

"Jeeze, I am starting to get concerned about this Bruce Willis obsession. Have you actually seen any of my movies?" Nicholas asked her.

143

"I've seen a couple but I might have to revisit them to refresh myself. I am definitely thinking of renting 'Katie does Kansas'" Freya replied.

"Perhaps we could watch that one together" Nicholas suggested.

"Kinky" Freya responded.

"Stop that Miss Johnson, I'm in a wet suit, a very tight wet suit" Nicholas told her.

"I am envisaging it, tell me you have flippers on" Freya said.

"I do............OK I admit, I don't but I wasn't lying about the wet suit. I'm over in Kouloura" Nicholas told her, speaking of the small bay near Kassiopi.

"It's lovely there, really quiet" Freya responded.

"It was, until we arrived. So where are you?" Nicholas inquired.

"I'm at 'Banas', just having a coffee. There's a couple of guys from Channel 290 tailing me around. I'm having to hide behind the menu every time they walk past" Freya told him.

"You're kidding me? Do you want me to organise someone to be with you?" Nicholas asked her.

"God no! I mean that would be 3 people following me about then" Freya said.

"I'm so sorry, just try and pretend they aren't there" Nicholas spoke.

"There were more photographers outside Emma's office earlier, one of them had a camera I would kill for, top of the range, only just come on to the market. It seemed a total waste to be using it to try and photograph me" Freya told him.

"How many were there?"

"Um, seven? Eight? Plus me makes nine. Did you see a British paper today? We made page 7" Freya announced.

"Did they get my good side?" Nicholas asked.

"No, you had your trousers on remember" Freya joked.

"I'm sorry about the photographers, once they latch onto something there is no stopping them" Nicholas told her.

"It's OK, I am a master of disguise" Freya replied.

"So are you busy tonight? Do you want to do something?" Nicholas asked her.

"Tonight? I thought we were going out tomorrow, I've got a notepad here organising everything" Freya fibbed.

"Oh tomorrow is still on, I just thought that if you hadn't got plans we could meet up tonight" Nicholas told her.

"Well I didn't have plans up until about an hour ago but now I'm working" Freya said.

"Working? Taking photos?" he queried.

"No, waitressing. Emma's a bit off colour at the moment so I said I would do tonight for her" Freya informed him.

"Waitressing where?" Nicholas asked.

"At 'Petroholis Restaurant' at the harbour, Emma's boyfriend owns it with his parents, they do fantastic meatballs" Freya told him.

"Sounds good............hey Martha, could you make a dinner reservation for us tonight, about 8.00 at 'Petroholis Restaurant'" Nicholas called to his assistant.

"Oh my God no! Don't do that, it isn't fair" Freya exclaimed.

"Is it the only way I am going to get to see you tonight?"

"Yes"

"Well then you leave me with no choice. I shall see you later tonight, make sure you are wearing a proper traditional waitress outfit though, like in the movies, I want to see stockings and a frilly apron" he teased.

"And you can call me Katie" Freya replied.

"See you tonight" he ended.

"Bye" Freya said and finished the call.

Freya smiled as she put the phone back down on the table. It had been a good conversation and proved that she hadn't imagined the night before and he definitely wanted to see her again.

She took another sip of her coffee and then ducked her head down onto the table as she caught sight of the Channel 290 crew heading up the road towards the restaurant.

Her mobile phone began to ring and she turned her head to see who was calling. The name 'Russell' was flashing on and off. God, what did he want? She hoped he had got

146

her message tell him their relationship was over. She pressed 'ignore' and sat up, just in time for flashes to go off in her face. People were pointing and calling, their faces pressed up against the glass of the window.

"Bloody Hell, how did that happen?" Freya asked herself as she picked up a menu and put it up to her face.

Freya spent the rest of the day sat on a sun lounger at 'The Calypso Apartments' with her sunhat on and a white 'Calypso Apartments' t-shirt on over the bikini Emma had made her buy at Agatha's. 'The Daily News' was not the only newspaper she was appearing in, much to her horror. The same photograph of her and Nicholas was also in 'The Today', 'The Herald' and 'The Spectator'. They had described her in one paper as 'Nicholas Kaden's female companion' and in another as 'Nicholas Kaden's love interest'. The third described her as 'the first woman, excepting co-stars, to be seen out with the Hollywood actor in over three years'. All three newspapers had asked for people to contact them if they knew who she was. She hoped no one who really knew her did.

She had paid Spiros, one of 'The Calypso's' waiters, 100 Euros to keep away anyone with a camera trained in her direction. She had also told him to keep the non-alcoholic cocktails coming at regular intervals.

She had eaten a Full Monty breakfast at lunchtime and when she had been reading the agony aunt column in 'The Herald' she had polished off a tuna and mayonnaise wrap.

It was now half past four and she was due at the restaurant at six o clock. She took a sip of her cocktail and then her mobile phone rang.

She looked at the display and saw the name 'Barbara' flash up. It was her mother calling. It was such a shock

147

Freya nearly dropped the phone into the drink she was also trying to keep hold of. What was she going to do? She hadn't spoken to her in over a year. Perhaps if she ignored the call it would just go away. She could press 'ignore' but then she would have to listen to a message from her later. She pressed 'accept' and put the phone to her ear.

"Hello"

"Hello darling, how are you?" her mother's voice spoke.

"Fine. And you?" Freya responded.

"I'm fine thank you, so how are things?" Barbara Smith-Andrews asked her.

"Oh you know, the same as usual, work, work, work" Freya replied.

"Really. So where are you now? On an assignment?" Barbara questioned.

"Yes I'm at this little junior school, you should see the little sweethearts, I tell them to say 'cheese' and they all say 'Dairylea'" Freya spoke, sitting up on her sun lounger.

"Which school is it? Perhaps I know it" Barbara continued.

"All Saints" Freya replied.

"Darling, why do you always treat me like an imbecile? Haven't I always told you you get your brains from me?" Barbara spoke.

"No, you've always told me I never apply myself to anything and what a disappointment I am" Freya answered.

"Since I married Robin I've always ordered a newspaper, I like to keep abreast of current affairs while I'm eating my grapefruit of a morning. Well since I have been slowing down and preparing for retirement I take three newspapers, 'The Daily News', 'The Today' and 'The Spectator'" Barbara told her.

"Get to the point mother" Freya said with a sigh, knowing now she had seen the photograph.

"You're in Corfu, there's a photograph of you in all three newspapers with Nicholas Kaden, the actor" Barbara announced.

"Is there? Are you sure it's me? Nicholas who?" Freya responded.

"Nicholas Kaden, the actor who won an Oscar for his performance in that brilliant World War II film about the Nazi who helped some of the prisoners escape, what was it called?" Barbara asked her.

"'Turncoat'" Freya answered, already bored with the conversation.

"Yes, that was it, 'Turncoat'. So, are you dating him? You're holding hands" Barbara wanted to know.

"Mother why are you calling me?" Freya asked her.

"To see how you are and to see what is happening in your life"

"So you can tell the ladies down the golf club" Freya stated.

"No"

"Well the truth is it's all a bit delicate really, for me and Mr Kaden. See, I don't take photographs for a living anymore, I'm actually an escort to the stars. Last week I accompanied Tom Selleck to a black tie charity dinner hosted by your friend Donald Trump" Freya spoke, flicking through her newspaper as she did so.

"I am trying to build bridges here" Barbara said.

"No you're not Mother, you've just discovered that my life is a little more interesting than it was the last time you spoke to me, which was about a year ago, and you just want to feed on the information to tell your pals at the golf club" Freya snapped.

"It hasn't been a year" Barbara said quietly.

"I'll give you a clue, the last time I spoke to you it was about six weeks after my 29th birthday and hey Mum, guess what? I was 30 four days ago, thanks for the card and flowers" Freya said.

"You know I've never been one for birthdays" Barbara spoke.

"Except when it comes to your own"

"So are you dating him or not?" Barbara queried.

"Tell the Golf Club Gals I have Nicholas Kaden on week days and Clint Eastwood at weekends, that has to be worth a couple of gins" Freya replied.

"I don't know how you ended up this way Jane" Barbara spoke.

"Yes you do, you know exactly how I ended up this way. Goodbye Mother" Freya said and she ended the call.

Every time they spoke it was harder and harder for Freya to believe that her mother was her mother. There was not a maternal bone in her body and she had absolutely no concern for anyone but herself. Freya felt nothing for her. Her mother was Mrs Superficial.

At six o clock Freya was at 'Petroholis Restaurant' being given instructions by Mrs Petroholis. Freya was trying to listen to what she was being told but she was also pulling hard at the white shirt she was wearing. It was far too tight across the chest. The only godsend was that it was buttoned up at the back and not the front. The skirt was on the snug side too and Freya was glad she wouldn't be sitting down in it at all.

"Now all you have to think about is taking the orders, Yiannis and Mr P will do the rest. Is OK?" Mrs Petroholis asked Freya.

"Yes, that's all fine, table numbers are clearly marked, Melissa and Leandros know everything if I have any questions" Freya said, speaking of the other servers.

"Good, good, so, come, we have a drink before we open" Mrs Petroholis spoke and she led Freya over to the bar area.

She poured out two small glasses of retsina and gave one to Freya.

"Yammas" she said knocking her glass with Freya's.

"Yammas" Freya repeated and downed the liquid.

"Drinking before you work huh?" Yiannis spoke as he appeared from inside with a large metal container filled with condiments.

"It's your mother, she made me" Freya answered.

151

"You should be quiet, I know exactly how much red wine goes into the cooking and how much does not" Mrs Petroholis told her son.

"Busted" Freya whispered to Yiannis.

"Oil and vinegar, all tables" Yiannis spoke and he passed the heavy tray to Freya.

By eight o clock that evening Freya had served thirty tables of people. Waiting tables was coming back to her. She had quickly recalled that hot soup could scald, ice cream had to be put in a cold dish, not one straight from the dishwasher, and main courses were generally served after starters. However, despite the mild mishaps she had collected 40 Euros in tips.

It was an extremely warm evening and the nylon skirt was making her awfully itchy. She had been forced to tie her hair back with an elastic band and the tendrils which had escaped were now being held back by bulldog clips.

There had been two photographers outside the restaurant since opening. They had taken photos when Freya had spilt ice cream over a three year old boy and when she had broken off the cork in an expensive bottle of red wine. In the end Freya had taken them out some drinks, heavily infused with Yiannis' prescription eye drops. They had left within the hour.

"One garlic bread, one loukanika, one taramasalata and one humous. Is there anything else I can get you? Freya spoke as she put plates down in front of a table of customers.

Her attention was quickly drawn away from the table to the entrance of the restaurant where a group had gathered and cameras were beginning to flash. It was

Nicholas, accompanied by Hilary, Martha, Gene and Bob. Freya's lips tightened at the sight of the latter two as she had hoped to avoid them for as long as she was able.

"Excuse me, could we have another bottle of white wine please?" the gentleman at Freya's table asked her for the third time.

"I'm sorry, of course, I'll just get that for you" Freya said and she left the table and headed for the kitchen.

"Oh Mrs P, do I look a fright?" Freya questioned as she tried to see her reflection in the door of the stainless steel fridge.

"You look like you are working hard which is how a waitress should look" Mrs Petroholis replied.

"I look terrible" Freya announced with a sigh.

"You look even more terrible if table 16 no get their steaks" Mrs Petroholis spoke and she handed Freya two plates and two dishes of vegetables.

"Sorry, OK" Freya said and she headed out of the kitchen again.

Nicholas and his group were sat only a little way from the entrance to the kitchen, as the back of the restaurant was a lot more private than the front or sides. This was due to the fact that the front and sides all had open access to the harbour.

Freya delivered the food for table 16 and passed Yiannis on the way.

"Your friends at table 2 have asked for you" Yiannis spoke with a wink.

"Something wrong with your eye Yiannis?" Freya asked him.

"Yes, you took the last of my eye drops" he answered.

"Could you deal with table 25 then, they want another bottle of medium white" Freya told him.

"No problem, I'll do it, go on" he urged her.

Freya took a deep breath and headed towards the table where Nicholas was sat. As she approached, Nicholas stood up, left the table and went towards her. He was wearing a light blue cotton shirt and pale blue jeans with sandals.

"Hey" he greeted and he kissed her cheek.

"Hi" Freya replied, feeling herself blush.

"You look harassed" he remarked, holding her hands.

"I'm fine, we're just really busy tonight, as you can see. I didn't realise you were bringing Dumb and Dumber with you" Freya said, indicating Bob and Gene.

"No well neither did I, it was supposed to be Martha and I talking through a couple of things and then Hilary invited herself and wherever she goes Gene and Bob aren't far behind" Nicholas replied.

"Can I spit in their soup?" Freya asked him.

"Of course, I would expect nothing less after what they said about you" Nicholas answered.

"No Roger? Who's guarding your body?" Freya wanted to know.

"I was rather hoping you might" Nicholas replied with a smile.

"Unfortunately I already have a job tonight and as that is the case I'd better take your order" Freya said, getting out her notepad and pen.

They went back to the table and Nicholas retook his seat.

"Hello again everyone. Shall I get you some drinks while you look at the menu?" Freya asked the group.

"What does everyone want?" Nicholas asked them all.

"I will have a gin and tonic with no ice and a dash of lime, in a tall glass with a slice of lemon" Martha spoke as Freya jotted it down.

"I'll have a beer, make it a LARGE one" Gene spoke.

His comment and emphasis on the word 'large' made Bob start laughing so much he had to cover his mouth with his napkin.

"Is something funny?" Nicholas asked them, fixing them both with a stare.

"No Nick, not at all, sorry, Gene was just referring to something we were discussing last night. I'll have a large beer too" Bob answered hurriedly.

Freya looked up from her notepad and glared at Gene, knowing that what Bob had just said was rubbish and they were referring to her size.

"Freya, I'll have a mineral water" Nicholas told her.

"Still or sparkling sir?" Freya asked him, looking up from her pad again.

"Bubbly works best for me" Nicholas replied with a smile.

"I'll have the same" Hilary answered, moving her chair closer to Nicholas.

"Fine, good, well I'll go and get your drinks and I'll be back for your food order in a few minutes" Freya spoke politely and she left the table and headed for the bar.

If she managed to get through the evening without punching Gene or Bob it would be a miracle. She gave the drinks order to Leandros and ate an olive from the small pot on the bar. She had to maintain a calm exterior, particularly as she was working for Mr and Mrs P, she didn't want to let them down.

Freya collected the drinks from Leandros but just as she was about to move away, she caught sight of a condiments tray at the corner of the bar. It was just too tempting. She took a container of pepper and shook a good portion of it into Gene and Bob's beers. She stirred the drinks with a straw and then carried the tray over to the table.

"One gin and tonic with no ice, with lime and a slice of lemon in the tallest glass we have, two beers and two mineral sparkling waters" Freya said as she put the drinks down in front of everyone.

Gene took a swig of his drink and looked at the liquid with suspicion.

"It's Amstel, is that OK for you? I could get you a Mythos, which is a local lager, if you would prefer" Freya spoke with a smile of helpfulness.

"It's fine" Gene answered.

"Right, is everyone ready to order or shall I give you a few more minutes?" Freya offered.

"I think we're good right?" Nicholas asked everyone.

No one disagreed.

"OK I'll have *tzatziki* to start with followed by the meatballs which I hear are the restaurant speciality and for dessert............well I haven't quite made my mind up about that yet" Nicholas spoke and he gave Freya a suggestive look which made her cheeks redden again.

"Just a small Greek salad for me" Hilary spoke.

"And for main course?" Freya questioned, looking up at the actress.

"That is my main course" Hilary answered.

"Oh sorry, I do apologise, one Greek salad. And for you Martha?" Freya asked.

"What would you recommend?" Martha questioned, looking up at Freya with cold eyes.

"The meatballs for main and for starter the local sausage *loukanika* is very good or the pastry parcels filled with cheese, that's called *tyropita*" Freya told her.

"And which items on the menu are low GI?" Martha asked with a smile.

"I'm not sure on that but all of them are definitely 100% BL" Freya told her.

"What is that?" Hilary questioned.

"Bloody Lovely" Freya answered, much to Nicholas' amusement.

"I'll have the pastry parcels and the meatballs" Martha told her and snapped her menu shut.

Freya turned to Gene next.

"And for you?" she asked through gritted teeth.

"I'll have the melon, followed by chicken *souvlaki* with vegetables and roast potatoes, tell the chef not to overcook the meat......oh and I would like a large portion" Gene remarked with a straight face.

Bob coughed loudly into his napkin, hiding his face.

"What the Hell is wrong with you two?" Nicholas asked, raising his voice.

"It's a private joke, sorry, we shouldn't be so rude" Gene responded.

"No you shouldn't" Nicholas agreed.

"It's OK Nick, let them have their fun. What would you like a large portion of Bob? Hair perhaps? Shall I see if I can rustle up a toupee for you?" Freya asked him.

"Now wait just a minute" Bob spoke, throwing his napkin on the table and starting to rise from his chair.

"No, you wait. I realise that for whatever reason, probably something relating back to your childhood, that you have an issue with my size, but we all have to get through this evening without falling out. I am sure that you don't want any negative publicity for the film, so let's cut out the wisecracks and we will all get along fine. Anymore use of words such as 'big', 'gigantic', 'gross', 'enormous', 'large' or 'prize pig' and I will knock you both into the middle of next week, publicity or no publicity. Do I make myself clear?" Freya spoke calmly, smiling at them both as she finished the sentence.

"Crystal" Gene muttered under his breath.

"Good, so Bob, what will it be?" Freya asked.

"Same as Gene" Bob replied hurriedly.

"Good choice. Right thank you for your order, I will bring out the starters as soon as they're ready" Freya spoke.

She walked away quickly. Those guys were utter creeps. She made her way towards the door to the kitchen but just as she was about to push the door open someone took hold of her arm.

"Hello Freya"

Freya turned around and saw Russell stood in front of her. Her mouth dropped open and she just stood there, rooted to the spot, unable to speak.

"What are you doing here?" Freya asked, her thoughts being blurted out before she could stop them.

"Well that's not really the greeting I was hoping for but I understand that you are mad at me at the moment. I probably look awful don't I? You won't believe it but I've been travelling since this morning. I was delayed in Gatwick for four hours, and I've nearly worn through my shoes traipsing around 'Tie Rack'" Russell told her with a sigh.

"What are you doing here?" Freya repeated.

"I could ask you the same question. Are you waitressing? You look uncomfortably trussed up in that blouse" Russell said and he made a move to brush his hand down the front of her shirt.

"Get off me" Freya hissed and she took two steps backwards away from him.

"Look Freya, I know you're upset with me, but I'm here to make things right again. I thought if I took some proper time off work we could have some quality time together" Russell spoke.

"For the third and final time, what are you doing here? Didn't you get my message?" Freya questioned, backing away even more.

"Yes I got your message, but I know what you're like when you're angry, you need a bit of time and space to think about things. That's why I left it a few days before I came over, so you could calm down. But I'm here now and I'm ready to talk things through if you are" Russell continued.

"I said I never wanted to see you again, I needed no time to think about that statement and I haven't changed my mind since" Freya told him.

"Come on Freya, there isn't anything that can't be fixed if you want to mend it enough and I want to make things work between us. Look, I'm totally shattered and could really do with a drink, come and have a drink with me. Hey Yiannis, good to see you, do you think we could have a bottle of white wine?" Russell called as Yiannis appeared from the kitchen.

"I don't want a drink, I'm working, Yiannis, stay where you are" Freya ordered.

"Look I know I've been a complete idiot, I hold my hands up and admit that but Freya, we need to talk it through, just give me a chance to explain" Russell begged.

"I've got nothing to talk about with you" Freya replied.

"We have a relationship to talk about" Russell responded.

"No, we had a relationship, or so I thought, you blew that" Freya told him.

"I admit, I've made mistakes, a lot of mistakes, but surely we can work through this, I mean we've been together a long time, it seems stupid to just throw that away" Russell continued.

Freya looked over at Nicholas' table and could see that he was looking over at what was going on between her and Russell.

"As far as I am concerned there is nothing worth salvaging from the last eighteen months. And if I am honest, I don't even think you realise the reason I broke up with you" Freya told him.

"Of course I know why you broke up with me, you found out about me and your mother" Russell said matter of factly.

In that split second, after he had said the words, Freya felt all her energy drain from her body. She could almost feel herself whitening. Her legs felt devoid of stability and her heart slowed to minimal output. She just stared at Russell unable to believe what he had just said.

"You and my mother" Freya repeated, her voice shaking.

People were continuing their meals all around her but to Freya the restaurant had fallen silent. Her head was filling with a hundred and one thoughts, like a huge balloon ready to burst.

"I thought you knew, I thought you'd found out. When you didn't turn up at the restaurant I presumed something must have happened and then you didn't return my calls and......"Russell stuttered, realising that Freya had had no idea, judging from the look on her face.

"You and my mother" Freya spoke for the second time.

"It was a stupid, stupid fling and when I met her I had absolutely no idea she was your mother, I mean how would I have known? You don't have any family pictures around, you never even speak about your parents" Russell began to blab.

All Freya could feel, as Russell carried on talking, was fear deep in her gut, rising up through her body like it was going to engulf her. He knew. That was why he was here begging for forgiveness. He knew and he could see an opportunity about to slip away if he didn't try and make amends. He didn't love her, he hadn't ever loved her and she would lay a bet that her mother had got bored with him approximately six weeks ago when he had returned home with flowers and takeaway food and charmed her back into bed.

At that moment she hated Russell almost more than she had hated anyone before. He was still talking, on and on about how he had met her mother, how her mother had pursued him and how he hadn't wanted to betray her. But it was all floating over Freya's head. He was threatening her whole existence now, everything she had worked so hard for. She could feel herself losing control.

Before she could consider the implications, as the red mist descended, Freya pulled back her arm and punched Russell square on the jaw. He staggered backwards and fell into a table of four, scattering their drinks and meals and knocking over their bottle of wine which smashed and broke, sending shards of glass flying across the floor.

Nicholas immediately rose from his seat and hurriedly made his way across the restaurant towards Freya. Martha immediately left her chair and trotted after him.

"You make me sick! You are disgusting! I don't know how you had the nerve to come here" Freya spat as she shook with anger.

"I think you've broken my tooth" Russell exclaimed as he got to his feet, holding his face.

"You're lucky that's all I've broken" Freya screamed at the top of her voice.

"Look, I came here to apologise, I came here to try and make things right between us" Russell told her.

"Make things right between us? After what you've just told me?! Are you out of your mind?" Freya continued to scream.

"And what about all the stuff you haven't told me?! Eighteen months together and you never told me who your parents were or even your real name" Russell yelled back at her.

"Shut up! Just shut your mouth Russell or I swear to God I will shut it for you!" Freya shouted, almost hysterical and unable to stop herself from reaching out and nudging Russell towards the exit.

"Then I think we had better talk don't you?" Russell suggested, standing his ground, unwilling to leave.

"Get lost!" Freya yelled and she pushed Russell hard in the chest. In an instant reaction Russell snapped and pushed Freya back. She lost her balance and fell against the wall scraping her arm down a sharp corner of the brickwork. It stung and she sat on the floor, nursing her arm and trying to regain some composure.

"Hey, what the Hell is going on?" Nicholas questioned, grabbing hold of Russell by the arm.

"Oh Freya, here he is, right on cue, the gallant knight in shining armour I have had to see in all the national papers holding hands with you, Mr Kaden" Russell mocked, shaking Nicholas' arm off.

"Nick, come back to the table" Martha ordered.

"Freya, who is this? Is this your ex?" Nicholas queried as he helped Freya to her feet.

"Her ex? I'm an ex already am I Freya? It didn't take long to wipe out a year and a half did it?" Russell responded.

"And how much of that year and a half have you spent screwing other people?" Freya yelled.

"I think you had better leave" Nicholas ordered Russell.

"I think you had better keep out of stuff that doesn't concern you" Russell retorted.

"Nick, please come back to the table, this not helping anyone" Martha spoke.

"Russell, I think you should go, now is not the time for talking" Yiannis told him as pleasantly as he could.

"You heard the man" Nicholas said to Russell.

"I am not going anywhere until Freya agrees to talk with me" Russell stated, staring at Freya who was still nursing her wounded arm.

"I have nothing to say to you" Freya responded through the tears that were beginning to prick her eyes.

"Then you leave me with no choice but to tell everyone here everything I know" Russell said loudly, to ensure he received maximum attention.

No one was eating anymore, everyone was staring at the scene being played out before them.

At that moment Mrs Petroholis emerged from the kitchen wondering why none of her orders backing up in the kitchen were being served.

"Yiannis, what is happening here?" she inquired.

"I'm sorry Mrs P, it's my fault, I...." Freya started, trying to conceal her bleeding arm and to stop it from dripping on the floor.

"Ah this is nice isn't it? All these people running to stick up for you Freya. Have you lied to all of them too or is it just me you couldn't trust?" Russell asked her.

"Russell, please, if I meant anything to you, please don't do this" Freya begged him, tears in her eyes.

"Right that's it, I've had enough of this" Nicholas said, his patience snapping.

In one swift move he grabbed hold of Russell, pushed him out of the restaurant and onto the street. Freya, Martha and Yiannis hurried after him and all the customers turned towards the scene.

The paparazzi had regrouped outside the restaurant when Nicholas and his entourage had arrived for their meal and they were quick to get their cameras into action as the actor appeared in the doorway bundling someone out onto the road.

"I think Freya has made it quite clear that she has nothing left to say to you" Nicholas spoke when he and Russell were outside.

"I think it is in 'Freya's' best interests to listen to what I have to say to her" Russell responded as Freya, Martha and Yiannis joined them out on the road.

"Nick, please, just leave him, please" Freya pleaded, taking hold of Nicholas' arm.

"You do not have to speak to his guy if you don't want to, I won't have him threatening you" Nicholas spoke, looking to Freya.

"Tell him Freya or I will" Russell warned her.

"Freya, just say the word and I will get rid of him" Nicholas said, still looking at Freya.

"Either you agree to meet with me and talk or we get this all out in the open, right here, right now, in the middle of the high street, in front of your new boyfriend and all these journalists. Five seconds, 5, 4" Russell spoke, beginning a countdown.

"Alright! Alright! I will meet with you, just please go now, I don't want the Petroholis' to suffer, please Russell" Freya begged, crying hard as she was almost overcome by panic.

"Oh Freya, I don't think I have seen you look so out of control" Russell said, watching as Freya whimpered and clutched at her bleeding arm.

"Listen, you've got what you came for, now just leave" Nicholas ordered him.

"Gladly. By the way, I am staying at the 'Dolmas Apartments', room 3, just give me a call when you are ready to talk" Russell told Freya.

Freya managed a nod and watched as a smirk crossed Russell's face. Then, satisfied with the night's conclusion he turned to make his way back up the main street towards the town square.

Freya looked at Nicholas almost apologetically, not knowing for the moment what to do or say.

"Are you OK? Let me see your arm" Nicholas ordered, taking Freya's arm and looking at the wound through the rip in her shirt.

"I think we should return to the restaurant and try to diffuse the situation as quickly as possible" Martha decided.

"Just shut up Martha. That doesn't look nice, I think the only place we are going to is the hospital. Get Mikey on the phone and get the car here!" Nicholas ordered.

"It's fine, a small dressing and it will be OK" Freya insisted, not wanting to make a fuss.

"You're going to the hospital, no questions" Nicholas stated firmly.

Just under two hours later Freya and Nicholas were in a cubicle in Corfu Town's hospital. The doctor had assessed

Freya's arm and had decided that it did require a couple of stitches. They were now waiting for the nurse to come to suture it.

Freya was sat on the edge of the bed, holding on to a dressing she was pressing over the wound.

"You OK?" Nicholas asked her.

"I'm tired, but I'm sure feeling drained of energy is natural when your dirty laundry has been washed in public" Freya answered.

"So what is the deal with you two?" Nicholas asked her, running his hands through his hair.

"What do you mean?" Freya replied.

"Well is it really over between you or are fights like tonight normal practice and it's all going to be forgotten tomorrow?" Nicholas queried.

"Is it really over?! He's slept with my mother for God's sake, of course it's over" Freya told him.

"He did what?!" Nicholas exclaimed in horror.

"Look, it's really over between Russell and I, but given tonight's performance, I would understand if you want to retract the intention of another date with me" Freya spoke, swallowing a lump of regret which had formed in her throat.

Nicholas sighed and sat down in the chair next to the bed.

"I'm sorry you got involved, I had no idea he was going to turn up" Freya spoke sincerely.

"It's OK" Nicholas insisted.

"But you are having second thoughts about me. It's alright, I completely understand" Freya said with a nod.

"I'm not having second thoughts, if you tell me it's over then I believe you" Nicholas responded, looking up at her.

"What he wants to talk to me about, it isn't like you think" Freya spoke, her voice faltering slightly.

"Listen, we all have a past and I don't want you to feel that you have to tell me anything you are uncomfortable with right now. If there are things you need to sort out with Russell then that's fine, but I won't have him threatening you like tonight, unless you tell me it's none of my business and then I will butt out completely" Nicholas told her seriously.

"No, I want it to be your business, well, you know, I....I don't want to lose the start of something, with you" Freya told him.

"Good, because what I would really like to do is spend some time with you, where we can get to know each other without anything else getting in the way, like my fame and your ex and the past. I am only interested in the present and the future, the here and the now. I'd like us to just try and be two ordinary people for the next couple of weeks and see where we go from there" Nicholas told her.

Freya reached for his hand with her good arm and softly brushed his fingers with hers.

"I would really like that too" she admitted.

Nicholas looked at her and Freya could sense the tension in the moment. She reached up and touched his cheek with her hand, drawing his face towards hers. Nicholas leaned forward in the chair and then hurriedly retreated as the door of the room was flung open and a nurse carrying a suture kit came in.

"This would never happen in the movies" Freya remarked with a smile.

"You're kidding me, it happens in at least five of my movies" Nicholas replied.

"And in what scene do you usually get to kiss the girl?" Freya wanted to know.

"Rarely before the end" he answered.

"I am not waiting that long" Freya told him.

Just under an hour later Nicholas and Freya were back in the car beginning the return journey to Kassiopi.

"So does this qualify as our second date?" Freya asked.

"Yes but I have to say it is probably the lousiest second date I've been on. You get injured, I eject someone from a restaurant and we spend three hours driving to and from the hospital" Nicholas spoke.

"It's romantic in a strange way, a bit like something that would happen in an episode of 'Moonlighting'" Freya told him.

"Jeeze Freya, you and Bruce have some long term thing going on. I think I feel more threatened by him than I do by Russell" Nicholas remarked.

"Well isn't it better that you know about Bruce and I now rather than finding out later?" Freya replied.

"He's actually a really nice guy" Nicholas told her.

"So you do know him! Oh my God Nick, you really are famous" Freya announced.

"But not that famous as I don't have his number in my cell remember" Nicholas spoke.

"True, I forgot about that.....and you really don't have to feel threatened by Russell..........oww" Freya yelped as the car hit a bump in the road.

"You OK?" Nicholas asked, steadying her.

"Yeh, stupid bloody Russell, I managed to get to 30 and not have any stitches at all and now, a few days in, I have three of them. You had any before?" Freya inquired.

"Any what?"

"Stitches, you look like someone who probably fell out of a few trees when he was growing up" Freya spoke.

"I've had a few" Nicholas answered.

"Oooo where? Do you have any good scars? I bet you have some great scars" Freya spoke.

"Not really, sorry to disappoint" Nicholas replied.

"Well maybe you could show them to me sometime" Freya suggested.

"Maybe" he agreed with a smile.

The car pulled up outside 'The Calypso Apartments'.

"Well, it's been an interesting evening" Freya remarked with half a smile.

"You could say that and I am beginning to think that every second with you is destined for drama" Nicholas responded.

"I'm sorry" Freya answered, dropping her head.

"I was just kidding, it's OK, I told you, starting now we'll forget all about everything else and just have some time getting to know each other" Nicholas spoke and he took some of her hair, which had fallen out of the bulldog clip, into his fingers and gently tucked it behind her ear.

Freya felt herself shiver at his touch.

"Listen, are you going to be OK here on your own?" Nicholas asked her.

"Yes, I'll be fine" Freya insisted.

"I don't want to rush things you know and spoil it" Nicholas stated seriously.

"You mean you don't want to come up to my room and make out in synch with the couple in the room above" Freya translated.

"Well it would be kind of like being at an orgy" Nicholas agreed.

"And you would know? I knew those Hollywood parties were wild" Freya replied.

"You'd better believe it" Nicholas said with a grin.

"So are we still going out tomorrow? Freya asked him.

"I hope so. Are you telling me you haven't organised things yet?" Nicholas asked her.

"As it happens I have and where we are going there shouldn't be a photographer for miles, apart from me of course" Freya told him.

"Which is a good idea seeing as tonight's fracas is going to be all over the papers tomorrow" Nicholas said with a sigh.

"Well I do hope they captured my punch because it was infinitely better than your shove" Freya remarked.

"I can't deny it, you've obviously had a lot more practice"

"I am going off you Mr Kaden and I was just beginning to like you" Freya told him.

"You were?" Nicholas asked, edging closer towards her.

"Yes" Freya answered.

She could see his breathing had quickened and her heart was in absolute overdrive. She was looking at him, he was looking at her. She leant forward and then Mike the driver spoke through the intercom.

"I'm sorry Mr Kaden but I just thought I would mention that there are now a dozen or so photographers with their lenses trained on the car"

The moment had been interrupted again.

"Have you seen 'Notting Hill'? Well Hugh Grant and Julia Roberts get to kiss in the very first scene. You should do more films like that, the timing might rub off" Freya told him with a sigh.

"OK Mikey, we're just leaving" Nicholas spoke.

"Meet me tomorrow, outside 'Harry's Place', about ten o clock, I'll pick you up from there" Freya told him.

"OK, well, I'll see you tomorrow" Nicholas said.

He leant forward and kissed her cheek, stroking the hair at the back of her head.

"Bye" Freya responded, squeezing his hands.

She got out of the car and shut the door behind her. Flashes started going off immediately but she stood her ground and watched the car drive away up the road.

"Freya! Freya! How's your arm? Did you need stitches? Is it true you were engaged to Mr Buchanan?" one of the reporters shouted.

Freya turned away from them, not speaking and began to walk into 'The Calypso Apartments' complex. All she was glad about was that they were still calling her Freya.

Chapter Eight

For the second time since she had arrived in Corfu, the shagging pair in Room 320 did not wake her. This time though, it was because she was awake before them. Her arm had been painful in the night. It had been hard to get comfortable and eventually, having managed only three hours sleep, she had got up at 5.00am.

It was still dark so she made a cup of tea and put the light on on the balcony. The air was fresh and there was a mist over the mountains in the distance which suggested another warm, humid day ahead. Freya sat down and rubbed her sore eyes. So much had happened in the past few days, it was hard to get her head around it.

Her and Russell finishing, Emma being pregnant and her meeting Nicholas. Especially her meeting Nicholas. She knew that she shouldn't be attracted to him, for lots of reasons, the ridiculous bet that had started it all, the timing, Nicholas' lifestyle, particularly his lifestyle. She loathed the excessiveness of it all and the desperation of the people in his world, their drive to have more and more of everything and anything, just because they could. It was wasteful, it was unnecessary and it was everything she had given up.

But she knew that it wasn't the lifestyle that made him attractive to her, it was the way he was with her. He listened to her, he voiced his own opinions but he didn't shout hers down, he was compassionate, he shared her sense of humour and he seemed to have a free spirit, just like she did.

Russell turning up had been a shock. She had not expected him to be bothered enough by her ending things to turn up. Little had she known that the only reason he had turned up was because he didn't want to lose her now he had discovered she might be some sort of meal ticket. He knew about her now and he had obviously kept it to himself for at least six weeks. But Freya knew that would not last, no matter what he wanted to discuss with her. It was a ticking time bomb that she could do nothing about, except to wait and see if it all blew up in her face or not. She knew that if she and Nicholas were to have a chance of a relationship she needed to tell him the truth. But she wasn't sure she could.

She found it so hard. She had only told one man about it, he had been the only man to meet her family and it had ultimately led to her downfall. Now her two worlds had collided again in spectacular fashion. She hated her parents, they disgusted her. All they had ever cared about was money and status, the very things that mattered least to Freya.

"I didn't wake you did I?" Freya asked when she had called Emma on her mobile phone later that morning.

It was now eight o clock and Freya had showered and dressed in ¾ length jeans and a navy blue vest top.

"No, I've been washing tablecloths since half past six. How are you? How's your arm? Yiannis has told me everything, I can't believe I missed it, it's probably the most excitement the restaurant has seen since I have been working there and where am I? In bed asleep" Emma stated, disappointedly.

"The arm is sore, I didn't get a lot of rest" Freya spoke.

"I'm not surprised with all that happening. Yiannis said that Mrs P was having a hissy fit about the broken glasses up until most of the customers from last night booked again for tonight hoping for a repeat performance" Emma spoke.

"I must go and see her later and apologise" Freya remarked.

"I wouldn't worry, she is seeing the Euro signs in the situation" Emma assured her.

"So what exactly did Yiannis tell you?" Freya inquired.

"That that creep Russell has been sleeping with your mother. Did he get that right?" Emma asked.

"Yes, he did, it's true. So you were right about him seeing someone else, albeit you didn't guess it would be one of my close relations" Freya answered.

"Oh God. I was sure he must have misheard. How awful" Emma said.

"I know, I've scrubbed myself raw in the shower, it kind of feels like I've slept with her myself" Freya remarked.

"Oh Freya, I don't know what to say" Emma admitted.

"It's OK, I'm dealing with it. What worries me more is that she told Russell the truth about me. I don't think she knew he was in a relationship with me but she obviously told him all about her only daughter. Although it is surprising she would wax lyrical about someone she has virtually disowned" Freya announced.

"Oh my God, no, oh Freya, after all these years" Emma said, concern in her voice.

"I know, I'm so scared I feel sick. And the worst thing is, with all the press sniffing around because of Nick it is only a matter of time before someone picks up on it or Russell decides to make a few quid, which I think he has set his sights on getting from me" Freya spoke.

"What are you going to do?" Emma asked.

"I'm not entirely sure yet but I think I am going to have to do something I haven't done before, I think I am going to have to tell Nick before someone else does" Freya said with a heavy sigh.

"Oh Freya, maybe if you speak to Russell and reason with him no one will have to know anything and everything can go back to normal" Emma suggested.

"Well he was all for telling everyone in Kassiopi last night. He wants to meet with me to talk about it but I know what he wants, he will want money for his silence. It will be money I don't have and even if I did have it I don't think I can trust him. Oh I don't know, it's all a bloody mess, my feet are starting to get itchy and if I don't make a decision soon I am going to be hailing a cab to the airport again" Freya told her.

"Oh no you don't. Perhaps this is a good thing, maybe if the truth does come out you can finally put it all to rest once and for all" Emma suggested.

"I don't know, I can't see my parents wanting me to reappear on the scene" Freya stated.

"Who cares about them? You hate them, why should you care what they think?" Emma asked.

"I don't care what they think, I care that they will cause me no end of problems if it is all brought up again now, after all this time" Freya said.

"Well you know I am with you 100% whatever you decide to do" Emma told her.

"Thanks Em" Freya replied.

"So, are you seeing Nick today?" she inquired.

"Yes, I'm going to show him the lake at Korisson. I figured the paparazzi wouldn't find us down there" Freya told her.

"I wouldn't bet on it. How are you getting there?" Emma asked.

"Motorbike" Freya announced and smiled to herself.

She could see that Nicholas was already there waiting as she rode up the main road from Kassiopi towards 'Harry's Place'. He was wearing a white t shirt and black cargo style shorts and he had sunglasses on. She pulled the motorbike up beside him, turned off the engine and removed her helmet.

"Good morning" she announced with a smile.

"Hey, look at this thing, she's a beauty" Nicholas remarked, admiring the motorcycle.

"She's nice isn't she? The best the Kassiopi Bike Rental shop had to offer. No Harleys I'm afraid, but you can see the similarities" Freya spoke as she got off the bike.

"Yeh, lots of chrome, two wheels, she's fine" Nicholas told her.

"Well I'm glad you're making friends because you are going to have to drive. My arm started hurting the minute I left the harbour" Freya admitted.

"That's OK, as long as you don't mind wearing the pack" Nicholas spoke and he indicated the rucksack he had in his hand.

"That's fine. Shall we go? I am ever fearful that photographers are going to jump out of places you would never expect them to be" Freya said, putting her helmet back on and getting back on the bike.

"Yeh, me too. Mmm is this my helmet? Very Seventies" Nicholas said with a smile as he prepared to put it on.

"I thought Eighties actually, it reminded me of CHiPS. Now if they ever make the film you should be the new Eric Estrada" Freya told him.

"With Bruce Willis as Jon Baker? You just want to see us in those tight uniforms. So where are we headed" Nicholas asked as he tightened up the helmet.

"South. Now come on Poncherello, step on it" Freya replied.

Nicholas started up the engine and set off up the road.

They headed south and travelled down through the resorts of Ipsos, Dassia and Gouvia and then on to Corfu Town which was by far the most congested, with lots of city traffic.

Freya was enjoying the scenery immensely. She had only hired a motorbike once on Corfu, which was some years ago now and it was far more enjoyable with a partner than it was on your own. She was also enjoying being at close quarters to Nicholas. He had a solid build, slim but muscular with a broad back and well defined shoulder and arm muscles. Like it or not, he was every inch the archetypal movie hero.

They reached Limni Korissia in a little under two hours and parked at the edge of the lake.

"God it's beautiful here" Nicholas remarked as he took his helmet off and viewed the landscape around him.

"This, well scenery like this, is the whole reason I got into photography" Freya told him as she unstrapped the bag on the back of the bike and removed some bottled water.

"Seeing this today I can understand that" Nicholas replied.

"Here" Freya said and she passed him the bottled water.

"Thanks"

He drank some of the water and passed it back to Freya.

"Well, what I thought we would do is have a walk around the lake so I can take some pictures and then we can find a nice spot and eat the picnic I've prepared. You might have to carry the basket though because I'm injured" Freya told him.

"No problem, it sounds great" Nicholas answered.

"Good, well, let's go" Freya said excitedly.

"Hang on, just one second. I've got something for you" Nicholas said.

He picked up his rucksack and produced a plastic bag from inside it.

"A present?" Freya inquired.

"Well I know it was your birthday the day we met and I just thought I'd get you something. Here" Nicholas said and he gave her the bag.

"You shouldn't have bought me anything.............Oh my God, oh Nick, this is the same one that that guy from Channel 290 had" Freya exclaimed as she produced a leather case, knowing from the outside that it contained a camera.

"It should be, I had to phone the network and ask what kind of cameras they were using these days" Nicholas admitted.

"You didn't! Oh God, this is the best present I've ever had" Freya exclaimed as she continued to admire it.

"Do I take it you like it then?" Nicholas spoke with a smile as he enjoyed her enthusiasm.

"It's amazing, it's fantastic, thank you so much........let me take a shot of you" Freya said as she set the camera up and aimed it at him.

"I thought you said no photographers would find us today" he joked.

"I don't count because I won't be selling any I take of you to feed the gossip hungry masses" Freya told him.

"I'm shy" Nicholas responded.

"Come on Mr Big Movie Star, give me a movie premiere smile..........gotcha!" Freya said as she snapped him.

"Now your turn" Nicholas said, trying to take the camera from her.

"No, I'm sorry you can't give someone a present and ask for it back so soon" Freya told him and she practically ran away toward the lake.

"To not let me share would be selfish and cruel" Nicholas called, chasing after her.

"I've always been cruel and selfish, anyone will tell you" Freya replied.

"Come here, let me take your photo" Nicholas insisted and he took hold of the camera and wrestled it from her grasp.

"Only if you promise to let me have Claude back straight away" Freya bargained.

"You've named the camera" Nicholas remarked.

"I name all my cameras, now do we have a deal?" Freya asked.

"Claude is all yours for the rest of the day" Nicholas agreed.

"OK, well come on, get on with it, my face hurts if I smile for too long" Freya spoke as she smiled for him.

"That's nice, really good, so now with your top off honey" Nicholas said, zooming in on her chest.

"Give Claude here, topless shots are purely for the bedroom" Freya said, snatching back the camera.

"I'll remember that" Nicholas replied and he took hold of her hand.

They began their walk around the freshwater lake which was only separated from the sea by sand dunes and grassland. Freya pointed out the bird and plant life she was familiar with, having visited the lake on several occasions, and took photographs when something particularly caught her eye.

"What's your film about?" Freya asked Nicholas as they walked.

"Where did that come from?" Nicholas asked her.

"Well it just struck me suddenly that I don't know the name of this film you are making or what it's about and I really think I should. What's the plot?" Freya inquired.

"Oh it's really thin and flimsy" Nicholas admitted.

"So why do it? I would have thought you could pick and choose your films now you are where you are, at the top of the acting tree" Freya spoke.

"I can and I do the majority of the time. But the parts I enjoy getting stuck into aren't necessarily the kind of role people want to see me playing so I have to take that into consideration. So I do a few big budget action films which pleases the fans and then I do more serious and demanding roles in smaller budget films for me" Nicholas explained.

"So what's this one about?" Freya asked.

"It's called 'Captive'. I'm the hero – obviously – and Hilary is my love interest....."

"Obviously" Freya added.

"My character, Nathan, has got into trouble with a nasty Mr Big who is played by Bob"

"Ironic" Freya replied.

"And basically Hilary's character gets kidnapped and Nathan decides in his wisdom to go and get her back without telling the cops" Nicholas explained.

"That sounds like a bit of a rip off of 'Commando'" Freya announced.

"You like Arnold Schwarzenegger too?" Nicholas asked.

"I have his entire catalogue on DVD" Freya told him.

"We seriously need to talk about your film library" Nicholas remarked with a smile.

"I do have one of your movies, 'Turncoat'" Freya admitted.

"And did you enjoy it?" Nicholas asked her.

"I wouldn't say I enjoyed it, I cried most of the way through it. But I really lost it when Boris got killed at the end. I was sort of expecting it but I was still surprised when it actually happened" Freya told him.

"Good, that was exactly the idea. So how was my performance? Any room for improvement?" Nicholas inquired.

"You won an Academy Award for that role, you don' t need me to tell you how good your performance was" Freya replied.

"Maybe I do" Nicholas responded.

"Well, I thought you played the character with sensitivity. You made him appear vulnerable even when he was torturing people which is completely admirable. But I think, what I liked best was the way you made him a real person with all the complicated feelings that real people have. I mean he was a vile, evil Nazi, but by the end of the movie I was sympathising with him. I mean it wasn't really about the war or him being a Nazi, I thought it was really about the fact he started out as just an every day person. He was just an ordinary man in an extreme situation having to make decisions about right and wrong and trying understand his humanity" Freya told him.

"That is the best synopsis I've heard, you totally got the film. Do you know when I won the Oscar I wasn't even sure whether the people that nominated me even understood what it was really about" Nicholas spoke.

"Everyone has a unique interpretation of things, perhaps it doesn't matter whether they did or not" Freya said.

"I think everyone has a bit of Boris in them, someone scared of their past, uncertain of their future, struggling to make sense of life, I know I have" Nicholas admitted.

"Me too but I think I will hold off on torturing anyone today" Freya spoke with a smile.

They found a shaded area close to the lake and Freya laid down the blanket she had packed. Nicholas sat down and watched as Freya busied herself getting out containers of food.

"Won't you let me help? I feel redundant just sat here watching" Nicholas told her.

"No, it's fine, all under control, besides you would only peek. Now, if there's anything you don't like I apologise but I'm not as financially able to order an entire shop like you" Freya spoke.

"There's not much I dislike, apart from sushi, you don't have any of that do you? I'm not a lover of cold fish, it's just wrong" Nicholas told her.

"No cold fish. Now, before we eat I've prepared a little quiz" Freya announced and produced a piece of paper.

"A quiz" Nicholas remarked.

"Yes, I thought it would be a fun way for me to get to know more about you" Freya carried on.

"Now this isn't fair. You should have mentioned this last night, given me some time to prepare my questions" Nicholas spoke.

"But it was my date to organise and you sprung surprises on me" Freya reminded him.

"Well I'm not answering any of those questions unless we turn them round and you have to answer them as well" Nicholas insisted.

"Perhaps I should have mentioned this last night and that would have given me time to prepare my answers" Freya responded.

"That's the deal, so are we agreed?" Nicholas asked as Freya sat down cross legged in front of him.

"I'm not used to having someone boss me around" Freya admitted.

"Me neither" Nicholas replied with a grin.

"Oh go on then, I'll answer the questions" Freya agreed reluctantly.

"Good, well go on, shoot, because I'm starving" Nicholas told her.

"OK, right, Question One, date of birth and star sign" Freya asked.

"October 21st 1970, Libra"

"36 this year" Freya said, writing on her paper.

"Hey are you taking notes? Are you sure you're not a reporter?" Nicholas remarked.

"Don't freak out! I'm ticking off the questions as I ask them that's all" Freya responded.

"Go on, your birth date, 21st June 19?"

"Actually its 20th June 1976, Gemini" Freya told him.

"But you said your birthday was the night we met at the restaurant" Nicholas commented.

"It was a second birthday to make up for the awful one I had had the day before" Freya informed him.

"And here was I thinking it was only the Queen of England who had two birthdays" Nicholas remarked.

"Me and Lizzie....OK tell me about your marriage?"

"Well my wife's name was Lauren Germaine. She's an actress, you might have heard of her, although she hasn't worked with Bruce or Arnie as far as I am aware. Anyway, we met in 1998, we married in 1999 and we divorced in 2001. We shouldn't have got married, it was too quick, and as I told you before, we wanted different things" Nicholas told Freya.

"Were you in love?" Freya asked him seriously.

"I thought so at the time, but no, I don't think we were in love. She's married now, has two children. A lot can happen in five years" Nicholas told her.

"Yes it can" Freya agreed.

"So have you been married? Got children?"

"No, never been married, no children" Freya responded.

"Been close?"

"Not really" Freya replied.

"But you've been in love" Nicholas stated.

"Yes, once, a long time ago. I was young, we both were and it probably wouldn't have worked out anyway" Freya said thinking back.

"What happened?" Nicholas asked her.

"We are digressing. This is not on my list of questions" Freya told him.

"You didn't specify that digressing was forbidden" Nicholas replied.

"Are we in the courtroom Mr Harvard? This is my date remember" Freya spoke.

"Look, like I said last night, it's OK, if you're uncomfortable talking about it" Nicholas spoke.

"It was a long time ago that's all..............pets?" Freya asked, moving on the questioning.

"No, I don't stay in one place long enough to take care of a pet. You?"

"No, I'd probably end up killing a pet because I would forget to feed it or walk it or something. I don't have any plants in my house for that same reason" Freya said.

"Because you would forget to walk them?" Nicholas questioned with a smile.

"Exactly. So, now we are on to stays in hospital. Ever been sick?" Freya asked him.

"How did we get from pets to hospitals?" Nicholas inquired.

"Well I wrote some of the questions yesterday before I got stitches in my arm and then the rest I wrote afterwards when I had trauma on my mind" Freya informed him.

"I see" Nicholas spoke.

"So have you ever been ill or had an operation or broken something interesting? You must have a medical story to tell, everyone does" Freya told him.

Nicholas took a deep breath and Freya noticed him stiffen and look slightly uncomfortable.

"We don't have to do that question, it was stupid and you probably don't want to hear about the time I broke my arm falling off of a lorry" Freya started, trying to ease his obvious anxiety.

"No. It's OK. I said I would answer the questions and although we haven't known each other long I do trust you" Nicholas spoke.

He ran his hand through his hair and took a sip of water from the bottle.

Freya sat still and waited to hear what he was going to say. She had no idea what was coming.

"I had cancer" Nicholas said seriously.

"Oh my God. Are you OK?" Freya announced in horror.

"Yes, I was given the all clear three years ago" Nicholas informed her.

"Well why did I not know about this? I mean you are always in all the newspapers all the time and OK I wouldn't read every article on you but you pick up most things by them being announced on TV and stuff, I would have remembered hearing something like that" Freya spoke.

"It wasn't in the papers. No one knows about it" Nicholas said with a deep breath.

"What? What do you mean no one knows about it? I've seen the photographers tailing you, they would print anything about you, something like that would not escape their notice" Freya asked in bemusement.

"I mean you're the first person I've told" Nicholas stated.

"The first girl you've dated that you've told?"

"No, the first person I've told, period" Nicholas spoke, his eyes fixed on the ground.

"And this happened when? Four years ago? And you told no one, went through it alone" Freya exclaimed in amazement.

"Yeh" Nicholas responded, taking another sip of the bottled water.

"I don't believe it. How can you go through something like that and no one know? I mean, were you working on a movie at the time? Where did you go? How did the press not find out?" Freya questioned.

"I went to Canada for my treatment, I checked into the hospital under an assumed name and I locked myself

191

away from everyone and everything and just focussed on getting through it. Part of me wanted to tell my brother, the other part didn't because I knew what would go through his mind. He had lost his parents and now he was going to lose his brother. He's married now, with a daughter, but he's still vulnerable because of what he went through back then. He didn't need something like that to worry about" Nicholas attempted to explain.

"I don't know what to say, I mean it was incredibly brave but also incredibly stupid, you should have had support" Freya insisted.

"I didn't want to burden anyone with it and also, I think if I had actually said the words to someone it would have made it seem real. As it was, I kind of tied it up inside me and it became like an internal battle of wills between me and the cancer" Nicholas spoke.

"But you're OK now? Completely clear" Freya checked.

"Yes I'm OK, I have to go and have checks every now and then but at the moment it's all good" Nicholas responded.

"So where was it, the cancer?" Freya asked him.

"The location of the cancer was another reason why I chose not to tell anyone............it was testicular cancer" Nicholas stated.

Freya remained quiet, letting him continue.

"I didn't want anyone to know because how many action heroes would carry on selling movies if their audience knew they only had one ball" Nicholas spoke matter of factly.

"They had to remove it" Freya spoke.

"Yeh, which freaked me out to begin with, but the people I met at the hospital, people with other types of cancer were going through so much more than me. I had no right to feel sorry for myself. Plus they did a pretty good job with the prosthesis" Nicholas told Freya honestly.

"I don't know what to say, to go through that on your own, I don't know how you did it" Freya admitted.

"It was my choice, I used keeping it a secret as a weapon against the disease. I think it helped me remain focussed on living my life rather than dwelling on the fact that I had something that could kill me" Nicholas explained.

"Well, I admire you for getting through it. Can you still have children?" Freya asked him.

"Yes, they tell me one compensates for the loss of the other so to speak. This is embarrassing isn't it?" Nicholas remarked with half a laugh.

"I'm not embarrassed. You lose Bert you still have Ernie, there is almost always one half of the duo who is better anyway. Take Starsky and Hutch, what was the point of Hutch? Or Laurel and Hardy, Laurel just got on my nerves" Freya told him.

"I can't believe you are comparing my testicles to Starsky and Hutch" Nicholas said with a loud laugh.

"There could be worse comparisons" Freya insisted.

"So do you think you would like kids one day?" Nicholas asked.

"I don't know. I mean I can't even look after a pet or a plant, what would I do with a baby?" Freya asked him.

"We could get a nanny" Nicholas responded with a smile.

The significance of the use of plural was not lost on Freya and she smiled back at him.

"So, you and Hitler eh? I hope having one ball is all you two have in common" Freya joked.

"Well actually I was thinking of growing one of those little moustaches" Nicholas answered.

"Can I end our relationship now?" Freya questioned in jest.

The quiz came to a rapid conclusion once Nicholas had confessed about his cancer and they eat some of the picnic. Freya then produced a cotton napkin and a plastic tub.

"One last game" she announced.

"This is the very last time I let you organise a date, it has been like a TV challenge show" Nicholas informed her.

"Here, put on your blindfold" Freya urged him.

"And you promise there is no cold fish?" Nicholas asked her.

"I promise, just some lovely Greek delicacies and you have to guess what they are" Freya told him.

"Fine but how is this game going to work for you? I can't blindfold you, you know what you packed in the container" Nicholas spoke.

"Put your blindfold on, come on it will be fun" Freya insisted and she held the napkin to Nicholas' face and moved to tie it around the back of his head.

"Don't run off and leave me here, I am no good with directions, I'll fall into that lake and be eaten by whatever lives in it" Nicholas told her.

"Sshh, open your mouth" Freya ordered.

He did as he was told and Freya put in a large black olive.

"Now, don't chew, just hold it in your mouth and wait a few seconds, OK, now suck slowly, don't chew, just suck" Freya spoke as she watched the olive move around in his mouth.

"It's an olive" Nicholas said as he ate.

"Yes, but doesn't it taste better with your eyes closed? You can eat it now but don't forget to spit the pip out" Freya ordered.

Nicholas swallowed the olive and spat out the stone in the bushes.

"Now, try this" Freya spoke and she put a cube of feta cheese into his mouth.

"It's salty, creamy and crumbly, definitely feta cheese. This is too easy" Nicholas told her as he ate.

"It isn't about getting it right, it's about experiencing the taste differently" Freya said.

"OK, sorry, what's next? Is it something sweet?" Nicholas asked, opening his mouth in anticipation.

"See I told you this would be fun. Now this is one of my favourite Greek specialities Nick and you are just going to love it" Freya spoke and she picked up a piece of seaweed from the container.

"I can't wait" he replied.

Freya put the cold, wet, green sea plant in his mouth and tried to hold in her laughter.

"Oh my God, what is this? It's wet and cold and chewy and it tastes salty and rubbery. Am I supposed to have this in my mouth?" Nicholas questioned as he struggled to chew and looked uncomfortable.

"Oh you're so funny! Your face!" Freya exclaimed as she laughed out loud, unable to control herself any longer.

"Have I really got to eat this? What is it? It's disgusting" Nicholas remarked.

"No don't swallow it, you can spit it out, take your blindfold off" Freya spoke through her laughter.

"What the Hell was it? Seaweed! Urgh God, it's probably been swimming around with excrement for the past year" Nicholas spoke, hurriedly swilling his mouth out with water.

"What are you insinuating about the Aegean?" Freya asked.

"God that was awful, but I'm glad it gave you some laughs. Your turn now, so you had better put this blindfold on" Nicholas said and he put the napkin over her face and tied it up.

"No seaweed left I'm afraid, give me the feta first, I'm ready for it" Freya announced enthusiastically.

Nicholas looked at her, waiting expectantly and smiling excitedly.

"Tell me when you want me to open my mouth" Freya told him.

Nicholas leaned towards her.

"About now" he spoke in no more than a whisper.

He touched her lips with his and Freya flinched slightly in surprise. His lips felt soft and moist and she immediately opened her mouth as he moved further towards her, kissing her deeply. Freya reached out for him, taking hold of the hair at the back of his head and pulling him towards her. She did not want this moment to end.

When Nicholas did pull away Freya was breathless and still blindfolded.

"Please tell me that was you and I haven't just embarrassed myself with a Greek farmer or something" Freya spoke.

"Take your blindfold off and I'll kiss you again so you can check" Nicholas told her.

Freya removed the napkin from her face and smiled at him. This time she moved towards him and pulled him towards her to kiss him again.

There were no photographers, no entourage, no crazy ex-boyfriends, just Freya and Nicholas, in each others arms beneath the Corfiot sun.

"It's so peaceful here" Nicholas remarked to Freya a little later.

Freya was laid back on the grass with her head in his lap. Nicholas had been gently stroking her hair for the last half an hour and Freya had not felt so completely content in a long time. The sun was making her warm all over and Nicholas' fingers softly brushing her scalp was starting to make her feel deliciously sleepy.

"Mmm peaceful, it's nice to be away from everything" Freya agreed.

"Is that why you came to Corfu? To get away from everything?" Nicholas asked her.

"Yes. I'm a bit impulsive, if you hadn't guessed already. I decided I needed a break and I wanted to see Emma, so I got on a plane" Freya told him.

"But things back home are OK? Your business and everything is going good? You've got no worries?" Nicholas asked her.

"No. Where is this coming from?" Freya asked him and she immediately sat up, feeling less content.

"Something Russell said last night that's all. He said had you lied to everyone or was it just him? If you are in any way financially tied to that jerk just let me know" Nicholas told her.

"I'm not financially tied to anyone" Freya stated firmly.

"I'm sorry, I said I wouldn't pry didn't I?" Nicholas responded.

"You did and honestly, I'm not in any trouble. Do I look like the kind of girl who gets in trouble?" Freya questioned with a tongue in cheek smile.

"I don't think I need to answer that" Nicholas told her.

"My worries are historic, I promise" Freya replied.

"Good. So, how would you feel about accompanying me to Athens on Friday? I've got to attend a dinner for the Greek dignitaries to thank them for allowing us to film here. It will be a honey pot for the press, there will be hundreds of them and it will mean me spending an hour or so signing autographs and posing for pictures with fans on the way in. But on the upside, there is a five course meal albeit we will probably be sat somewhere near Gene and Bob. And there are speeches, including one from me" Nicholas explained.

"And the good points?" Freya asked.

"I thought the five course meal would have done it for you, it's the only thing I'm looking forward to" Nicholas admitted.

"Can I wear a blindfold?" Freya inquired.

"I think questions would be asked. There are other pros apart from the food. We get to travel by helicopter and we get the penthouse suite in one of the best hotels in Athens" Nicholas told her.

"Stay the night?" Freya asked him.

"Yes" Nicholas replied, looking at her.

"Perhaps a blindfold will have a place in the evening after all" Freya responded with a grin.

"So is that a yes?" Nicholas inquired.

"It's a yes as long as you promise to keep the sharp cutlery away from me if Fred and Ginger make any 'large' comments" Freya responded, referring to Bob and Gene.

"It's a deal" Nicholas agreed.

"What is Martha going to say?" Freya asked him.

"She is going to freak but hey, I like living dangerously" Nicholas told her and he leant forward to kiss her again.

Chapter Nine

It was almost five o clock when Nicholas and Freya arrived back in Kassiopi.

They returned the motorbike to the hire shop and tried to make their way through the village as discreetly as possible.

"Shall we get a cup of tea? Do you want to come back to 'The Calypso?" Freya asked as they walked along, hand in hand.

"Yeh sure, coffee would be good and........" Nicholas spoke.

He broke off as his mobile phone began to ring.

"I'm sorry I'd better get that" he apologised and opened the phone up to answer.

They stopped walking and Freya immediately began to feel that everyone was looking at them. People were definitely slowing down in pace as they passed them, pointing and whispering. Freya could only assume that they were quietly debating what they should do in the light of being yards away from a celebrity.

"Does it have to be tonight? No I know..... I guess so ....yes I realise that, OK....... yeh OK, I'll be ready.......yes, I'll see you" Nicholas spoke into the phone and then ended the call.

"You're working tonight" Freya stated when he turned back to her.

"Yes, plans have changed and they want to shoot some stuff tonight, I'm sorry" Nicholas spoke.

"That's OK" Freya replied.

"I wish I didn't have to film. I wanted to take you out to dinner, talk some more and hopefully make out some more" Nicholas told her with a smile.

"Well hold that thought, maybe we can do it tomorrow night. I mean you are here to film, not be distracted by the likes of me. I will find some way to amuse myself, I'm sure I won't be invited to waitress again but there are nightly quizzes and karaoke competitions to enter around here" Freya reminded him.

"Why don't you come with me to filming?" Nicholas suggested, holding both her hands.

"Oh I don't know, where is it? What would I do? You weren't thinking of making me a runner or a grip? By the way, what is a grip?" Freya questioned.

"The only gripping I had in mind didn't involve cameras or lights............it's up at the fort, there will be about a million people running around after the director and Martha will be there running around after me and Bill and Ted will be there" Nicholas said, speaking of Bob and Gene.

"Are you trying to make this an attractive scenario?" Freya asked him.

"You'll get to see me probably forgetting my lines, definitely forgetting my actions but when it's over we can do whatever you like, have something to eat or go for a drink or ...." Nicholas began.

"Bit of Greek Dancing at Zorba's?" Freya suggested.

"If that is really what you want to do I'm happy to watch you" Nicholas answered with a smile.

"And if I come to filming am I going to have to watch you and Barbie fawning all over each other?" Freya asked, speaking of Hilary.

"If I remember rightly there isn't any 'fawning' at the fort but what's with the feeling insecure? I thought I made my intentions clear earlier" Nicholas spoke, slipping his arms around her.

"Yes, you're right, why should I feel insecure? I mean look at Hilary and I, both identical, practically separated at birth with our svelte figures and supermodel looks" Freya spoke sarcastically.

"She spends over an hour in make up before we shoot anything, she has to have three hair stylists and you've seen her eat, I've taken more food home in a brown bag" Nicholas told her.

"And I guess the little she does eat probably ends up down the toilet" Freya answered.

"Exactly, there would be no playing food games with her" Nicholas added.

"You would definitely get bored of tasting lettuce. 'Now Nick, I can't make up my mind, is this Kos or Iceberg?'" Freya joked.

"So are you going to come?" Nicholas asked Freya.

"Can I see if Emma can make it? It would be so up her street" Freya said.

"Sure, she can keep you company and cover your eyes when we do the cliff top sex scene" Nicholas replied.

"And she can help me heckle, it is OK to heckle isn't it?" Freya queried with a grin.

"I think you know the answer to that one" Nicholas answered smiling.

It was already half past seven when Freya and Emma made their way through the village towards the path which led up to the ruined fort. Emma had been ecstatic when Freya had said they had been invited to filming, for a prompt start at seven o clock. But she had managed to get herself involved in serving at the restaurant and had to be practically dragged away.

"Will you stop running? We're not that late, they aren't going to refuse us entry if we aren't bang on time. I am dating the star of this movie" Freya called, trying to tug Emma back and slow her down.

"I'm sorry I made us late, the restaurant is so busy lately it's all hands on deck" Emma spoke as she tried to catch her breath.

"But it can't go on Em, not with you in a delicate condition, it's too much working night and day, you have to tell Yiannis" Freya said seriously.

"I know, I know but it just never seems to be the right time" Emma complained.

"There never is a right time believe me" Freya stated with a sigh.

"I take it you didn't tell Nick about you then" Emma said.

"I couldn't. I'm pathetic, I mean he was so honest with me, telling me things he said he hadn't told anyone before and I thought about it and I just couldn't bring myself to do it" Freya explained with another sigh.

"Oh Freya" Emma spoke.

"We kissed Em and it was amazing and I just couldn't spoil it and I just knew it would if I did, so I didn't" Freya told her.

"Do you think it is going to be serious between you?" Emma inquired.

"I don't know, I mean we've only just started but I know I do feel at ease with him, you know, like I can be me" Freya admitted.

"Then you have to tell him and I think he would prefer to hear it from you than from someone else" Emma spoke.

"I know, it's just difficult, it's been so long since I left it behind, I just want it all to stay in the past" Freya answered.

"I bet you do" a voice suddenly spoke.

The sound of Russell startled Freya as she had been completely unaware of anyone walking behind them. Both Freya and Emma stopped where they were and turned around to face him.

"Don't mind if I join you do you? Apparently the fort is the place to be tonight, some sort of movie being filmed and the word in the village is that it's free hotdogs for everyone. You know I can't resist a freebie" Russell spoke, beginning to walk alongside the two women.

"Look, what are you doing here? I said I would talk to you and I will, but not tonight and not here" Freya said.

"Well perhaps time is starting to become an issue for me" Russell responded.

"Now you listen to me, I never thought you were good enough for Freya and you are really showing your true colours now. Don't you dare pressurise her" Emma ordered him.

"Oh Emma, do I take it that you have been privy to Freya's deception?

"Freya hasn't deceived anyone. The reason she was probably economical with the truth with regards to you is because she obviously didn't feel she could trust you and isn't that proving to be a spot on judgement?" Emma spoke, angered by Russell.

"You've changed Emma, not so shy anymore, I can only assume you have spent too much time in the company of Miss Opinionated here" Russell responded.

"Just stop it Russell, this has nothing to do with Emma, just get it over with, how much do you want?" Freya wanted to know.

"You think I want money? Whatever gave you that idea?" Russell questioned.

"Well I realise that I haven't seen my mother for a year or so and I am sure she has been surgically and cosmetically enhanced into looking half her age but I am relatively sure that the only reason she turned your head was because she has a Swiss bank account. And as you have been servicing her in the bedroom and my mother is generous with cash when it comes to getting what she wants I am also assuming that she tipped you well, probably well enough to enable you to reacquaint yourself with your bookmaker" Freya began, watching Russell's expression.

"Your mother is a very accommodating woman" Russell responded.

"But she also gets bored very easily and, believe me, you are not the first younger man she has entertained in this marriage or her previous marriage. She can't help herself you see, she likes pretty things and everything has its price. How do you feel about being one of her pretty things Russell?" Freya inquired.

"It was a mutual admiration and we both got what we wanted" Russell replied.

"Until she moved on to the next one, I take it that's what happened. Or did you just get greedy and she thought it was time to move on to someone with less financial ambition? Either way, she ended it didn't she, which meant goodbye to your betting fund" Freya carried on.

"There was a little more to our relationship than just a shared love of the good life, she is actually good fun, uninhibited, carefree. It was a shock in more ways than one to find out that you were her daughter, I can only presume you take after the old man" Russell responded.

"How dare you!" Emma exclaimed immediately, her voice full of emotion.

"It's OK Emma, let Russell have his say, it will be the final conversation he ever has with me. How much do you want to keep your mouth shut and to keep the bookies from your door?" Freya wanted to know, maintaining her calm.

"I want £25,000, that's all. Give me that and your identity stays in the past" Russell informed coolly.

"What?! You are joking!" Emma exclaimed in horror.

"Do I sound like I am joking? Do you really think I would have travelled over here if I didn't have to?" he retorted.

"And if I don't get you the money?" Freya asked.

"If you don't get me the money I will sell your story and the truth about who you are to the highest bidder. And there will be bidders Freya, particularly now you are moving in celebrity circles" Russell spoke with a smirk.

"You evil shit" Emma stated, before she could stop herself.

"I will take that as a compliment. So, Freya, what's it to be? A quiet settlement or you, me, Mummy and Daddy sharing the front cover of 'Hello' magazine?" Russell wanted to know.

"I don't have twenty five grand, you know that" Freya managed to speak.

"But you have at least two men in your life who could easily provide that sort of money and I'm not fussy how you get it. Ask Mr Kaden, ask Daddy but if you don't get it, your world is going to come crashing down" Russell warned.

Freya took a deep breath and then she nodded at Russell. A smile of satisfaction appeared on his face until Freya spoke.

"No" she said.

"I'm sorry, did I hear correctly? Did you say 'no'?" Russell asked, his expression darkening.

"Do you want me to say it again for you? I said 'no'. You are not getting a penny out of me. If you think I am going to pay you anything after I have wasted eighteen months of my life with you then you really are a mug" Freya informed him.

Russell pursed his lips, considering what to do and say next. Along with anger and almost contempt in his face, Freya saw utter fear and anguish in his eyes and could only assume that he really was desperately in debt to someone.

"Now you've heard what Freya has said why don't you piss off back to where you came from" Emma ordered bravely.

Russell turned, as if to leave, and then, overcome with rage he turned back and pushed Emma hard, making her stumble over and land on the ground.

"You bloody idiot! What have you done?" Freya shrieked and hurriedly bent down over Emma who was sitting on the ground looking shocked.

"You should keep the bitch on her leash" Russell spat angrily.

"She's pregnant for Christ's sake! Go and get some help" Freya screamed, overcome with fright for her friend.

Russell's expression changed and his pallor paled as he realised what he had done and the seriousness of the situation. He put his hands to his head and just stood still like a frozen statue.

"The baby" Emma said in nothing more than a whisper, looking up at Freya with panic in her eyes.

"I know, I know, does it hurt anywhere?" Freya asked her hurriedly.

"I don't know, I'm not sure but I think I'm bleeding" Emma stated as the tears began to fall and she started to breathe heavily.

"No, no you're not, everything is going to be fine................for God's sake Russell either go and get some help or piss off!" Freya exclaimed as she began to rifle through her handbag to find her mobile phone.

Shocked back into the situation Russell turned on his heel and hurried down the pathway back towards the village.

Freya opened her phone and called Nicholas.

"Hello is Nick there?...............yes I know he is filming but this is an emergency, it's Freya Martha and I need to speak to Nick................please, for Christ's sake, just get him..................forget it"

Freya ended the call and contemplated what to do for a few seconds. It was useless to call an ambulance, they were miles away from the nearest facility and the nearest hospital was in Corfu Town. She needed transport immediately.

"I'm going to lose the baby aren't I?" Emma stated, going very pale.

"No! Emma don't be silly, it's going to be fine. Look, don't move, just stay there, I'll be back" Freya spoke as positively as she could.

She set off up the hill towards the fort as fast as she could. She hadn't wanted to leave Emma on her own but she needed to get hold of a car. The nearest person who had a car was Nicholas and if anyone could rustle a car up in a few seconds it was him.

By the time she reached the area in which they were filming she was sweating, out of breath and in absolute panic.

The crowd around the security cordon was ten deep, she couldn't see anyone she knew. It was pointless calling Nicholas' phone again and she didn't know what to do. She had to do something but what?

Just as fear was rising in her stomach, threatening to actually make her vomit she saw Roger, Nicholas' bodyguard, at the edge of the cordon. She had never been so pleased to see someone in her whole life but she still had to attract his attention.

"ROGER! ROGER!" Freya yelled at the top of her voice, waving both her hands in the air was wildly as she could.

"Get out of the way! I was here first, you can't just push in you know" a woman who Freya had ended up standing next to yelled at her.

"Piss off will you, this is an emergency. ROGER!! ROGER!!" Freya shouted hysterically.

She put her fingers to her lips and whistled as loudly as she could. The high pitched noise was enough to make Roger look up from what he was doing and see her waving and shouting.

"ROGER I NEED HELP" Freya screamed.

Without hesitation he ducked under the cordon and hurried through the crowd towards her, pushing people aside as he did so.

"Move aside please, move aside Sir, move aside............Freya, what's going on?" Roger greeted when he eventually reached her.

"Roger I need the car, it's an emergency, my friend Emma, we need to get to the hospital now" Freya babbled hurriedly, emotion rising rapidly.

"Fine, where is she? Let's go, I'll call Mike" Roger said and he followed Freya towards the way back down from the fort.

"Hi Mike, look can you get to the path at the entrance to the fort right now, we're going to Corfu Town" Roger spoke into his mobile phone as he hurried behind Freya.

Emma was sat in the same spot but was being comforted by two passers by who Freya could only assume Russell had called to come to her assistance.

"Emma it's going to be fine, Roger's getting the car and we'll be in the hospital in no time, Mike is a fantastic driver, no one could get you there quicker or safer" Freya assured her and she put an arm around her shoulders as she sat down on the floor next to her.

"I think it's going to be too late" Emma spoke, wiping her nose with the back of her hand.

"No it's not, don't say that, it's going to be fine. I promise you" Freya said, trying to hide her fears.

"Don't make promises you can't keep Freya" Emma told her.

"I don't make promises I can't keep, it's going to be fine, it has to be fine.........where is Mike?" Freya asked, looking up at Roger.

"He was just at the harbour, he won't be long..............here he is" Roger announced as the black Mercedes arrived and pulled up next to them.

"We need to make a stop at 'Petroholis Restaurant'" Freya told Mike as Roger picked Emma up from the ground and put her gently down in the back of the car.

"You're going to get Yiannis? But he doesn't know" Emma reminded Freya.

"Well I think it's time he did because you need him right now............Roger can you tell Nick what's going on?" Freya asked him.

"Sure" Roger agreed.

"Step on it Mikey" Freya ordered as she got into the front of the car and made the dividing screen fall so she could keep an eye on Emma.

"I'm scared, I don't want to lose this baby, no matter where it was supposed to come on my list" Emma announced.

"I know" Freya replied and she bit her lip.

A little life was hanging in the balance because of her and her secrets and her stupid past. It suddenly put everything into perspective.

It was just over an hour before the group reached the hospital. Freya sat alone in the corridor, staring at the white wall in front of her. Yiannis had gone as white as the wall when Freya had burst into the restaurant and told him Emma needed to go to hospital. Freya didn't know what his reaction had been when Emma had told him about the pregnancy as she had shut the dividing screen and given them some privacy on the journey into the capital.

Freya was terrified for Emma and she knew she had caused this situation. Bloody Russell, bloody parents, bloody bloody past. She didn't care anymore, about anything, the only thing that mattered to her now was Emma and Yiannis' baby.

As the door of the room opened Freya rose to her feet and held her breath. Her heart was racing, she was mentally praying over and over in her head and her fingers were crossed together behind her back so tightly they hurt.

Yiannis came out into the corridor and Freya couldn't tell from his expression what the news was. Her heart thumped against her chest and she felt physically sick like never before.

"She's fine" Yiannis stated.

"And the baby?" Freya asked, swallowing a lump in her throat.

"The baby's fine too. Heart is beating normally and all is OK" Yiannis announced.

"Oh thank God! Oh Yiannis, I'm so so pleased" Freya said, almost hysterical with relief.

She threw her arms around him and held him close to her.

"You are going to make a wonderful father" Freya told him sincerely.

"Thank you" Yiannis answered, tears in his eyes.

"Can I see Emma?" Freya asked, wiping at her eyes and trying to compose herself.

"Yes, they are going to keep her overnight to make sure all is OK and I am going to stay too" Yiannis told her.

"OK, well I'll just be a minute and then I'll leave you two alone" Freya spoke.

She wiped her eyes again and took a deep breath before she opened the door of Emma's room and entered.

Emma looked pale and washed out, hardly standing out against the white bed sheets. There was a doctor in the room, pressing buttons on the machine next to the bed.

"Hi" Freya greeted.

"Hello" Emma responded.

"Please, no stay too long, she needs rest" the doctor told Freya as he headed towards the door.

"I promise, two minutes, that's all" Freya assured.

The doctor left the room and Freya sat down in the chair next to Emma's bed.

"The baby's fine" Emma informed her.

"I know, Yiannis told me, it's fantastic news" Freya spoke.

"You kept that promise. I'm sorry if I was horrible to you earlier, I was just so scared" Emma told her.

"You weren't horrible to me, although God knows you should have been. It was all my fault and I would never have forgiven myself if anything had happened to you or the baby" Freya spoke, holding her friend's hand.

"It wasn't your fault it was that shit Russell" Emma said with a sigh.

"Who was here being a shit because of me, who was threatening me because of my stupid past. Well that is something that is never going to happen again" Freya told her seriously.

"You aren't going to pay him that money are you?" Emma spoke.

"No, I'm not going to pay him the money, like I said I don't have the money. But I'm not going to have him blackmail me either, if it isn't him doing the blackmailing it will be someone else some other time and for what?" Freya asked.

"So you can still be Freya" Emma reminded her.

"I'll always be Freya Em, I always was on the inside" Freya insisted.

When Freya got outside the hospital she switched on her mobile. It rang straight away and there was a message from Nicholas.

"Hi Freya it's Nick. Roger told me Emma's sick and you've gone to the hospital. If you want me to come there just call me and I'll come. I know you might not be able to call, what with hospital protocol, but just call as soon as you can and let me know you're OK and that Emma's OK. OK, bye"

Freya sighed. This was going to be hard. She pressed 'call' on Nicholas' name and heard the phone ring.

"Freya, are you OK?" Nicholas asked, answering the phone almost immediately.

"I'm fine and Emma's fine and the baby is fine" Freya told him.

"The baby? She's pregnant? Well what happened?" Nicholas questioned.

"Nick I need to see you" Freya stated seriously.

"OK, sure, get Mike to bring you to the villa. Are you sure you're OK?" Nicholas asked her.

"Yes, I'm OK, but we need to talk" Freya told him.

"That sounds very serious" Nicholas said.

"I'll see you in about an hour" Freya spoke.

"Sure, see you" Nicholas replied.

Freya ended the call and looked up at the sky. Clouds were forming, the air was cool and it looked like it was going to rain.

The torrent had started by the time she arrived at Villa Kamia. It was not just drizzle or a light sharp shower, this rain was torrential and the sky indicated that there was a distinct possibility of thunder.

There were photographers outside the villa and they started taking pictures as the car approached. Freya was glad she was hidden behind the privacy glass as she didn't much want to be seen by anyone, let alone the world's press. Mike drove through the villa gates and stopped outside the front door.

"Mike, thanks for everything tonight, I'm sorry about messing you about again, I don't usually spend so much time in the hospital" Freya told him.

"It's no problem, I'm just glad things worked out OK for you and your friend" Mike replied.

"Me too. I'll see you" Freya spoke and she got out of the car, shutting the door behind her.

She hurried up the steps to the front door and knocked. Nicholas opened the door and let Freya step in out of the rain. The photographers again took photos long range from the gate, which was thankfully partially blocking their view.

"Hey you're soaking, let me get you a towel" Nicholas said as Freya entered. After shutting the door he went to fetch one.

The entrance hall led into an open plan living and dining area. The floors were marble and the walls cream. There was an eight person dining table with leather high backed chairs in one area and a brown suede corner group sofa absolutely covered in cushions in another area with a giant plasma screen on one wall.

Freya bypassed it all, hardly taking her surroundings in. She didn't stop walking until she had reached the patio doors through which there was a view of the swimming pool, jacuzzi and lastly the ocean.

Freya took a deep breath and was ready to begin when Nicholas re-entered the room.

"Here, let me dry your hair" Nicholas said, going towards her with the towel.

"No it's fine" Freya insisted, moving away from him.

"This isn't sounding too good. What's happened since I left you this afternoon, you were happy then, really happy" Nicholas spoke, standing still.

"My best friend nearly lost a baby" Freya replied, tears already brimming in her eyes.

"I know but you said everything was fine, that Emma and the baby were fine" Nicholas replied.

"They are, but she wouldn't be in hospital if it wasn't for me and my stupid deception. Russell met up with us on the way to the fort, he wanted money to ensure my past stayed in the past. Anyway, the upshot is that he pushed Emma and she fell. She was trying to protect me, like always, but this time I should have been protecting her and I didn't" Freya said and she began to pace around nervously.

"Tried to blackmail you? I am getting this right?" Nicholas asked, astounded.

"Yeh, but it isn't the fact that he wanted £25,000 that's made me angry, it was the way he hurt Emma and how close I came to losing her the most precious thing in the world. So, I've decided it can't go on, I have to face things and I'm going to start doing that tonight. Which is why I'm going to tell you" Freya stated, nervously playing with her hands.

"Freya why don't you sit down? I can get us a drink" Nicholas began.

"No, please, let me get this out, before I change my mind" Freya begged, breathing erratically.

"I've said to you before, you don't need to tell me anything you don't want to. The last thing I want to do is make you feel uncomfortable" Nicholas reminded her.

"I have to do this Nick, for Emma, for me, for us" Freya stated seriously.

Nicholas sat on the edge of the sofa and watched her as she walked up and down.

"Right, well, where to start? OK, my name isn't Freya Johnson. Well, I mean, it is my name now but it wasn't my birth name. My real name is Jane Harriet Lawson-Peck. My father is Eric Lawson-Peck of Lawson-Peck Industries" Freya stated in a rush.

"The billionaire" Nicholas said simply.

"Yes, that's him. The entrepreneur, the charmer, the man of the people" Freya spoke.

Nicholas remained silent, letting Freya continue.

"I was born into this wealthy, luxurious world where my parents stamped their feet and people dropped everything and came running. The problem was I didn't fit into that world. I didn't understand the need for 36 pairs of shoes, 34 of which I never wore, I didn't care that my father had six cars, all custom made. And I didn't understand why my mother never wanted to spend time with me. I spent my childhood escaping from nannies, a different one every month. I'd climb out of my bedroom window, shin down the tree, go through the hole in the hedge I'd made and meet up with Emma to go to the cinema or bowling, normal things that normal people do. My closest companion in that house was Joseph the butler. All I really wanted was a mother and father who loved me but all they cared about was spending and buying and Prada and Versace" Freya carried on.

"Freya, I..........." Nicholas started, rising to his feet.

"No, please don't interrupt me now, I want to tell you it all. Where did I get to?" Freya asked him.

"You used to escape from the house and meet up with Emma" Nicholas prompted.

"Yeh, we used to go bowling. Well when I was sixteen I met a boy at the bowling centre. His name was Jonathan and I thought he was the most amazing looking guy I had ever seen. Of course, being quite a large girl then and having a hang up over my size, I didn't think I had a chance with him. Ring any bells? Anyway one day, we ended up together in the queue to get bowling shoes and we spoke and we laughed and the next time I went bowling it was a date, with him. I used a fake name even back then but when we started to get serious and I realised that I was starting to love this guy I told him the truth about who I was. And once he knew the truth and he said he loved me and he didn't care who my parents were, he asked me to marry him. I said yes and I decided to take him to meet my parents. I didn't want to but he said it would be OK and I trusted in him and I trusted in us. And, believe it or not, they were completely normal with him! We ate Chinese takeaway on normal dinner plates, not the bone china, and they asked him about his football team and college, not in a 'what do you want to do one day son' kind of way but just in a generally interested kind of way. I thought that finally some of what I had been telling them about the way they treated people had sunk in. Ha! More fool me! I mean for half a second I believed my life was going to change and Jonathan and I were going to have this perfect, normal happy life ahead of us. I should have known better. The very next day my father went to Jonathan's college and he gave him £30,000 and told him to leave the area and have no contact with me ever again" Freya carried on.

Her breathing had quickened, her chest was tight and her eyes were now spilling tears as she continued to pace about the room.

"That was the last time I ever told anyone my real name" Freya said and she paused for breath.

"My God" Nicholas remarked.

"Yeh, some story huh? Well there is a bit more. I've saved the best bit till last. After Jonathan left I thought my life was going to end. I was locked up in that fortress of a house, with my 36 pairs of shoes, going out of my mind, with parents who couldn't care less whether I was alive or not as long as I behaved well at dinner parties. So one night when they had gone to some gala dinner or other I found myself in the house, on my own, surrounded by all the glitz and chintz, the chandeliers, the sheepskin rugs, the antiques and 18th century paintings and I just broke down. I broke down because I realised that everything I was looking at meant more to my parents than I did. And that really hurt. So, what did I do? I went out to the garage, I got some petrol destined for the fleet of ride on mowers and I doused the house with it. I started with my mother's walk in wardrobe and ended with the hideous tiger skin rug in the lounge. I walked out of the front door, I set fire to one of my mother's hideous fur stoles and I tossed it back into the house and watched the whole lot burn" Freya spoke.

She was visibly shaking as she remembered the night, she felt cold now and her chest ached as she thought back to the pain she had felt at that time.

"My parents arrived back from their meal to see half the neighbourhood and three fire engines outside the smouldering house and my mother got out of the car, another fur stole hanging from her neck and said 'Oh my God Eric, I didn't put the diamonds back in the safe'. There was me, sat with the fire crew, wrapped in a blanket, and she was concerned about her bloody diamonds" Freya spoke, pausing to wipe her eyes.

"Freya, come and sit down" Nicholas begged.

"No, I must finish this. So anyway the fire brigade obviously found out it was arson and my father was furious, blaming the staff and then trying to think of someone who had a grudge against him, which of course was most of the people he had ever had business dealings with. And then I told him it was me. I told him I had torched everything precious to him to make him realise that these things meant nothing and he could just go out and replace them, but I was precious and he had hurt me by taking Jonathan away. I mean, what seventeen year old was going to walk away from £30,000 when he realised my parents were never going to give our relationship a chance anyway. He didn't have a choice. I told my father he couldn't do that to people and he shouldn't be doing it to his own daughter" Freya said.

"What did he say?" Nicholas asked.

"He didn't say very much, he let his actions speak for him. He beat me, which I knew he would, and then he pressed charges against me for arson. He did it to scare me, because a week before the court date he said that if I agreed to go away to some posh college and to have no more contact with Emma he would drop the charges. I said no. I mean Emma was all I had, she still is all I have, I couldn't lose her. So I went to court, I pleaded guilty and I got a year in prison" Freya stated, hugging herself as she paced.

"Jeeze Freya, you went to jail" Nicholas exclaimed in horror.

"Yeh, I did nine months. My mother visited three times in those nine months, her and my father got divorced while I was in there. I've not seen him since that day in court and now I've found out my mother has been shagging Russell the meagre relationship that we did have has bitten the dust. Emma came to see me every weekend she could while I was inside, she was my lifeline and that is why she is so precious to me" Freya said with a heavy sigh.

"So you changed your name when you got out" Nicholas guessed.

"Yes I became Freya Johnson. I chose Freya because it was the name of this very pretty, very slim, popular girl at school and Johnson was the surname of Joseph the butler, I thought it was fitting. So after that, I went to college, I learnt photography and I got a job with a small newspaper which gave me the experience I needed to get a bank loan and set up my own business. It wasn't the easiest thing to achieve with a criminal record though" Freya told him.

"I can imagine" Nicholas responded.

"So now you know who I was and what I did and why I'm like I am, this big, loud, larger than life person who runs away when things get too much and who has been keeping this secret for what seems like forever" Freya concluded and she hurried past Nicholas, heading for the front door of the villa.

"Where are you going?" Nicholas asked as he rushed after her.

"I'm going back to 'The Calypso' to pack. I'm going to go tomorrow, I've just done too much damage here one way or another. I was supposed to be anonymous forever, that isn't going to be the case anymore" Freya said as she pulled open the door.

"Freya don't be stupid, it doesn't matter, come back inside, we need to talk" Nicholas spoke, following her down the steps.

"I've said all I wanted to say, my throat is dry and I'm all talked out" Freya stated, the rain soaking through her thin top as she made her way to the gate.

"Well I haven't done my talking yet" Nicholas told her and he grabbed her arm and pulled her quite forcefully back towards him.

"I'm sorry if I've misled you, I think if there was anyone I would have confided in, without my hand being forced, I think it might have been you. I don't know when I would have got the courage to tell you but I think I would have, I hope I would have" Freya told him.

The rain was relentless, which was probably why the photographers were no longer in attendance and Nicholas and Freya were both in short sleeved tops getting completely drenched.

"Will you stop this? You're not going anywhere, I've heard what you've said and I'm old enough to be able to make my own decisions about people based on the present, the here and now, because that is what is important. How many times have I said that to you since we met? God Freya we all have a past, you know some of mine but not all of it, I've done some stupid things I'd like to erase. Granted I never got round to torching the family home but I might have, given the right provocation" Nicholas spoke.

"This isn't a joke you know" Freya retorted.

"I know it isn't a joke and I can't imagine how you have felt carrying this around for so long but did you really think it would change my opinion of you?" Nicholas asked her, holding her arms and forcing her to look at him.

"I don't know. I didn't think. All I know is how it might change things for me. It's been 11 years and although I try to pretend it's all behind me, there isn't a day goes by when I don't think about it. And I am scared that everything I have made for myself and everyone who knows me as Freya are going to look at me differently because I lied to them, because I am not who they thought" Freya spoke, the words choking in her throat.

"Listen to me Freya. When I met you it was like this whirlwind coming into my life. I've never met anyone like you before, you have an amazing spirit, you captivate everyone you come into contact with. I don't care if you are Freya or Jane or Peggy Sue or Bill Clinton's lovechild, you are you and everyone will realise that. And it's you, the Freya I have only known for a few days, that I am already falling in love with" Nicholas announced.

Freya looked at him, lost for words. The rain had soaked them both in a matter of minutes and both raindrops and teardrops were clouding her eyes.

"Say something" Nicholas begged, breathing deeply as he looked at her.

"I'm not Bill Clinton's lovechild" Freya said before she could stop herself.

"Well thank God for that because I have to tell you, although I said it would be OK I do have to draw the line somewhere" Nicholas responded with a smirk.

"I'm scared" Freya admitted with a shiver as the dampness of her clothes began to affect her.

"Come here, I've got you" Nicholas spoke and he drew her into his arms.

He held her close to him as the rain continued to fall on them. Freya closed her eyes and felt him stroke her wet hair and she clung it him, feeling truly protected for the first time in her life.

Chapter Ten

Freya was woken by the sunlight. When she managed to open her eyes she could see it was filtering through the shutters at the end of the room. She sat up immediately and looked around. She did not recognise it but it was certainly a step up from her room at 'The Calypso'.

She saw her clothes, still looking damp, hanging up on the front of the wardrobe and she remembered then where she was. She had spent the night at Villa Kamia.

Wet from the awful storm her and Nicholas had gone back into the villa and talked. There had been few light moments as she detailed her relationship with her parents and Nicholas had told her exactly how difficult it had been coping with the loss of his parents and raising his brother.

They had drunk brandy and coke, they had watched the lightening from the verandah and then............ what had happened then? Freya wracked her brain, putting her hands to her head. She didn't remember this bed, nothing about it was at all familiar.

She lifted up the duvet and saw that she was wearing a dark blue long sleeved shirt which she could only assume was Nicholas'. But how did she get it on? Did she take her own clothes off or did she have assistance?

Nicholas was in the lounge when she came downstairs, still wearing the shirt she had woken up in. He was dressed in linen trousers and a white shirt and was sat on the sofa scribbling in a notepad. He looked up and stopped writing when he saw her.

"Hey you're up, come and sit down, want some coffee?"

"I'm a tea person actually and normal tea, none of that fancy stuff" Freya told him as she crossed the room to join him.

"Very English" Nicholas said and he kissed her lightly on the lips.

"What are you writing?" Freya asked him as she sat down on the sofa.

"My speech for the party on Friday" Nicholas replied.

"You mean you don't have someone to do that for you?" Freya questioned.

"I do, but I decided that this one is going to be a bit different" Nicholas answered.

"I do hope it's nothing controversial or Martha will never allow it" Freya spoke.

"That is why Martha is getting the uncontroversial one to look at and this one stays with me" Nicholas replied with a smile.

Nicholas made the tea and they sat outside on the patio to drink it. It was a glorious morning, the storm of the night before and the rainfall had made the air fresher and less humid. However it was still Corfu in June and the sun was already up in a cloudless sky which promised a warm day.

"I think I drank too much last night" Freya admitted as she took a sip of her tea.

"Yeh me too, I have a very dry throat" Nicholas agreed.

"I don't really remember going to bed" Freya stated nervously.

"Oh" Nicholas answered, disappointment in his voice.

"Oh God, we didn't did we? I don't remember, oh God how awful, I....." Freya started, feeling very flustered.

"Hey, I'm kidding, nothing happened. I leant you a shirt because your clothes were wet, you got changed and then you fell asleep on the couch. I carried you up to the guest room and that's it" Nicholas told her.

"Carried me! You carried me upstairs! You carried me upstairs and you had been drinking! My God, are you OK?" Freya asked him.

"It was fine, I work out remember and I only dropped you twice" Nicholas joked.

"Well I'm sorry I crashed out, it was a difficult night and I was just so tired" Freya answered with a sigh as she remembered everything that had gone on.

"I know, it was quite an evening all in all. By the way, filming went awful last night, so now we're even more behind, which I should be annoyed about but I'm not because it means we get to stay on Corfu a bit longer" Nicholas told her.

"How much longer? Freya inquired.

"Two weeks, maybe more, how about you?" Nicholas asked.

"I don't know. I spoke to my assistant yesterday morning, before we went out, and he seems to be handling things, although he did say that there had been a significant increase in bookings since my photograph was printed in the tabloids" Freya responded.

"Who said there was such a thing as bad publicity" Nicholas told her.

"Yeh well, wait until Russell tells everyone who I really am and that I went to prison, I don't think that news is going to give your movie anything but bad publicity" Freya stated with a sigh.

"No one is going to hear anything from Russell" Nicholas spoke, taking a sip of his tea.

"What do you mean?" Freya asked him.

"Do you really think I am going to let him get away with threatening you?" Nicholas asked her seriously.

"Nick this isn't 'The Sopranos', you don't have to arrange for someone to bump him off, this is Russell we're talking about not some gangster" Freya reminded him.

"He tried to blackmail you and he hurt Emma, nearly causing her to lose her baby, you want me to let that go?" Nicholas queried.

"It isn't your decision to make, it's mine and I will deal with it" Freya told him.

"I was going to give him the money" Nicholas stated simply.

"What?!" Freya exclaimed in horror.

"Well what's twenty five grand if it means he will shut up and leave us alone?" Nicholas stated.

Freya just looked at him, a shocked expression on her face. She put her tea down on the table and stood up.

"Did you not listen to a word I said last night? Using your money like that, to make people go away is exactly what my parents did" Freya stated and she turned away from him and began to walk back towards the villa.

"Freya, wait" Nicholas called and he hurriedly got up from the table and followed her.

"I don't believe you said you're going to give him the money, like by doing that it's all going to disappear. Don't you understand? Now that Russell knows it isn't ever going to go away, because the cat is out of the bag and things can only snowball from here" Freya shouted, tears springing to her eyes.

"Freya, I'm sorry, I didn't mean it like it came out, you know the money isn't important to me" Nicholas said as he attempted to defend himself.

"There is a vast difference to it not mattering and it not being important. You can't say you don't care about it and then use it to get what you want" Freya told him as she climbed the stairs to the bedroom.

"No, you're right" Nicholas agreed, following her.

"I'm going back to 'The Calypso'" Freya said as she took her clothes down from the wardrobe door.

"Don't go like this, I'm sorry, it was a stupid idea, perhaps offing Russell might have been a better plan" Nicholas said, watching her as she shook her clothes out to ascertain if they were dry enough to wear.

"Maybe" Freya agreed, stopping what she was doing and looking at him.

"I don't want to fight and you are right about the money. I

can't change the fact that I have it but perhaps I can start to use it differently" Nicholas spoke.

"If I had £25,000 to throw around I would give it to Emma to pay for her wedding. After all she's done for me over the years she deserves to have the perfect day" Freya announced with a sigh.

"Well maybe I can help there" Nicholas suggested.

"I don't want a handout from you" Freya responded.

"I wasn't offering you one, I thought we could agree a fee for you to take some photographs of me" Nicholas told her.

"Why do you want me to take photos of you? You have people snapping you all the time" Freya reminded him.

"Not photos like this. I want you to take pictures of me no one has seen before, real photos.........nude photos" Nicholas told her.

"You want to pay me to take kinky photos of you in the buff" Freya spoke.

"Just like I would pay anyone else, except of course I wouldn't normally take all my clothes off" Nicholas replied.

"What if I'm not that sort of photographer?" Freya asked him.

"It would mean a lot to me if you did it and it would pay for Emma's wedding. It wouldn't be me flashing my money around, you would have earned it" Nicholas said.

"£25,000 is too much" Freya stated.

"Then name your price"

"£15,000 and I'm only inflating my fee because it isn't my usual line of work and it is for Emma" Freya agreed.

"Then we have a deal? How about this afternoon?" Nicholas suggested.

"Fine" Freya answered.

There was an awkward silence.

"Look, I know how important it is that you distance yourself from the life you had with your parents, but you can't keep thinking that everyone who has wealth is like them. I was only thinking of paying Russell to protect you and maybe that is the wrong thing in your eyes but the gesture was made with the best intentions. He hurt you Freya and he wants to broadcast private details about your life, I don't think I would be normal if I didn't feel anger at that" Nicholas told her sincerely.

"No I know, I overreacted, I'm sorry, it's just last night, reliving it all again..... it still hurts. And I told you about it because I trust you more than I've trusted any man in my life before, which is completely crazy because we've known each other barely a week" Freya admitted.

"I am not like your father Freya, I'm not going to ask you to fit into my world" Nicholas told her.

"I don't think I can fit into your world" Freya said a little sadly.

"Well that's fine, I respect that, but perhaps my world can fit in somewhere around our world" Nicholas suggested.

"Our world" Freya stated.

"Yeh, you see I'm really not the holiday romance kind of guy" Nicholas responded with a smile.

"No?" Freya queried said smiling back.

"No" Nicholas told her and he took hold of her hand, pulled her towards him and kissed her.

Nicholas had filming for the rest of the day on Mount Pandokrator so Freya returned to 'The Calypso Apartments' to shower and change into some clean clothes. She should have felt liberated and unburdened having told Nicholas things she had never told anyone before but it now felt like she was just waiting for events to blow up, it wasn't a case of if now, but when.

She had tried to telephone Emma to see how she was but her phone was switched off. Freya assumed from that, that Emma was still at the hospital. She decided she would go to 'Petroholis Restaurant' for lunch later and see if there was any news then.

After her shower she had telephoned Russell. It had been a quick conversation asking him to meet her at 'The C Bar', which was where she was now. It was eleven o clock and she was waiting for him to arrive.

In front of Freya, lying on the table, was a plain white envelope with nothing written on the front. Freya picked it up and tapped the corner of it on the table, mentally going over its contents.

She saw Russell as he arrived at the entrance to 'The C Bar'. He looked terrible. His hair was dishevelled and he had bags under his eyes. Seeing him now, Freya felt almost sorry for him. He had obviously got out of his depth with a bookmaker. He had been in debt before, at the beginning of their relationship, but then he had had a large win which cleared his bills and he had vowed not to gamble again. At the time Freya had believed him but once a gambler, always a gambler. It had obviously become an obsession or it was an uncontrollable addiction.

Russell met her gaze and moved to join her at the table.

"I got you a beer" Freya stated, indicating the bottle on the table.

"Thanks, look, about yesterday........is Emma OK?" Russell asked in subdued tones.

"Yes and the baby is fine, no thanks to you. What has happened to you Russell? Pushing people around to get what you want? Begging for money?" Freya asked him.

"It isn't through choice" Russell responded, sitting down and straight away taking a swig of the beer.

"So you are in debt? Bookmaker or loan shark? Why the Hell didn't I know about this? How long has it been going on? Why didn't you talk to me about it instead of shagging my mother to keep up the repayments?" Freya questioned.

"I made you a promise I wouldn't gamble again, how could I tell you?" Russell answered.

"That's so lame Russell, was our relationship really that bad that you couldn't tell me you were in trouble?" Freya wanted to know.

"Is there any point discussing this now?" Russell replied, unwilling to answer.

"No I suppose not" Freya agreed.

"Is that envelope for me?" Russell asked her.

"Yes it is, here" Freya said and she slid it over the table to him.

"Who signed the cheque then? Kaden or Daddy?" Russell inquired as he tore open the envelope eagerly.

He pulled the envelope apart and produced a sheaf of A4 paper and a business card.

"What's this? Some sort of joke? I thought you said you had the money" Russell questioned as he took the paper out.

"No, I said I had what you wanted and there it is. That is my life. In those notes are all the details of my life as Jane Lawson-Peck, things even my beloved mother would have been unable to tell you" Freya announced.

"And the business card?

"Sandra McNeill from 'Shooting Stars' magazine might give you a decent price for an interview and the information, or you are welcome to sell it to the highest bidder. Just be sure that whoever you choose to tell prints only the facts, because if I read anything inaccurate, like how fantastic you were in bed, be sure that I will sue your arse" Freya told him.

"So you've told lover boy have you?" Russell asked as he took another swig of his beer.

"Yes" Freya replied.

"But you could never find the opportunity to tell me" Russell stated.

"Is there any point discussing that now?" Freya retorted.

"Perhaps neither of us trusted each other enough" Russell answered.

"Obviously not" Freya replied.

"Your mother has no idea who I am by the way. She doesn't know about us" Russell told her.

"That's a shame, it would have given us something in common after all these years" Freya said.

"I did love you" Russell spoke honestly.

"No you didn't, you thought I was large and ordinary. I heard you at the restaurant on my birthday, discussing it with the barman called Milo" Freya informed him.

"What?" Russell asked.

"I heard you describing me, I was stood behind you Russell, I heard what you said and I saw the hand actions" Freya stated.

Russell didn't respond.

"Well, you've got what you came for" Freya spoke, indicating the envelope.

"Yes, I suppose I have" Russell agreed and he rose to his feet.

"We're done then" Freya stated finally.

"I'm on the first plane home" Russell spoke with a nod.

"Have your pick of CDs from the flat and drop the keys into Simon at the studio" Freya said, unable to meet his eyes.

"I'll see you" Russell spoke and slipping the envelope into the back pocket of his jeans he headed for the exit of the bar.

Freya watched him go and couldn't help feeling a little sad. How could a year and a half of her life with someone amount to so little?

From where she sat she had a view of 'Petroholis Restaurant' and she watched as a taxi pulled up and Emma and Yiannis emerged from it. Freya knocked back the remainder of her drink, hurried from the bar, and made her way up the road towards them.

"EMMA!" Freya called as she rushed along.

Emma and Yiannis stopped outside the restaurant and waited for her to reach them.

"Oh, let me just get my breath back, how are you?" Freya asked as she took gulps of air when she had finally got to the couple.

"I'm fine, just a bit bruised" Emma responded.

"And the baby?" Freya inquired.

"Is absolutely fine and everything looks normal. We saw the heartbeat on the monitor and it was amazing" Emma told her, looking at Yiannis.

"Oh my boy and Emma! You make me grandmother! Come here, come here!" Mrs Petroholis shrieked as she came out of the restaurant to greet them.

She enveloped Emma in a bear hug which nearly squeezed all the breath out of her and then she let go, and turned her attentions to her son. Mrs Petroholis hugged him tightly too and exchanged words in Greek.

They both then disappeared into the restaurant leaving Freya and Emma alone.

"I'm sorry again, for Russell and what he did, I feel completely responsible and......"Freya began, still feeling that she had not properly made up for events.

"Stop it Freya, you aren't responsible for Russell. I think Yiannis might want a few words with him though" Emma spoke.

"Russell's gone and he won't be coming back" Freya stated.

"And he went without a fight? After all the threats last night?" Emma exclaimed in surprise.

"Well yes, kind of" Freya replied, holding back from telling her friend she had handed him her life history on a plate.

"And Nick?" Emma queried.

"I told him. Everything" Freya said with a deep breath and then a smile.

"Oh Freya, how do you feel now?" Emma asked.

"Strange. Relieved in a way, terrified in another" Freya replied.

"And what did he say?" Emma wanted to know.

"He said he wants to see my prison tattoos" Freya joked.

"Stop it! I was being serious" Emma told her.

"He said he was falling in love with me" Freya spoke.

"Oh my God! Oh Freya! I would jump up and down but Yiannis would probably have a fit. So, how do you feel about him?" Emma wanted to know.

"Well, I know I really like spending time with him and he knows everything about me now. I don't know, things like this don't happen to me. I'm a bit scared to like him too much in case I jinx it. I mean, look at him Em and look at me. Hollywood actor, someone who shops in 'Evans'" Freya stated, holding her arms out.

"I won't have this again Freya, you are amazing and Nick obviously likes what he sees, physical stuff is all superficial anyway" Emma spoke.

"What did I do to deserve a friend like you?" Freya asked.

"You must have put up with a lot of grief in a past life" Emma told her.

"Yeh, I must have" Freya agreed.

"Girls! Girls! Come, come, we have champagne to celebrate my grandchild! Emma, you have sparkling water. Come sit down! Come! Come!" Mrs Petroholis called, beckoning to them both.

"She is not going to leave me unattended for the next seven months" Emma said quietly to Freya as they moved towards the restaurant.

"It could be worse, she might let you off working the restaurant so much" Freya suggested.

"Oh I doubt it, Yiannis has already told me she nearly gave birth to him in the middle of preparing a moussaka and that she used to have him in a carry pack on her back in the kitchen until he could walk and then basically, after that, he was serving tables" Emma informed her.

"You'd best start reading the menu to your bump then, get it in training" Freya suggested.

"I'll read it in Greek and English, make sure it's bilingual when it comes out" Emma replied.

"Just teach it the basics. 'More please', 'beer' and 'can I have a room for tonight', those phrases have seen me through" Freya told her.

Emma took hold of Freya's hand and gave it a squeeze.

"I am proud of you for telling Nick. I know what that means to you and I know how hard it must have been" Emma spoke.

"Well it wasn't as hard as it is going to get. I have a feeling by tomorrow the tabloids are going to have a field day. God! Get me inside, there's a film crew heading down here, all lenses aimed at me" Freya shrieked and she ducked behind Emma and began to walk backwards into the restaurant, pulling Emma with her.

"My baby is going to have a celebrity godmother" Emma announced as she let herself be moved along by Freya.

"Godmother?" Freya said.

"If you want to. I can't think of anyone better to guide my baby along life's path" Emma told her as Freya ducked behind a plant.

"I would be completely honoured but are you sure? I mean, what with 'everything'" Freya said crouching down behind one of the restaurant tables.

"'Everything' as you put it is 'nothing'. We've been best friends forever, who else am I going to ask?" Emma asked as Freya started to crawl along the floor towards the kitchen, keeping an eye on the camera crew.

"Someone who hasn't been in clink?" Freya suggested.

"Experiences enrich people, a godmother needs to have led a varied life to be able to counsel and advise" Emma insisted.

"Then that's me, varied life, photographer, ex-con, appearance in 'The Daily News'. Christ, they're coming in, I'll come out when they've gone" Freya exclaimed and she hurried into the kitchen, nearly bowling over Yiannis and Mrs Petroholis in the process.

It was a little after five when Freya arrived at Villa Kamia wearing the apron and headscarf she had borrowed from the restaurant to disguise herself. It had been a hectic day trying to avoid the cameras and she hadn't wanted to take any chances in being spotted now.

"Have you come to cook for me?" Nicholas inquired, looking in amusement at her outfit as he opened the door to her.

"You're not funny! This is what hanging around with you has lowered me to" Freya spoke, taking off the headscarf and hitting him on the arm with it.

"They've gone from outside for now. I sent Mikey out in the car and they chased it down the road" Nicholas told her and he leant forward and kissed her lightly on the lips.

"Haven't they learnt anything?" Freya asked him.

"Don't knock it. At least we have a bit of privacy" Nicholas replied.

"Yes we do. So, where shall I take you?" Freya inquired suggestively and she produced Claude from her bag.

"I thought outside but you're in charge, I'll let you decide" Nicholas told her.

"Fine, but no funny business, this is a professional shoot and I expect you to be professional" Freya warned him.

"I love it when you boss me around" Nicholas replied with a smile.

Freya entered the house and followed Nicholas through the rooms and out onto the patio at the back of the villa.

"Want a drink?" Nicholas offered as he picked up a bottle of wine from the large glass garden table.

"Mmm, well usually I don't drink while I'm working but I would hate for you to have to drink the entire bottle alone" Freya responded as she sat on the edge of the sun lounger and began to fiddle with the settings on her camera.

"You're always thinking of me, it's sweet............here" Nicholas said and he gave her a full glass.

"Thanks" Freya replied and she took a sip of the cool liquid. It was just what she had needed.

She looked up at Nicholas, taking in what he was wearing, how he looked and the position of the sun. It was something she did every day but this time it felt different. Her subject meant a lot to her. She swallowed and tried to compose herself.

"OK. Unbutton your shirt, and lose the shorts" Freya told him as she stood up and began moving furniture around the patio.

"You're direct, I like that" Nicholas replied, smiling as he began to undo his shirt.

"I'm a professional, you're paying me remember and I am going to give you some quality photographs, so less of the glamour model and more of the real you" Freya told him.

She couldn't help but watch as he unbuttoned his top and took off his shorts. He stood in black Calvin Klein jockey shorts with his shirt open and Freya had to bite her lip to remain focussed. This was going to be a difficult assignment.

"Over there. By the gate. Just pretend I'm not here. I want you looking out at the ocean" Freya said, indicating where she wanted Nicholas to stand.

"Just looking at the sea? You don't want me to do anything else?" Nicholas asked her.

"Nothing else, just look out to sea, clear your mind of me with the camera and just focus on the horizon and what that brings to mind, pretend I'm not here" Freya ordered him as she got herself into position.

"OK" Nicholas agreed and he turned to face the sea.

Freya took a deep breath and watched him. She saw him close his eyes and then refocus. She was so intent in watching him that she almost forgot what she was supposed to be doing. She put her camera to her eye and looked at him through the viewfinder.

He had an amazing presence, his height, his stature, the way he held himself, it was no wonder the camera loved him. Freya moved to the side of him, taking photographs of his profile, then to the front, from an angle, focussing on his face, the great bone structure he had, the firm jaw.

He looked wrapped up in his thoughts as Freya continued to photograph him. He had huge eyes which seemed now to be full of thoughts. Large deep blue eyes with those almost never ending eyelashes.

"And now, look straight at the camera, don't smile, just look" Freya ordered, not removing the camera from her face as Nicholas turned to her.

She looked at him through the camera, his open shirt, his expression full of reticence. Freya wondered what he was thinking of. She took more pictures. She eventually took the camera away from her face and smiled at him.

"And relax.........how was that?" Freya asked him.

"Different, a bit strange, it was weird not smiling" Nicholas replied.

"I'm sure you have thousands of photos of you smiling" Freya reminded him.

"Yes I do.........so what next?" Nicholas asked her.

"By the pool I think" Freya told him and pointed in the direction of the swimming pool and the side she wanted him to stand.

She watched as Nicholas walked over to the side of the pool. Freya positioned herself across the pool opposite him and checked the scene through her camera.

"You want these photos to be intimate yes? Explicit?" Freya asked him.

"Yes" Nicholas agreed.

"Then you had better take off your clothes" Freya said with a nervous swallow.

"OK" Nicholas replied.

He undid the button of his shirt and took it off, tossing it towards the sunlounger.

Freya tried to busy herself choosing options on the camera but she couldn't help but look at him. She noticed he was hesitating, his breathing rapid, he seemed nervous.

"Are you sure you want to? I mean we don't have to do this we could......" Freya began, trying to ease the tension that had developed.

"It's OK. I have to do this. It's fine" Nicholas responded.

He pulled down his underwear and discarded it. He stood at the edge of the pool, completely naked and Freya's breath caught in her throat. She had photographed nudes before, at college, but this was completely different. She hadn't quite expected the sight of him to affect her so much.

"Um, I, er, I want you to assume the pose like you're going to dive into the pool. Arms up straight, palms together, tension in the torso and legs, slightly up on your toes" Freya told him, turning her face away from him.

"Like this?" Nicholas asked as he adopted the position.

Freya turned back to face him and saw he had done exactly what she had asked him to do.

"Yeh, like that" Freya answered and she put her camera up to her face and began to photograph him.

She was sweating. She could feel the beads appearing on her forehead. She moved around the pool taking his image from various angles, trying to treat him as just a subject but feeling something quite different.

"So have you taken many pictures of naked men?" Nicholas asked her.

"Some. Most of them were over sixty. Keep still for a minute" Freya ordered as she walked towards him, zooming in.

"Sorry, it's just I think I need a cold shower" Nicholas admitted.

"Oh OK, well you can get in the pool in a second, just look at me now" Freya said, moving closer to him.

Nicholas reached out and took hold of her hand.

"Put the camera down" he urged.

"I said we had to be professional about this, this is a proper photo shoot you're paying good money for" Freya spoke, trying to ignore the fact that his body was just inches away from her and he was naked.

"Look at me Freya" Nicholas spoke in barely more than a whisper.

"I am looking at you and I'm getting some great shots" Freya answered.

"Not through there, put Claude down for a second" Nicholas repeated and he took the camera from her.

"We haven't finished yet" Freya told him, feeling slightly uncomfortable.

"Why don't you take your clothes off?" Nicholas suggested, running his hand down her arm.

"Oh I don't think I make as good a physical specimen as you do" Freya answered with a nervous laugh.

"Why don't you let me be the judge of that" Nicholas suggested, holding both of her hands and looking at her intently.

She closed her eyes and swallowed, feeling the warmth of his hands in hers. She became almost light-headed as she felt him unbutton her top. She trembled as he loosened her bra and removed it from her shoulders.

"You are beautiful Freya" Nicholas spoke as he looked at her.

Freya shook as she looked back at him, her top bare, her nipples unforgiving in their obviously aroused state. She put her arms around him and drew him close to her, feeling the firmness of his body against her.

She kissed him roughly, unable to stop herself from wanting him any longer. With one quick movement he picked her up almost effortlessly and unspeaking, carried her into the villa.

He had taken her to the master bedroom and laid her on the bed which was covered in soft cushions and throws. Freya had looked up at him, bent over her, nude, breathing erratically and she had felt something inside her quake with anticipation. She had realised that she could have laid there and looked at him forever.

He had kissed her from head to toe, his mouth covering every part of her body, his lips tasting every inch of skin. Freya had never experienced such torturous pleasure.

She remembered now, closing her eyes, how he had pulled her towards him until he was inside her and it had taken her breath away. She had clung to him, wanting to pull him deeper and deeper into her. She had kissed his face, his neck, his broad shoulders, his chest and his stomach. She had felt him shudder as she had moved her mouth lower, moistening every part of him until he could bear no more.

He had made her feel like she was going to burst with emotion as they made love. Her hair had been damp, she had felt hot all over, yet she had shivered with satisfaction. She had felt his heart quicken as she held him tightly to her and then all of a sudden her whole body had been filled with a wave of emotion so powerful it made her feel like she has having the nicest of heart attacks.

She hadn't been able to move or breathe, she had lost control and had let out a cry of delicious anguish as the wave rolled over her like a giant tsunami. She had felt delirious, her head had felt like she was drunk, like a huge ball of candyfloss, unable to function properly.

Now, laying in Nicholas' arms it all seemed like a wonderful dream or a film scene she was replaying, like watching someone else playing her part.

Freya turned to look at him to make sure it was real. He ran his hand through her hair and then ran a finger over her lips. She took hold of his hand and kissed it.

"So these other naked men you have photographed, have you ended up in bed with any of them?" Nicholas asked her.

"Um, one or two. I'm sorry, were you supposed to be my first?" Freya answered with a grin.

Nicholas propped himself up, his head resting on his hand, elbow on his pillow, looking at her.

"You're my first" he spoke seriously "in a way"

"What do you mean?" Freya inquired.

"I haven't slept with anyone since the surgery" Nicholas told her.

Freya looked at him and saw the emotion in his face and she leant forward and kissed his mouth tenderly. She ran her hand through his hair and down his cheek. There was no need to say anything, she knew what it had meant to him.

"I keep wanting to pinch you to check you're real" Freya admitted to him.

"I feel the same. I keep thinking what if I had turned down this movie or it had been set on another Greek island, we might never have met" Nicholas said, taking her hand in his.

"I'm scared" Freya said suddenly, as he feeling rose in her.

"There's nothing to be scared of. I really want this to be the start of something real, something serious. I don't know how we are going to sort out the logistics of it all but I really want to try" Nicholas told her.

"I don't know what to say, everything has happened so fast" Freya spoke with a sigh.

"Yeh I know but I am a great believer that if something feels right you shouldn't let the grass grow. Life is too short" Nicholas replied.

"I know. It's just so much has happened to me in the past week and I know that if we are together, people are going to scrutinise me and us, particularly in the light of my true identity becoming public knowledge" Freya said.

"But I've told you, I don't care about any of that. Let people scrutinise, let them say what they want, none of them matter" Nicholas insisted.

"I just don't want to let you down. You know me, the way I am, I'm not sure I can let comments run off me" Freya told him.

"You mean if someone hollers 'Freya hey, over here, how did prison affect you?' or 'Freya, is it true that you have helped Nicholas in providing background and insights for his next role as a man on death row' you might turn around and punch out the journalist instead of just smiling for the camera?" Nicholas asked her.

"That is as good an example as any" Freya agreed.

"I told you before, I don't want you to change or fit into my world. I want you, as you are and nothing more. And if you really feel the need to wipe out a cameraman or two believe me there are ways and means" Nicholas assured her.

"There's something you should know" Freya spoke seriously.

"Go on" Nicholas urged.

"I gave Russell details about my past life, told him everything there was to know, including some rather damning stories about my father. I told him he could sell it to the highest bidder in exchange for leaving us alone" Freya told him.

"You didn't have to do that" Nicholas said.

"No I know I didn't. But it wasn't giving in to him, I haven't given him any money directly but perhaps 'Shooting Stars' magazine will be foolish enough to pay his debts off for him and I won't have it on my conscience. And seeing as I have given him the details myself there is a small chance the truth might get printed, not a distorted version" Freya spoke.

Nicholas held her hand tightly in his.

"Now I know it is coming I can be ready" Freya said.

"And we can handle it together" Nicholas spoke, squeezing her hand.

"Mmm, starting with the dignitaries' dinner" Freya reminded him.

"Don't worry about that. Believe me, once I have done my speech the press won't be talking about your past" Nicholas insisted.

Chapter Eleven

It made the Friday edition of 'Shooting Stars' magazine. There were two photographs of Freya on the front cover. One was the picture of her and Nicholas taken outside 'Harry's Place' and the other was her prison mug shot.

There were also more pictures inside, of her parents, of her as a child accompanying them to the races at Royal Ascot and two photos that she had taken for clients, Lake Coniston in Autumn and Class 11A of Hildon Comprehensive School.

Freya was sat with Nicholas and Emma at 'Petroholis Restaurant' reading the article over breakfast. Outside, the building was surrounded by photographers taking pictures. They had tried to come onto the premises but Mrs Petroholis had quickly shown them the door and banned them from entering, so they had set up camp across the street instead.

"Well, that's that then" Freya stated, letting out a breath and moving her chair back from the table slightly.

"I don't think it's that bad, it does only tell the truth so I suppose Russell does have a crumb of decency about him" Emma stated.

"More likely he didn't want to be sued. Cute hair in that picture by the way" Nicholas commented as he pointed to a photo where Freya had pigtails.

"They could have got one of me on my gold diamond encrusted potty surely. And don't think I'm joking" Freya remarked, trying to make light of the situation. There were tears building in her eyes.

"Hey, come on, we knew this was coming. It's all out there now, it's done" Nicholas said, putting his arm around her which prompted immediate action from the photographers.

"Yeh I know, it's just that I should have held off a bit longer, they are all going to be there tonight, shouting questions and taking pictures and wondering what the Hell you are doing with me" Freya stated, suddenly becoming overwhelmed by everything.

"I promise tonight will be fine, you've got to trust me, I wouldn't lead you into the lions' den" Nicholas assured her.

"Perhaps I shouldn't go" Freya suggested.

"No! That would be like saying you were ashamed of who you are" Emma told her.

"I am! That is what hiding my identity was all about, I was ashamed" Freya admitted.

"Of what? Of having been to jail?" Nicholas asked her.

"A little, but more so of being the child of Mr and Mrs Lawson-Peck. If only I could change my genealogy" Freya said.

"You can't change that but you can change how you deal with it. You have got to face this head on, no more running away" Emma spoke determinedly.

"God, when did you get so wise?" Freya questioned with a sigh.

"Emma's right, you've got nothing to be ashamed of and I'm not going to hide away. I want you there tonight, I want you to hear what I've got to say when I address the guests" Nicholas told her.

"I am starting to get concerned about this speech and I suspect if Martha knew what you have planned she would be positively panicked" Freya spoke.

"She worries too much.........shall we have another coffee? I've got twenty minutes before the car comes" Nicholas said, checking his watch.

"I'll get some" Emma said, immediately rising from her chair.

"No, no, sit down, I'll get it and I'll see what is taking Yiannis so long unloading that delivery" Nicholas said, getting to his feet and heading towards the kitchen.

"Freya, he's so nice" Emma spoke as soon as Nicholas was out of earshot.

"He isn't just nice, he's amazing in every way. I just can't believe him" Freya admitted, smiling at her best friend.

"Is it serious? I mean it seems serious but, you know, he lives in America and........."Emma began.

"And I don't. I know, I don't know to tell the truth, we're just making the most of every day..................we slept together" Freya admitted with a blush.

"Oh my God! When?!" Emma exclaimed loudly.

"Ssshh, it was Wednesday. It was perfect, it was so perfect it made me cry. God, I sound pathetic, like a part in one of his films" Freya said with a tut.

"Oh Freya you have no idea how happy I am for you" Emma said, smiling at her friend.

"And he knows the truth about me which means no more deception, it's just too perfect" Freya said nervously.

"Now stop it right now, you cannot keep thinking that just because everything is going well that something is going to go wrong" Emma said, almost angrily.

"Why not? It's the story of my life" Freya replied.

"No. This is the story of your life, right here in black, white and colour and it's all out for public consumption, nothing is going to go wrong" Emma assured her.

"OK" Freya answered, sounding less than convinced.

"So what are your plans for today?" Emma asked her.

"I've got a car taking me to Corfu Town to get something to wear for tonight's dinner. I was going to wear the black dress I bought from Agatha but it's a really posh do and I don't want Hilary Polar to upstage me" Freya told her.

"Impossible" Emma answered.

"But I won't be gone all day and I thought you might help me with my hair and then we can look through some bridal magazines and start planning your wedding" Freya spoke, taking another roll from the plate and spreading it with jam.

"Oh Yiannis and I have talked about that and we are going to wait until after the baby is born. We're going to save up and Mr and Mrs P have given us quite a large sum of money to put towards building our house" Emma informed.

"That's great news but why wait? You told me you wanted to get married before the baby is born" Freya reminded her.

"Yes I know but it doesn't matter" Emma spoke, in a less than convincing tone.

"I know it does, you told me that too. Here" Freya spoke and she passed Emma a slip of paper.

"What's this? Oh my God! Freya? This is a banker's draft" Emma stated, looking at it in disbelief.

"Made payable to you. It's for the Euro equivalent of £15,000. It's a thank you from me to you for all you've done for me over the years, all the lies you've had to tell and all the unexpected visits I've made that you never moaned about. You're my best friend Emma and I love you" Freya said, becoming emotional as she spoke.

"Oh Freya, I can't take this, it's too much" Emma spoke, astounded by the sum of money she was holding.

"It isn't a handout from Nick, I earned it, in the most pleasurable of ways, but I earned it all the same and it was always going to be for your wedding, like I promised" Freya told her.

"I don't know what to say" Emma said as tears formed in her eyes.

"Say I'm going to wear something classy and stylish and nothing pink" Freya answered as she ate some of the roll.

"I was thinking of chocolate for the bridesmaids" Emma admitted.

"Now you are talking, chocolate and I have a long and well established relationship" Freya replied with a smile.

It was ten o clock when Nicholas' car came to pick Freya up at 'The Calypso Apartments'. There was a crowd of people around the vehicle as soon as it pulled up and as

Freya hastened towards it, all eyes and cameras were on her. She still hated it but was becoming strangely accustomed to it.

Mike was at the door to open it for her and Freya ducked to get in. Then she stopped and hesitated, as she saw someone else was already sat in the back seat.

It was Martha, dressed in a stern looking black trouser suit.

"What are you doing here? Mike's taking me to Corfu Town" Freya told her.

"I know, get in" Martha ordered, not even turning her head to look at Freya.

"I don't remembering asking for a guide" Freya replied, still not getting in and now being jostled by people wanting photographs and autographs. Poor Mike was doing his level best to keep his hat on his head.

"And I didn't ask to have my workload trebled. I think we ought to discuss this" Martha said and she slammed a copy of 'Shooting Stars' down onto the leather seat next to her.

"Shall I autograph it for you?" Freya suggested, still unmoving.

"For God's sake, get in the damn car!" Martha yelled and she leant forward, grabbed hold of Freya's arm and forcefully pulled her inside the vehicle.

Mike hurriedly shut the door and Freya was left on the back seat, nursing her injured arm.

"What the Hell did you do that for? You know I have stitches" Freya exclaimed as she examined the wound.

"It seemed to be the only way to get you in here. Go ahead Mike" Martha called to the driver.

"If your plan is to kidnap me can you use something other than duct tape because it brings me out in a rash" Freya replied.

"Oh everything is one big joke to you isn't it?" Martha began.

"I don't know what you mean" Freya replied.

"What on Earth do you think is going to happen to Nicholas' image after this?" Martha questioned and she tapped the magazine with a well manicured finger.

"This has nothing to do with you" Freya told her.

"It has everything to do with me. I am paid to look after him, to ensure his image is protected and to be honest, since you somehow managed to involve yourself with him, everything I have been working so hard to maintain is suddenly in jeopardy" Martha spoke seriously.

"What are you talking about?" Freya questioned.

"I'm talking about this article in this magazine, I'm talking about Nicholas racing off to the hospital with you when he has other commitments, brawling in the street, inviting you to the function tonight when he should be escorting Hilary. You are, without doubt, an unsatisfactory influence" Martha concluded.

"You're flattering me Martha" Freya responded.

"See, here we are again, another joke! Don't you hear what I am telling you? You are not someone he should be associating with" Martha carried on, becoming increasingly agitated.

"For what reason? Because I'm not stick thin like Hilary? Because I've been in prison? It can't be because I am the daughter of Eric Lawson-Peck because he is money, which makes me money and you love money" Freya spoke.

"The fact that you are related to that clever, genial man, who I have had the pleasure to meet, is your one saving grace. But after all those vile things you said about him it is no wonder he disowned you" Martha continued.

"Those vile things, as you call them, were nothing but the truth of my life with him" Freya told her, her temper rising.

"My heart bleeds" Martha answered.

"You mean it would if you had one" Freya retorted.

"You can insult me all you wish, it won't be anything I haven't heard before. My primary concern is Nicholas' career and I want you to know that this sort of attention is not only unwanted but also damaging" Martha told her in serious tones.

"Then if I am so dangerous and such a bad influence why aren't you having this conversation with Nick?" Freya inquired.

"Because when you have known someone for as many years as I have known Nicholas, you get to know the strategies that work and the strategies that don't" Martha explained with a smug look on her face.

"I might have known you would have a strategy. So tell me, how many other women have you had this conversation with?" Freya wanted to know.

"A few. Not many in recent years I have to admit, but judge for yourself whether it was productive or not. Two Academy awards, twenty three films all grossing highly around the world" Martha spoke.

"He is in love with me" Freya told her plainly.

"Oh please! 'I love you' falls off an actor's lips so easily. They can't help it, it's the nature of the job, saying it over and over to one actress after another, reality and fiction are bound to get blurred" Martha said.

"What are you expecting me to do? Let him down tonight? Disappear back to England and pretend we never met?" Freya wanted to know.

"You're not slow to catch on, a quick mind is a plus in your favour" Martha responded.

"Do you really think for one minute that I am going to take any notice of what you say?" Freya asked her.

"If you care at all for Nicholas you will. He's 35 now, at the top of his career but that cannot last forever. There are younger actors coming up, getting the romantic leads he might once have had. To remain in the game he needs to be focussed, he needs nothing but good publicity and in this last week, thanks to you, he's had more bad press than he's had since I've been working for him" Martha said.

"You'll have to tighten his leash for sure" Freya answered.

"You cannot possibly think for one moment that you and he can have a full time relationship" Martha stated.

Freya didn't respond and Martha let out a cackle of laughter that vibrated through the back of the car.

"My God, you really do think that don't you?! Oh my, this is amusing. You haven't the first idea about his life and what his career entails. Things here in Corfu have been very casual, I admit, but that is unusual. His life is Hollywood, its non stop" Martha spoke.

"And he despises all that did you know? He hates the parties and the snobbery and the endless interviews, they bore him" Freya told her.

"Is that what he told you? And you believed him? Those parties and the interviews have helped to make him a superstar of epic proportion. He would be no one without the things that made him who he is" Martha said.

"I've heard enough" Freya stated.

"But have you taken any of it on board?" Martha asked.

"I am going to that party tonight, Nick wants me there" Freya told her.

"Fine, if you insist on putting yourself through it. But let me tell you this, you might have coped with a couple of paparazzi here, but that party and all the parties to come are like being in a zoo enclosure at feeding time. They say cruel cruel things Freya, about how you look, about who you are and about what you are. There would be daily reminders of what you've tried hard to forget" Martha told her.

"This conversation is over, you can leave now. Mike, stop the car, Ms Wilson is going" Freya called to the driver.

"Well don't say I didn't try and warn you. And good luck finding a dress, I hear there are one or two small boutiques that cater for the....how shall I put it? More voluptuous woman" Martha spoke as the car came to a halt.

"Thank you, now hurry up and close the door, we wouldn't want to draw any unnecessary attention to the fact that I'm kicking you out" Freya snapped.

Martha left the car and shut the door with a bang. Freya took a deep breath. No matter what she tried to tell herself, the conversation had unsettled her. She didn't know what to do.

She was still going over things in her mind as she walked through Corfu Town. She didn't know where she was heading. All she could think about was the way Martha had laughed about the prospect of her and Nicholas having a proper relationship. Perhaps she was right, after all, if anyone had told Freya the scenario a week or so ago she would have laughed too. What was she doing? She was getting involved in something she had always felt uncomfortable with. Nicholas lived in a completely different world to her, chock a block full of things Freya had escaped from when she left Jane behind.

She caught sight of her reflection in the window of a shop. She was huge, there was no denying it. What did he see in her? Actors didn't sashay up the red carpet with women her size on their arm.

Fifteen minutes later Freya found herself standing outside 'Agatha's Boutique'. She looked at the outfits in the window, almost in a trance, not really seeing them, not really looking at anything, just lost in her thoughts, trapped in consideration. What was she going to do? Go to the party? Not go to the party? Her mind was full but earlier this morning everything had been clear and she

263

had felt strong. She had felt sure of Nicholas and the feelings they were beginning to have for one another. But now all she felt was confusion.

"Freya?"

Freya was brought back to the present as she heard her name being called. Agatha was stood at the entrance to her shop, looking at her.

"Oh hello Agatha" Freya replied with a sigh.

"Why so sad? I see you in newspaper with very handsome man, the actor, there is party in Athens tonight" Agatha spoke as Freya went up the steps and joined her at the door.

"Yes and I'm supposed to be going but I'm in two minds. I don't know whether it's me" Freya told her.

"I no understand. What isn't you? The party? The handsome man?" Agatha queried with a furrowed brow.

"No, both those things are very me, I don't know, I'm just having second thoughts about certain things" Freya responded.

"Life is too short to think twice about things, always think about things with your heart, the brain it is not always working right, but the heart, it never fails you" Agatha assured her.

"You really believe that?" Freya wanted to know, looking seriously at the shop owner.

"Yes I do" Agatha answered sincerely.

Freya took a deep breath and thought about Nicholas, how much he was starting to mean to her. Was their relationship something she could just give up on before it had really been given a chance?

"God Agatha I need a dress for this party tonight, it's got to look fantastic, it's got to make me look somewhere near fantastic, I'm sorry it's short notice" Freya exclaimed hurriedly.

"Come in, I have the perfect thing" Agatha answered with a smile and she pushed open the door of the shop and ushered Freya inside.

At half past five that evening Freya grimaced as Emma put another grip into her hair. She flinched and yelped as it pinched her scalp.

They were in Freya's room at 'The Calypso Apartments' getting Freya ready for the party. The full length mirror had been covered by a sheet until the transformation was complete.

"Oh Freya, keep still! I'm nearly done, just a couple more" Emma said as she carried on doing Freya's hair.

"You aren't giving me a beehive are you?" Freya questioned.

"Yes of course I am. Seeing as you are going to be on the front pages of the papers tomorrow I thought you could make a style statement" Emma replied.

"I think I've made enough statements for a while" Freya answered with a sigh.

"There, I'm done. Now hurry up, go and get this dress on and I'll uncover the mirror" Emma urged.

"OK" Freya agreed and she disappeared into the bathroom.

"They were filming in the harbour again today, the whole place was cordoned off and there were guns and explosions, it was quite a show" Emma told her as she cleared away her hair brushes, tongs and grips.

"Nick said they were going to blow up a boat" Freya called back to her.

"Not his boat?" Emma queried.

"No, not his boat, a much cheaper one I hope..........OK, here I come" Freya said.

She opened the bathroom door and stepped out into the room. She was wearing a cobalt blue, knee length dress. It had a sash detail around the waist and a v neck shape.

Freya turned around and showed off the back, which was bare, apart from the twisted criss cross of the straps which ran from the bottom of her back to her neck. She was wearing gold high heeled sandals.

She looked at Emma who was sat motionless and completely silent.

"Well? Unveil the mirror, I want to see what you've done to my hair" Freya ordered.

"Freya, you look..........beautiful, really beautiful" Emma told her, standing up and going over to the mirror to remove the sheet.

Freya stood in front of the mirror and looked at her reflection. She could hardly believe she was looking at herself. Her blonde hair was pinned back from her face, a diamante clip holding the front in place. The back was knotted in a perfect twist with another diamante clip holding it in position.

The dress emphasised her bust in all the right ways, skimmed over her stomach and the sash detail detracted attention from Freya's width. The cut of the material meant that the dress hung in such a way that it actually elongated her. She looked almost slim! How could one dress manage that?

"Agatha is a genius isn't she?" Freya remarked as she turned from side to side, admiring herself.

"You look fantastic Freya, I could cry" Emma announced as tears filled her eyes.

"Those hormones of yours have a lot to answer for........what's the time?" Freya asked, seeing her watch wasn't on her arm.

"It's quarter to six, what time are you being picked up?" Emma inquired.

"Six o clock. We're meeting the helicopter outside the village. It's going to land in one of the fields near to Nikos Supermarket, it was the only place it could set down. God I can't believe I just said helicopter like it was getting a taxi or something. I've never been in a helicopter before, do you think it's safe?" Freya asked, picking up her watch and strapping it to her wrist.

"Probably a hundred times safer than driving on Greek roads. So, are you all set? Got everything packed?" Emma questioned, indicating Freya's overnight bag.

"Well it's only one night, I've got a change of clothes, Claude, my toiletries, what more does a girl need when she's staying in the penthouse suite?" Freya asked with a smile.

"I know what sort of freebies those places have, designer make up bag please and any expensive products going" Emma requested.

"I'm hoping for a new bathrobe" Freya replied.

Emma laughed and then threw her arms around her friend, hugging her tightly.

"I've never seen you look so happy Freya, enjoy every minute tonight" Emma ordered her.

"Well I'm looking forward to the hotel and the meal but the photographers....well I'll just have to deal with them" Freya spoke with a deep breath.

"There's nothing to be worried about anymore, the press will soon get bored of your story when the next bit of scandal comes along" Emma assured, holding Freya's arms.

"Yeh I know, it just brought it all back you know, my parents, prison, especially prison" Freya spoke, her thoughts drifting back.

"It's over now, for good. No one is going to think any differently of you. You didn't deserve to go to prison" Emma told her.

"Mrs P looked at me differently today. She tried to be the same with me but I saw something in her eyes, I am sure it was disappointment" Freya spoke.

"The only look in her eyes at the moment is fear at having me as her daughter-in-law sooner than she anticipated" Emma said with a smile.

"How soon? Does this mean you've set a date?" Freya asked excitedly.

Emma nodded.

"Oh Em, when? Tell me"

"Two months time, 22nd September. We're getting married in Our Lady of Kassiopi which, as you know, is Greek Orthodox, so that pleases Mr and Mrs P. Then we are having a blessing on the beach by my C of E vicar from home with a traditional Greek band and dancers and I'm thinking of having a big marquee down at the harbour somehow and inviting the whole village" Emma told her.

"That sounds perfect" Freya agreed with a smile.

"It wouldn't be happening without you" Emma said.

"Yes it would, Yiannis adores you, I just provided the means to ensure Baby P was legitimate, I couldn't let the poor kid be born out of wedlock" Freya joked.

Emma laughed and then Freya's mobile phone began to ring from inside her handbag, which was lying on the bed. Freya hurriedly rifled through it to answer it. She saw from the display that it was her mother.

"It's my mother" Freya said out loud as the phone rang in her hand.

"God what does she want? She has a nerve, don't answer it" Emma spoke, not wanting her friend's night to be spoiled in any way.

"I want to know what she's got to say, I'm intrigued. Hello" Freya answered, putting the phone to her ear.

"Jane, oh good, you answered. I didn't know whether you would, in the circumstances"

"Mother, please don't call me that name. I take it you've read the press today and you now know you've been sleeping with my ex-boyfriend"

"Er, yes, I don't know quite what to say about that. It all seems quite trivial compared to everything else"

"Does it? Well Russell didn't mention your sordid little frisson in the article so I'm sure you won't lose clients over it" Freya spoke.

"I've had your father on the phone today, I think he has been rather bombarded by the press"

"Am I supposed to feel concern?"

"Jane, he's furious with you, I don't think I've ever heard him this angry"

"Again, am I supposed to feel concern? It isn't my fault that this has all come out. You were the one who shagged Russell, which led him to finding out about me which, in turn, led me to have to admit to being related to that man. It isn't something I'm proud of, it isn't something I boast about"

"Some of the stories in the article were very descriptive Jane, unnecessarily so"

"Which ones in particular? The one where he beat me with his belt because my table manners were unacceptable or the one where he had Gloria the maid assaulted on her way home from work because she had brought my supper to my room when I had been banned from eating at the dining table?" Freya questioned.

"I think you misunderstood your father's intentions"

"Misunderstood them?! He is a monster Mother! He sent me to prison, I was his only daughter and I was only eighteen years old" Freya reminded her.

"I'm not condoning what he did back then but none of us want it brought back up again" Barbara stated.

"I'm sure you want to sweep it back under the Axminster but, as I said, it was your indiscretion that led to this" Freya spoke.

"Always blaming someone else aren't you Jane? Nothing ever lies at your door does it? I mean you blame my affair for this coming out but let's face it, if you weren't dating Nicholas Kaden no one would be at all interested in your life" Barbara stated.

"Christ! You can't seriously think any of this is my fault!" Freya exclaimed.

"It was you that set fire to the house" Barbara reminded her.

"Do you know something Mother? I really wish you'd both been in it" Freya spoke and she ended the telephone call.

Her heart was racing now and she sat down on the edge of the bed to compose herself.

"OK?" Emma asked tentatively.

"Yes I'm OK. I suppose I should have expected some comment from at least one of them" Freya said, putting her mobile phone away in her bag.

"Don't let it spoil your night, neither of them are worth it" Emma said.

"No, I know" Freya agreed.

"Well come on, chop chop, it's nearly six and you don't want to keep your Prince Charming waiting" Emma said and she handed Freya her small holdall.

"Do you know, I had to buy that bag today or my overnight stuff would have been taken to the penthouse suite in supermarket carriers" Freya told her with a smile.

"Here, on second thoughts, let me carry it, I might get in a photo if I take it to the car" Emma spoke, snatching the bag back.

"I think Roger's meeting me at the entrance but by all means you can escort me" Freya said smiling.

"Roger the big, strong, bodyguard, the real life Kevin Costner who picked me up like I was the lightest thing in the world and put me into the car before our race to the hospital?" Emma stated.

"That's the one" Freya replied.

Roger was waiting for Freya at the entrance to 'The Calypso Apartments', chatting to Spiros to pass the time.

"Hi Roger" Freya greeted.

"Hello Freya, hello Emma" Roger spoke with a smile.

"Hi" Emma replied.

The black Mercedes was waiting down the alleyway with a crowd of people around the car, some tourists, some photographers and even some locals who Freya recognised as working in the bars.

As soon as the crowd saw that Freya had appeared, all attention was diverted from the car to her. There was an automatic surge and suddenly it was pandemonium.

"Bloody Hell! I didn't realise it was going to be like this" Emma exclaimed as she was jostled about by people trying to get to Freya.

"Look, go back inside, I don't want you and Baby P getting pushed about. I'll see you tomorrow with the hotel freebies" Freya said, taking the holdall from her friend.

"OK. Have a fantastic time" Emma called and she watched as Freya and Roger got into the car.

A few minutes later the car pulled up alongside a black BELL430 twin turbine helicopter in a field just outside the village centre.

Freya and Roger got out of the car and Nicholas, dressed in a tuxedo, hurried to meet them.

"Hi" he greeted Freya, taking hold of both her hands and admiring her.

"Hi" she responded.

"You look amazing" he said, bringing her hands to his mouth and kissing them.

"And you have scrubbed up quite well too" Freya replied, taking in just how handsome he actually was.

"And so has Roger don't you think? Look at you man, you look dandy" Nicholas commented, pointing out his bodyguard's smart attire.

"I have already complimented Roger on his appearance tonight and he on mine" Freya informed him.

"Hmm, I think I might have to watch you two, too much mutual appreciation going on here" Nicholas joked.

"We share an admiration of Bruce Willis movies" Roger informed Nicholas.

"Damn that guy! I am starting to wish I was him" Nicholas responded as Freya laughed.

"We had better be going, we don't want to hit traffic at the other end" Roger told Nicholas as he checked his watch.

"You're right. So, are you ready?" Nicholas asked Freya.

"Yes" Freya replied.

"Then let's go" Nicholas said.

He held Freya's hand as they made their way towards the helicopter.

Freya couldn't believe how noisy it was in the helicopter once the engines were running. However, when they had taken off and Freya had remarked on this, Nicholas had insisted that the particular model they were travelling in was a lot less noisy than others he had been in.

"I have to do some interviews tonight, after the dinner" Nicholas spoke to Freya as they soared over the ocean.

"Oh, OK" Freya answered, a little disappointed.

"But, what I thought you might like to do was take some photos in Athens. So I've arranged for the driver to take you around the city, wherever you want. You have brought Claude with you haven't you?" Nicholas asked her.

"Claude has not left my side since he came into my life" Freya replied.

"Good, well I just thought it would be better than just waiting around or going back to the hotel on your own. I hear the Parthenon at night is really something" Nicholas told her.

"That would be good" Freya agreed.

Greece from the air was just as picturesque as from the ground. The whole ride was exhilarating and completely different from the flight experienced from an aeroplane. Freya felt more vulnerable in the helicopter but it was also exciting because it somehow felt that you were much closer to everything. It was like floating in a metal bubble.

They landed on the helipad of the Athens Palace Hotel just over thirty minutes after leaving Kassiopi and Martha was there to greet them.

She avoided eye contact with Freya and spoke directly with Nicholas.

"The car is waiting, this way. How was the flight?" Martha spoke, taking Nicholas' bag from him and leading them towards the roof exit.

"Good thanks, we enjoyed it didn't we Freya? Here, let me take that" Nicholas spoke and he took Freya's holdall from her.

"Yes it was fun" Freya answered.

"Good. Right, the itinerary is as follows.............we go now to The Plaza Hall, there is no more than an hour for meet and greet outside, the dinner starts at 8.30 and afterwards there are scheduled interviews with 'Film 2006', 'The News Channel' and 'Entertainment Now'"

Martha reeled off as the group descended the stairs and headed for the lift.

"OK fine. Listen I'll try not to be too long doing the interviews because I hear the penthouse has a waterbed" Nicholas whispered to Freya.

"But does it have a complimentary bathrobe?" Freya questioned.

"I almost guarantee it and hopefully some great towels. I have towels from nearly every Four Seasons hotel in my bathroom back home" Nicholas admitted with a grin.

"My God! You take the towels? That's stealing" Freya exclaimed in mock horror.

"I figured they were gifts. I took one, another appeared on my bed the next day, I didn't want to offend" Nicholas responded.

"You shock me! You are a towel thief!" Freya spoke loudly.

"Do you mind? We are trying to run through the evening's proceedings" Martha reminded them.

They left the hotel by the back entrance and got straight into the car that was waiting for them. Martha left them at this point and Roger got into the front of the car with the driver.

"How is Martha getting to the venue? Broomstick?" Freya questioned, turning to face Nicholas.

"I believe she has the deluxe model with twin twigs and turbo boost" Nicholas replied.

"I think my humour is lost on her" Freya spoke.

"She likes routines and itineraries, that's the way she works and she is good at her job" Nicholas told her.

"Yes, she certainly is devoted to the cause" Freya agreed.

"Is everything OK?" Nicholas asked, taking hold of her hand.

"Yes fine, well, actually my mother called me just before I left tonight" Freya admitted.

"And what did she have to say?" Nicholas questioned.

"Oh nothing really, just about how annoyed my father is with me, about the story being headline news and how all of this is my fault" Freya told him.

"Are you serious?" Nicholas asked her.

"It was what I should have expected, it just unsettled me that's all" Freya admitted.

"Do you want a drink?" Nicholas asked, opening the mini bar.

Freya nodded.

Nicholas poured them both brandies and handed Freya one of the glasses.

"You know, I can't help thinking that I'm ultimately to blame for your past coming out" Nicholas told her as he took a sip of his drink.

"Please tell me you haven't slept with my mother too" Freya responded.

"Not knowingly" Nicholas replied with a smile.

"Don't tell me, you think it's all your fault because you have catapulted me from mere obscurity, where I was just an average photographer disowned by her rich parents, to high profile celebrity in a week. And if we hadn't met no one would be at all interested in a girl from Clapham" Freya told him.

"Something like that" Nicholas agreed.

"Well, that's what my mother said. And in a way she's right, but do you know what? I am so glad I met you" Freya responded, looking straight at Nicholas.

"Me too" Nicholas replied and he put his glass down and leaned towards her.

Freya also put her glass down and moved towards him. She felt his lips on hers and she closed her eyes, drinking in the moment, as he kissed her.

The Plaza Hall was sixteen miles away from the hotel and it took the car just under half an hour to arrive there. The vehicle came to a halt and Nicholas asked the driver to give them five minutes before he opened the door.

"You do look so amazing tonight Freya" Nicholas told her, holding her hand and squeezing it gently.

"Thank you" Freya replied, accepting the compliment.

Nicholas took a deep breath and then looked at Freya with a serious expression on his face.

"When the driver opens this door it's going to go crazy, you know that don't you? There will be more photographers than you have seen in your whole life. You will be almost blinded by the flashes and there will be people screaming my name and your name, asking for us to turn this way and that. Don't let it freak you out. All you have to do is smile and hold my hand, nothing else" Nicholas told her.

"OK" Freya replied.

"But, more important than the not freaking out and the smiling, is that I want you to know that out there, it's all a show, it's all false. You and me, here, that's what's important, that's what's real" Nicholas spoke sincerely.

"Do you really mean that?" Freya asked him.

"Yes, you'll see, starting tonight things are going to be different" Nicholas assured her.

"OK" Freya answered.

"So, are you ready?" Nicholas asked her.

"As I'll ever be" Freya replied.

She took a deep breath and prayed she wouldn't fall over in her high shoes.

The driver opened the door and Freya nearly jumped out of her skin at the volume of the shouts and screams as she and Nicholas got out of the car and stood on the pavement.

There were, what seemed like, a million flashes going off and for a moment Freya was temporarily blinded and lost her ability to focus on anything. She had floaters and everyone looked blurred.

"OK?" Nicholas asked, squeezing her hand.

"Blind in one eye, deaf, but other than that I'm fine. Just don't walk too fast over that red carpet, new shoes" Freya responded over the noise.

"OK, just wait here with Roger while I sign some autographs. I won't be long I promise" Nicholas told her and he kissed her cheek.

The action prompted more flashes and a whooping of excitement from the crowd.

Freya watched as Nicholas went up to the members of the public who were all taking his photograph and calling to him. He shook their hands and posed for pictures and chatted to them, full of enthusiasm. Hilary, Gene and Bob were also going along the edge of the crowd signing autographs, but it was obvious Nicholas was the star attraction.

"So, how far away from you is he allowed to be before you have to rein him in?" Freya asked Roger as they both stood watching Nicholas.

"I like to keep a relatively close eye on him but tonight there is a team of security. See the guys in the dark polo shirts?" Roger pointed out.

"I see them. That one looks frighteningly like Vin Diesel" Freya spoke.

"A fat Vin Diesel" Roger replied.

"Vin Diesel having overdosed on doughnuts........speaking of food, I'm starving" Freya admitted, checking her watch.

"If it's any consolation you're not the only one, I missed lunch today" Roger told her.

"Then you must be looking forward to 8.30 more than me...........oh no, here comes the Wicked Witch, cover me" Freya said and she took a step backwards and tried to hide herself behind Roger.

"That will be all for the moment Roger, I think the security team have things under control here" Martha spoke as she arrived at Roger's side.

"Pardon me M'am but Nick has asked me specifically to remain with Miss Johnson until he is done" Roger replied, unmoving.

"Well perhaps you could leave her just for a brief moment so I might run through a few details with her regarding the evening's arrangements" Martha suggested with a firm, unfriendly smile.

"Whatever you have to say to me surely you can say in front of Roger. Don't you move Roger" Freya spoke, still trying to use the bodyguard as a human shield.

"May I start by complimenting you on your appearance tonight, I cannot imagine how long it must have taken you to get things just right" Martha spoke, her tone heavy with sarcasm.

"Well it took me about as long as it probably took you to cover up your crow's feet" Freya answered with a smile, seeing Roger tense himself as he tried to remain serious.

"One day your quick wit is going to land you in hot water" Martha retorted.

"I've been in plenty of hot water Martha and I have always managed to avoid getting scalded" Freya replied firmly.

"They make a lovely couple don't they?" Martha continued, trying to draw Freya's attention to Nicholas and Hilary, as she turned to look at them.

The two actors were stood together, smiling for the cameras and Hilary's arm was around Nicholas' waist.

"Did you know he got to choose his co-star for this film? He could have had anyone, and out of all the actresses we screen tested he decided on Hilary. Now why do you think that was?" Martha questioned, turning to look back at Freya.

"Britney unavailable?" Freya replied.

"I think it's because she is a star in the making. She looks like a star you know, blonde, beautiful, slim, elegant.........."

"Flat chested" Freya added.

"She knows how to play the game, she would be good for him" Martha carried on.

"Why are you doing this Martha? It's very embarrassing and as far as I am aware, you are not his mother. In fact I am not really sure who you are" Freya told her.

"I want you to realise that this flirtation you are having with his world cannot last. You are not what he needs in his life, look at what has happened since you met! I have had to do a major damage limitation exercise to stop this movie being hampered by talk of your private life, which is something no one would be at all interested in had you just stayed away" Martha carried on.

"Oh grow up Martha! Nick isn't some little boy who needs hand holding, he's a grown man, capable of making decisions himself. I haven't brainwashed him into wanting to be with me, I have no idea why he does want to be with me but he does and you should respect that" Freya told her angrily.

"Of course I am thinking of you in all this really. I mean how would it feel to have your life plastered all over the news and then to be cruelly dumped, having laid yourself bare for nothing" Martha spoke.

"Don't waste your time worrying about me, I suggest you start thinking about yourself. Perhaps begin by compiling your résumé, because one word from me about what you're trying to do and Nick will fire you" Freya warned.

"I wouldn't be so sure" Martha answered, unfazed.

"I told you about me and hot water Martha, not so much as a blister. How about you?" Freya asked sternly.

"I will see you inside. Roger, ensure the security team outside has been adequately briefed about arrangements for departure" Martha ordered and she left them, heading for the entrance of The Plaza Hall.

"Argh! That woman! If she was anyone else I would have punched them out" Freya remarked to Roger as she took a deep breath and tried to remain calm.

"I think the battle was won after you said 'flat chested'" Roger told her.

"You think?"

"I think you should tell Nick what she said" Roger spoke seriously.

"No! No, it's nothing. She doesn't frighten me and he's told me she is good at her job. I don't want to rock the boat. And please, I would be grateful if you would not mention it" Freya begged.

"Don't worry about me, I can't tell him. I'm like all three of those wise monkeys rolled into one. I see nothing, I hear nothing and I say nothing" Roger replied.

"OK, good. So, how long has he been with the flat chested, woolly brained bimbo now?" Freya asked, looking at her watch.

"About twenty minutes" Roger answered.

"Is that all? Do you think we can have our starters brought out? Or perhaps just some rolls? Or maybe the car could fetch us a takeaway" Freya suggested.

"I've never seen Nick go crazy for a girl before" Roger spoke again in serious tones.

"What do you mean?"

"Just that there have been a few women before, but with you, he's different" Roger stated.

"Has he said something about me? Come on Roger, what has he said?" Freya inquired, eager to know.

"Hey, I'm a wise monkey remember and I've said too much already" Roger told her.

"Damn those ethical monkeys...................hey do you have gum? Or a Twinkie! Bodyguards always have a Twinkie in their pocket in the films" Freya exclaimed.

"Purely fiction" Roger answered.

It was over an hour before Nicholas had finished autograph signing and greeting the crowd that had turned out in their hundreds to see him. Then it was handshaking with the dignitaries.

Once inside, The Plaza Hall was spectacular. The main room had a high domed ceiling and elaborate artwork surrounding it. Thirty tables, each seating six, were beautifully laid out and at the top of the room was a large stage with a lectern. Being projected onto the wall for all to see were clips from some of the filming of the movie in their original, raw, unedited state.

Much to Freya's dismay she and Nicholas were sat with Martha, Hilary, Gene and Bob. On the table directly next to them were some of the high ranking Greek dignitaries including the Mayor of Athens.

The food began to arrive shortly after they were seated, for which Freya was truly thankful for.

"I'm sorry it dragged on a bit" Nicholas remarked to Freya as they waited to be served.

"It was fine, there were a lot of people" Freya spoke, almost licking her lips with anticipation as the food came round.

"More than I was expecting, more wine?" Nicholas asked her, noticing that her glass was already half empty.

"Thanks. So does Martha have any idea you've altered the speech?" Freya questioned in whispered tones.

"No but it won't be long now until she does" Nicholas replied with a smile.

"So Freya, how have the press been treating you?" Gene questioned quite pleasantly.

Freya was taken aback at him having spoken to her and she wasn't quite sure how she should react.

"Well I haven't really been hassled by anyone today" Freya replied.

"Good. Still, there's plenty of time yet, seeing as the news has only just broken" he answered.

"I'm sorry, could you just clarify? Are you trying to sound supportive or are you still being an arse?" Freya wanted to know, sensing his comment was not well meant.

"Yes Gene, I would like to know the answer to that one myself" Nicholas stated, fixing Gene with a stare.

"I was just offering my support of course, and making conversation. Seeing as we have spent most of the day being asked questions about Freya, I just wondered whether she had received the same treatment that's all" Gene replied, drinking his wine.

"Freya's private life is not up for discussion tonight unless you also want to discuss yours" Nicholas spoke firmly.

Gene did not reply and Martha fixed Freya with a look that could have curdled milk.

"Was he telling the truth? Did you get asked questions about me all day?" Freya wanted to know.

"It wasn't as bad as he was making out. He's pissed because we had a fight at filming today" Nicholas spoke quietly.

"A fight!" Freya exclaimed.

"Not in the literal sense, more a battle of words. Their attitude stinks and I told Gene, and Bob, it was the last time I would be working with either of them" Nicholas informed her.

"Nick, I am grateful for you defending me but these people, they are your..............well I was going to say friends but perhaps that's the wrong choice of word. But you have to get along with them. And I am quite sure that

Gene and Bob will not be the last people to have a dig at me" Freya spoke seriously.

"Probably not, but I would expect it to be coming from the newspapers not from my colleagues" Nicholas said as he took a drink.

"There are people with prejudice everywhere you look, no matter what their profession" Freya told him and she glanced over at Martha who was talking with Hilary.

"A few more weeks and I will only have to see them at interviews and the premiere" Nicholas replied.

"Well then, you can manage to ignore the jerks for a little longer. See how far you've come putting up with their snide comments without any bloodshed, it would be a shame to spoil it now" Freya spoke.

"You're right" Nicholas agreed.

"Besides, if anyone is going to spread Gene's nose across his face it's me, although not in this dress, it cost far too much" Freya told him.

The food was delicious, the wine kept flowing and Freya even managed to make small talk with Hilary. It had been very basic but it had been conversation none the less.

After they had finished eating it was time for the speeches. A short bearded man of about fifty, dressed in a tuxedo, stepped up onto the stage.

"Who is that?" Freya whispered to Nicholas.

"That's James Peterson, he's the head of Global Pictures which is the studio making the film" Nicholas told her.

"I feel like I should have known that seeing as I'm dating you" Freya responded.

"I'll introduce you later" Nicholas promised.

"............we hope that tonight's meal and the entertainment goes some way to expressing our gratitude for your hospitality and your assistance over the past months. Your country is truly one of pure, unspoilt beauty filled with warm, generous people" James Peterson spoke.

Everyone applauded.

"Now I am going to hand you over to the star of the film, ladies and gentlemen, Mr Nicholas Kaden" James Peterson spoke.

The whole room again erupted into applause and Nicholas stood up, preparing to go on stage.

"Do I say break a leg or something?" Freya asked him as he took a sip of water.

"Not traditionally but on this occasion it is appreciated" Nicholas replied with a hesitant smile.

He left the table and walked towards the stage as everyone still continued to clap. He negotiated the steps and shook James' hand before preparing his notes on the lectern.

The applauding stopped and Nicholas looked out upon the guests.

"Good evening ladies and gentlemen, it's really nice to see so many people here tonight to share in this celebration. As James has already said, your country, in particular your islands, are a thing of beauty and we all feel extremely privileged to have been able to use such stunning locations for this movie" Nicholas began.

The guests applauded his show of appreciation.

"At this point I was due to tell you all a little bit about the film itself and the reason why Greece was chosen as the setting but a) I think it is obvious why Greece was chosen, the scenery is incomparable and the people are generosity itself and b) I've been told I only have a ten minute slot and what I really want to talk to you about tonight I consider to be a great deal more important than any film" Nicholas continued.

Freya looked over at Martha who was now scrambling for her bag. When she had located it she began frantically leafing through papers.

"I am going to talk to you this evening about something very personal to me and I am going to start by showing you a photograph taken by a very talented photographer, Miss Freya Johnson" Nicholas spoke.

The people in the room let out a united gasp as on the big screen appeared one of the photographs that Freya had taken of Nicholas at Villa Kamia.

It was a photograph of him, naked, taken from behind, looking out to sea. Freya had not seen the result of her session as she had had nowhere to access developing equipment. It was a good photograph, it was black and white and it showed off Nicholas' physique to perfection.

"What the Hell is going on? This isn't in the speech I have" Martha hissed as she carried on leafing through paperwork.

"It's a good photograph" Hilary remarked to the table in general.

"You mean he has a cute butt" Freya said to her with a smile.

"Well, I......."Hilary responded, trying not to blush.

Nicholas waited for the murmuring and surprised comments to die down before he recommenced.

"You are now probably wondering why I'm showing you a photograph of me, wearing nothing but a smile. Well it's one photograph of many that I have had taken to highlight a cause to which I am going to donate my $10 million dollar fee from this film" Nicholas carried on.

There were more gasps and whispers from the crowd at the show of generosity.

It was only at that moment that Freya realised what he was going to say to this room full of people. She held her breath and felt for him, standing on the stage alone, all eyes on him, people waiting to hear what he was going to say.

"I really don't want to make this a completely sentimental speech, but, I have been hiding something from everyone for quite a while now and up until recently I was happy to go on hiding it. But someone I met just a short time ago, has taught me a great deal about myself, about who I am, the position I am in and how I should be using that position to make a difference to others. So I am standing up here to tell you that four years ago I had testicular cancer" Nicholas announced.

There were no murmurs this time, just silence. Everyone was looking at Nicholas, unmoving, listening intently, observing his stance, waiting with bated breath, wondering what he was going to say next.

"There were approximately 9,000 cases of testicular cancer in the USA in 2004 and according to the latest figures this is on the increase. I guess, given the country's size, it doesn't sound like this affects very many people, but when you consider that these men are usually between 25 and 45 you will then understand that we are talking about partners, sons, husbands and fathers at the prime of their lives. The treatment for testicular cancer is extremely effective if it is diagnosed early enough. Ordinarily, surgery to remove the tumour is enough, however, in more extreme cases a combination of radio and chemotherapy can be used. The death rates are falling, but they could be reduced more dramatically if men checked themselves on a regular basis. Before I had cancer I never examined myself and it was only by chance that my tumour was discovered. I was lucky. But I do not want anyone to leave themselves to chance. Which is why, apart from donating my fee from this film, I am proposing to sell these rather intimate photographs of me to the highest bidder" Nicholas told the room.

Freya smiled. This was amazing, this was exactly how someone in his position, with all his wealth and fame, should be using his influence.

"$1 million" a voice shouted from the back of the room, amongst the press pack.

"$5 million" another voice called.

"Your generosity is appreciated but if you could just hold fire for the moment and place any bids with my PA Martha, she will be able to coordinate things" Nicholas spoke.

He took a deep breath and looked down at his notes.

"Well that is about all I wanted to say. I have some leaflets about signs and symptoms if anyone would like one. It is important to me that you don't feel sorry for me, I am not standing up here because I need a hug, I am one of the survivors. The purpose of my telling you my story is to raise awareness and hopefully some money to go towards research and care. Gentlemen I would like you all to check yourselves when you get home, ladies, check your men and just make sure that no one in this room, or anyone that you know, dies from embarrassment. Thank you" Nicholas concluded and he stepped away from the lectern.

Freya was first to her feet, clapping wildly and soon the whole room was filled with applause as everyone rose to their feet in admiration.

Everyone wanted to shake Nicholas' hand as he made his way back to the table and Martha was already being mobbed by people from newspapers and magazines as a bidding war on the photographs commenced.

"Nick, I had no idea" Bob commented as Nicholas returned to the table.

"Why would you? It's fine" Nicholas remarked and retook his seat next to Freya.

"Hey" he greeted with a smile.

"I have a bone to pick with you. You did not tell me you would be exhibiting my work tonight" Freya replied, smiling back at him.

"I wanted to surprise you" Nicholas answered.

"I don't think I was the only one to get a surprise, Martha went white" Freya told him.

"She looks kind of grey right now" Nicholas remarked, as he watched Martha frantically jotting things down on a pad of paper.

"You were wonderful up there, and what you're doing, it's just amazing. I know what it must have felt like, getting up there in front of everyone and talking about it" Freya told him and she took hold of his hand.

"It's because of you Freya, that I found the courage to stand up there and tell people about it. You've faced your demons these past few days and I know how hard that was for you. I thought it was about time I cleared out my skeletons too so that we can start with a clean closet" Nicholas told her seriously.

Freya smiled and squeezed his hand tightly.

"Come back to America with me" Nicholas stated.

"What?" Freya asked in shock.

"Come back to America with me, live with me" Nicholas repeated.

"I....." Freya began.

"Nicholas, could we just have some photographs of you holding up the leaflets?" one of the many photographers standing around the table asked as Roger and some of the security team tried to keep things in order.

Their conversation was interrupted by the need for almost everyone in the room to start snapping Nicholas. They all wanted a few words or more information about Nicholas' illness and there was no chance to continue speaking about Nicholas' proposal as the dinner party had descended into chaos.

Freya hadn't had a chance to answer the question and, if she was honest, she was quite glad they had been interrupted as she had no idea what her answer would have been. Freya watched him, having photographs taken and charming reporters, looking so at ease.

"Did you know? About the cancer?" Hilary's voice suddenly spoke.

Freya turned her head to look at the actress.

"Yes" she answered.

"Why did he not tell anyone?" she questioned.

"I don't know, perhaps living in his world, where image and perfection seems to be so important to everyone, he felt he couldn't tell anyone" Freya responded.

"But that's so sad" Hilary remarked.

"It's more than sad, it's bloody tragic and don't you think your industry should change? I don't want to get on my soap box here but perhaps if people were more focussed on people's personalities and not their appearance Nicholas might have felt able to share what he was going through and been able to ask for support" Freya stated.

"But unfortunately you can't look at a personality" Hilary responded.

"Not if you can't see beyond the superficial exterior of people. We are all in the same basic package Hilary, granted some of us have bigger ones than others, but it's what is inside that sets us apart" Freya spoke.

"I don't really understand you" Hilary admitted.

"No, I know you don't. But take you for example, great package, but wouldn't it be nice to actually eat?" Freya replied.

"I do eat" Hilary responded defensively.

"No you don't. I've watched you, you take a bite and spit it into your napkin, and then you push the food around your plate a bit" Freya told her.

"I do not" Hilary answered.

"Yes you do. Why? To stay thin?" Freya wanted to know.

"I do eat, just not very much, I've never been a big eater" Hilary responded.

"You keep telling yourself that" Freya replied, taking a roll from the basket on the table and taking a bite of it.

"I wouldn't get very many film roles if I looked like you" Hilary told her, taking a sip of her water.

"So you don't eat because you think you should conform to some ideal the industry has set for you, where you have to look like a Barbie doll. That is what I am trying to say. It was the same for Nicholas, the All-American action hero, he was so terrified of what people would think he didn't confide in anyone about his cancer" Freya spoke.

"That's just the way things are" Hilary answered, still nervously sipping at her tonic water.

"Well, I think it's wrong" Freya stated defiantly.

"Freya, the car is waiting for you to take you around the city" Roger spoke, appearing at her shoulder.

"Oh, OK" she replied.

Freya picked up her bag and made her way to the entrance of The Plaza Hall with Roger.

The flashbulbs went off one after another as Freya stepped out of the building and Roger walked her to the car.

"Nick is going to meet you back at the hotel, he said he will hopefully be done by 1.00. The driver's going to take you wherever you want to go" Roger informer her.

"Thanks. Listen Roger, when all the madness is over I would really like to meet your wife. Maybe we could have a drink or something one time" Freya suggested.

"I think she would like that" he agreed.

"See you" Freya spoke and she got into the car.

Chapter Twelve

Freya knew exactly where she wanted to go and that was The Parthenon. When she arrived at the monument it was lit up with warm yellow and orange light that filtered onto the ancient stones.

It had been built some 2500 years ago as a temple to the goddess Athena and had also been the Church of the Virgin Mary and a mosque, until it became an archaeological ruin after a gunpowder explosion in 1687 blew the roof from the building.

Freya had last visited the site many years ago but she annually visited the British Museum which still housed the 'Elgin' marbles. It was a beautiful sight and Freya was glad she had Claude to capture the scene.

She looked down from her position by the monument, onto the city and took a deep breath, drinking in its beauty.

What was she going to do? Everything in her life had changed in the space of a week but how did she feel about the change? Was it a change for the better? How happy had she really been before this week? Was she truly happy now? And, if she was happy then what had made her happy? The location? Being back in Greece had always made her happy. Was it being with Emma again, the faultless friend who was the only person she felt she could rely on? Or was it Nicholas? Sensitive, kind, refreshingly different Nicholas who treated her with respect, valued her as a person and made love to her like she was a Greek goddess. She had never felt that way with anyone before. She didn't really know the answer.

But what about his world? He came from a place Freya had thought she would never have to revisit. The wealth, the luxury and the pompous people in it. It came as part of his profession she knew and she also knew that he loved what he did, but did he care about her enough to understand that she really couldn't live under a microscope or in some gold covered, diamond encrusted cage of scrutiny.

He had said that he did understand, on countless occasions, and he had shown tonight that he now truly realised that the money could be used for so much more than buying flashiness.

But did he mean it? She wouldn't want him to give up being an actor, because that was what he was, but in reality could he really separate himself from the celebrity lifestyle? Would he be happy eating out at a burger bar or a drive through? Would they ever be able to go grocery shopping or to the cinema without having Roger go with them?

And what was America like to live in? She had never been there and she didn't even know whereabouts Nicholas lived.

And what about her business? It had taken all her guts and determination to build it up. It had taken a long time to acquire her good reputation and client base and, providing neither had been hampered by recent events, she didn't know whether she wanted to start all over again somewhere else.

She focussed Claude at the city scene below and took another photograph.

Her mobile phone rang from inside her bag. Freya put Claude around her neck and reached into her bag to answer it. The display was flashing with an unknown number.

"Hello" Freya answered.

"Hello Jane"

The sound of his voice sent chills right through her, paralysing her to the spot. It was Eric Lawson-Peck, her father.

Freya couldn't bring herself to speak. She tried to get something out but her voice was lost, disabled.

"I've been watching you on the news at the party in Athens. I must say that you have turned into quite the performer, perhaps some of the social skills coaching paid off after all" Eric spoke.

"What do you want?" Freya managed to say once she had caught her breath and swallowed the knot of nerves which had sprung up to her throat.

"What do you imagine I want Jane?" he asked her.

"This is about the magazine article" Freya guessed.

"How perceptive of you, yes, the magazine article and the various exerts of that article in every newspaper. The lies you told to this Russell Buchanan, whoever he might be" Eric continued.

"I haven't told anyone any lies" Freya stated simply.

"I think you have Jane. You don't really think I had the maid assaulted do you? Kind, sweet Gloria who always had time for you?" Eric spoke.

"You paid one of your heavies to beat her up" Freya said bravely.

"You heard me sanction this did you? Heard me tell someone to hurt poor Gloria?" Eric questioned.

"You organised it, you made it happen and that is as good as doing it yourself" Freya told him.

"And you have proof of this of course. I mean you wouldn't be so stupid as to accuse someone of something so serious and not have anything to back you up" Eric continued.

"I am not listening to any of this. You beat me, you hurt Gloria and you did countless vile and hideous things that I don't want to think about" Freya told him.

"You will listen to this and you will listen well. Your behaviour has again been completely unacceptable to me and I will not stand for it" Eric began.

"What are you going to do? Send me back to prison?" Freya asked him.

"You are going to print a retraction. You are going to say that this Russell character has misquoted you and you are going to set the record straight, exonerating me and telling everyone the truth, that I was a perfect father, a fine moral role model and that your 'breakdown' and prison episode was due to an upset when your boyfriend cruelly left you" Eric continued.

"You paid Jonathan to go away, just like you pay everyone to go away. I won't do it" Freya responded firmly.

"I would think a little more carefully about your reply" Eric spoke.

"I won't do it" Freya repeated, trying to sound unfazed by his threatening tone.

"Then you leave me with no choice. It's a shame really, he's actually quite a decent actor, I've seen a few of his films and I have also met that charming PA of his" Eric carried on.

"What are you talking about?" Freya questioned.

"Your boyfriend, Nicholas Kaden. It would be a shame for him to topple from that pedestal the world seems to have him on, particularly in the light of this news of his cancer. Cancer is a terrible disease, once you have had it it never really goes away" Eric continued.

"I have nothing left to say to you"

"It wouldn't take much to put a fly in the ointment, we are, as you know, a world obsessed by scandal. A rumour here, a rumour there, caught in possession of Class A" Eric spoke.

"You don't scare me" Freya responded bravely.

"Oh but I do Jane and I always have. That is how it should be with father and daughter. You should have been in awe of me, you should have shown me the respect I deserved" Eric told her.

"You are sick" Freya said as her eyes filled with frightened tears.

"And you know what I am capable of" Eric stated coolly.

"What has Nicholas done to deserve any of this?" Freya wanted to know.

"It isn't about him, it's about you. I learnt a long time ago that the way to hurt you is to hurt those you care about. Perhaps I have chosen the wrong target, maybe I would do better focussing on Emma" Eric replied.

"You leave Emma alone" Freya hissed.

"Come on Jane, I don't have time for this, what's it to be? A retraction? Or perhaps I could get someone to do a 'Gloria' on your boyfriend" Eric suggested.

"I've heard enough" Freya replied.

"I don't think you are listening to me you stupid little bitch! If you don't print a retraction I will have him hurt, really hurt. You think that pathetic bodyguard of his will keep him safe? I know more people in more places that he's had leading ladies. I will find him one night, on his own, and I will finish him" Eric stated viciously.

Freya didn't reply. She knew he meant it and she knew he could do it.

"We've broken up" she said as matter of factly as she could.

"Oh Jane, I admire your attempt but I have eyes, I saw you on television with him, you were so close it made me want to vomit" Eric told her.

"It's true, he's been screwing his leading lady, I just found out" Freya stated.

"Fine, if that's how you want to play it, then it's Emma, makes no difference to me" Eric spoke.

"No! Not Emma! Look please, don't do this" Freya begged in despair.

"A retraction Jane, by the end of next week" Eric ordered and he ended the call.

Freya was shaking as she looked at her mobile phone and realised what had happened. Her heart was racing, her head was spinning. There was only one option open to her now. She looked at her watch and decided it was time to go.

Freya got into the back of the car and shut the door behind her.

"Could you take me to the airport please?" she requested of the driver.

Freya certainly felt overdressed to be sat in Athens airport. Some people had pointed and stared at her earlier at the check in desk but now she was away from the main area, it was almost solitary. There was a flight to London at 2.30am and she was running away again.

It had been wonderful while it had lasted, being close to someone who seemed to really care, feeling beautiful inside and out, but it wouldn't have been like that forever. It had been a dream. A strange dream, some good bits and bad bits but now she had woken up and it was time to return to her reality which was her flat in Clapham and her business. Her things, the life she had built for herself.

Freya swallowed, less than an hour ago she had had a choice, now she was being made to choose. What would she had chosen for herself? Perhaps she would never really know.

As she contemplated what she would have decided, her mobile phone began to ring. It was Nicholas.

She didn't know what to do. She didn't know what to say to him but after everything, in particular his bravery on stage tonight, she knew she couldn't ignore him. He deserved more than that.

"Hello"

"Freya! Where are you? The driver said he took you to the airport. What's going on?" he asked, almost frantically.

"I can't live with you" Freya said, the words nearly choking her.

"Oh......I see.......well OK, that's fine, but we can talk about it can't we? Why are you at the airport?" Nicholas asked, trying hard to hide his disappointment.

"What is there to talk about?" Freya asked him.

"Well we need to talk about it, I mean we can work something out. I threw it at you, I know I did, and it was wrong. I was emotional because of the night and I jumped in" Nicholas told her.

"Martha says I will ruin your reputation. She says you would be better off with someone like Hilary" Freya stated as she searched for excuses.

"Roger told me what she's been doing. After tonight she's history" Nicholas responded.

"But Roger can't tell you what I said. He's a wise monkey" Freya spoke.

"Roger knows exactly how I feel about you Freya, he had to tell" Nicholas said.

"It wouldn't work, I can't be the doll on you arm that you need" Freya continued, still struggling with excuses.

"Who says I need a doll on my arm? Martha? Gene and Bob? Hilary? I want you on my arm, no one else" Nicholas insisted.

"But what if I can't do it? And I am sure people don't want to see you with someone like me" Freya carried on.

"I don't care about 'people' how many times do I have to tell you that? And what do you mean when you say 'someone like you'? Someone bright and intelligent and funny and beautiful, someone I really care about? That's exactly the type of person everyone should be with" Nicholas spoke.

"I'm going home" Freya told him.

"You're running away" Nicholas responded.

"I'm just going home. It's where I belong" Freya spoke.

"You are so used to running away you don't know how to stop, even when you have nothing left to run away from" Nicholas stated.

"That's not true" Freya insisted.

"Yes it is, you're scared. Scared to trust me, frightened that if you start believing in us it might actually happen" Nicholas carried on.

"What you are doing with the fundraising is fantastic, you don't know how much I admired you tonight" Freya told him.

"You are really ending this aren't you? After all we've been through together you're ending it" Nicholas spoke.

"I don't know what else to do" Freya admitted, the tears welling up in her eyes.

"Come back here and talk to me. I'll have a car pick you up, or I'll come there" Nicholas told her.

"No. My flight leaves in twenty minutes" Freya lied.

"Don't leave Freya, please don't leave" he begged her.

She could hear the emotion in his voice and it made her stomach contract with longing.

"Nick, I want you to know that I've never met anyone like you before. You are the only man that has ever made me feel special and you are such a good person. I just wish things were different" Freya began.

She stopped talking because she could not go on. Tears were running down her face, her throat was dry and she couldn't find the words she was looking for.

"Don't do this Freya, don't turn your back on me" Nicholas pleaded with her, his voice failing him as he tried to swallow his emotion.

"I have to, for your sake, I'm sorry" Freya insisted and she ended the call.

She dropped her head to her knees and burying her face in her expensive dress she sobbed, soaking the material with her tears.

Chapter Thirteen

Freya had played 'Turncoat' almost daily since she had returned to England two months ago. She knew it was unhealthy but she had wanted to see him to remember him.

She had eaten from every takeaway outlet in the area and had set up an account with 'Threshers'. She had had few assignments. She had done four weddings (no funeral) and was in the middle of some promotional pictures for a new 'Friendly Shoppe' which was opening soon.

The school photography had all but dried up which she could only assume was down to the fact that everyone now knew she had a criminal record. Although she had often felt like kicking a few of the children who insisted on picking their noses when she was ready to shoot, she would never have really harmed any of them, or set fire to them, not on a good day anyway.

It had taken a few weeks for the journalists to leave her alone. She had done an interview with 'Shooting Stars' magazine saying that Russell had misquoted her. She knew better than to disobey her father and she truly feared for Emma. It had been the sensible thing to do. She wasn't sure whether her father's squeaky clean image had been tarnished at all by the 'gossip' but she only hoped it had. So now she was a wayward rich kid who had a criminal record and told lies. And once upon a time she had briefly dated a Hollywood actor. It was quite a life synopsis.

The only reminders of her time with Nicholas were some photographs from Lake Korrison and the fact that old ladies occasionally stopped her in the street and asked where her handsome young man was. Although it hurt like Hell every time it happened, Freya had learnt to smile and nod and pat their arm.

She had bought a new mobile telephone which had been a necessity. Nicholas had phoned often and not always from his mobile, which meant screening the calls had been difficult. When she had answered and it had been him, the sound of his voice made her heart break and she was back to square one again, weeping into a pizza.

She had wept into a lot of pizzas lately. One large meat feast had got particularly damp when she had bought a copy of 'That's Entertainment' magazine and seen the photographs she had taken of Nicholas displayed for the world's consumption. The figure quoted as the donation going to Nicholas' testicular cancer charity was a cool $10 million. She was proud of what he had done and what he was going to achieve but it ached to no longer be part of his life and the photographs just seemed to mock her. She had held that body, she had cherished the person inside and she had had to let him go.

Tonight there was nothing on television again and Freya was not even in the mood for any of the 'Die Hard' trilogy. Arnie was doing nothing for her lately either and 'Turncoat' had been almost worn out. Besides, it only made her cry and she had done too much of that already.

Her mobile phone rang and Freya picked it up and checked the display. It was Emma.

"Hello Bride" Freya answered.

"Hello Bridesmaid, this is the Bride calling. Oh, you beat me to it" Emma greeted, disappointed Freya had ruined her joke.

"Sorry about that, so is this joke going to wear off when you are actually married?" Freya asked her.

"Yes, then it will be 'Hello Miss J, this is Mrs P calling'" Emma informed.

"It sounds like you are about to deliver the results of the Greek jury on Eurovision" Freya told her.

"Imagine me being Mrs P, I hope I don't end up looking like her" Emma remarked.

"Looking like her would not be good, cooking like her might be useful" Freya suggested.

"Anyway, enough of me, how are you doing?" Emma inquired.

"I'm fine, you're the one getting married at the weekend" Freya reminded her.

"I am aren't I?! I am so excited. My mum and dad arrived today for the start of the traditional Greek festivities. Apparently if I wasn't already pregnant villagers would come round and roll babies on our bed to promote fertility" Emma told her.

"Fancy" Freya responded.

"My mum is already driving me crazy with her fussing. She feels the need to check everything which is very annoying" Emma continued.

"Made lists has she? Did you never wonder where you got it from?" Freya asked.

"She's trying to take control. I'm just glad she doesn't understand Greek or I am sure her and Mrs P would be at loggerheads" Emma remarked.

"And how is Baby P doing with all this activity going on?" Freya questioned.

"I thought I felt it move the other day but apparently, according to this book I have, it's far too early to feel movement so it was probably just wind, which I seem to have a lot of at the moment" Emma informed her.

"Going to be jet propelled up that aisle are you?" Freya joked.

"I hope not" Emma replied with a laugh.

"Better steer clear of the beans" Freya suggested.

"I will. So what have you been doing with yourself since we last spoke?"

"Which was yesterday" Freya reminded her.

"Was it? Oh well, losing track of the days what with all the planning. Well what have you been doing today?" Emma asked.

"Taking photographs of hot dog sausages" Freya responded with a yawn.

"What? Oh the 'Friendly Shoppe' promotional posters" Emma guessed.

"Yes. I hope you haven't forgotten that 'there is always time to stop at a Friendly Shoppe'. Tomorrow it's photographing the management team with someone dressed up as a corn on the cob" Freya told her.

"It sounds fun" Emma responded.

"Who for? Me or the desperately broke guy dressed up in the sweet corn suit?" Freya questioned.

"I spoke to Nick today" Emma stated matter of factly.

Freya felt a stabbing pain in her chest the moment his name was mentioned. It was ridiculous, it was just a name but it evoked all sorts of memories and emotions and she immediately felt nauseous.

"Oh" was the one reply she could manage.

"He can't make it to the wedding. Apparently he has all this promotional work to do with the film, interviews and stuff that he can't get out of" Emma informed her.

"Well that's showbiz" Freya spoke light-heartedly.

"He asked for your number again. He always asks how you are and asks for your number Freya, I feel terrible not giving it to him" Emma stated.

"What do you want me to do about it? I don't make him phone you up, tell him to stop bothering you if it's that annoying" Freya commented.

"You know that wasn't what I meant, I just wish you would speak to him that's all. I wish you would tell him the truth about that phone call from your father because let's face it that is the only reason you are there and he is in America. You had something good together and you still could" Emma continued.

"I told you what my father said" Freya answered.

"I know you did but that was before you denied everything, anyway I still think you should go to the police about it, he threatened Nick and he can't get away with doing that to people" Emma spoke.

Freya didn't respond immediately. She had never told Emma that her father had in fact threatened her also. Emma had had enough to think about with the wedding

311

and the baby. That was why denying everything had been unavoidable.

"Em, he's above the law, you know that. I did what was best for everyone concerned. This way no one gets hurt" Freya spoke.

"Not physically perhaps but Nick is hurting. He obviously would never say anything but I can tell and I know that things with you aren't all that. Simon said you lock yourself in that dark room most days and don't come out for hours" Emma continued.

"You've been speaking to Simon, well remind me to fire him for being indiscreet" Freya snapped.

"Why don't you call Nick and just speak to him. Explain about your father, tell him you love him, make this right again" Emma suggested.

"He's probably with Hilary by now, they've been in the paper together every other day" Freya remarked.

"She's admitted she has anorexia. There was a big article about it in the paper and she is checking into an eating disorders clinic as we speak" Emma informed her.

"Well I can't say I'm surprised, but good for her, I hope it works. Look, I'd better go, I've got a pizza ordered and they will be here any minute" Freya spoke.

"Freya I just want you to be as happy as I am going to be on Saturday" Emma told her.

"I know you do but that is a hard task because on Saturday I doubt there will be anyone in this world happier than you" Freya reminded her.

"Everyone deserves happiness, no matter what your father may have told you" Emma insisted.

"Well, perhaps it wasn't just him. Maybe it just wasn't right, you know me, I'm not a red carpet, smile at everyone kind of person. Can you really imagine me having someone tell me how to look and another person to tell me what I can and can't do and never being able to puke up in public? It sounds all too like the life I had before, the one I set fire to" Freya said seriously.

"Freya, I just............" Emma began.

"Anyway, I am happy, in my own unique 'have takeaway and Dairy Milk be happy' kind of way............got to go, that's the door, listen, I will see you on Friday night for a few drinks before the big day" Freya spoke hurriedly.

"Mr P is going to pick you up from the airport. I can't wait to see you. Bye!" Emma ended.

"Bye" Freya replied and she ended the call.

Freya put the phone down on the coffee table and swallowed a lump in her throat. There was no one coming to the door.

Nicholas wasn't coming to the wedding. It was probably for the best. Now she wouldn't have to worry about feeling awkward or creating a situation that might interfere with Emma's special day.

But she missed him. She missed talking to him, missed holding him, just generally missed him in her life. She picked up the pile of photographs from the coffee table and leafed through them until she found the one she wanted. It was Nicholas at Lake Korrison, smiling at the camera, looking happy and relaxed, his dark hair flecked by the sun. It had been the very first photograph she had taken with Claude.

And then she could no longer bear to look at the picture. She cried loudly, almost hysterically, hugging the photograph to her chest. She led down on the sofa and buried her face into the cushion. She hurt so much.

Chapter Fourteen

"Emma, you mustn't move once you have the dress on, you do know that don't you?" Sue Barclay, Emma's mother spoke as Emma sat in front of the dressing table applying her make up.

It was the wedding day and Emma, Freya and Sue were in the room at 'The Calypso Apartments' where Emma had spent the night. They had had a champagne breakfast and were now getting Emma ready for her impending marriage.

"Yes Mum, I know I mustn't move but I need to put it on soon because I have to be ready when the wedding procession gets here in less than half an hour. Half an hour! Is that right?" Emma exclaimed, turning to look at Freya who was holding the next hairclip, ready to pin it into her friend's hair.

"Yes yes but half an hour is ample time to throw a dress on, now sit still and let me finish this" Freya ordered, getting ready to attack with another clip.

"Emma do keep still for Freya will you, because your hair has to be right. I remember when I married your father I had this irritating little curl that just wouldn't stay put and it was in all the photographs. It made me look like Medusa" Sue spoke.

"Please get her out of here for a bit. I am going out of my mind with nerves and she is making it worse" Emma whispered to Freya.

"Oh my God! Sue, I completely forgot, I left Emma's 'something blue' in my room. You couldn't just pop and get it while I finish fixing her hair could you? I'm in Room

365. You won't miss it, it's blue and it's on the bed" Freya spoke immediately.

"Oh yes, of course, I won't be long" Sue said and she hurried from the room leaving the two friends alone.

"Thanks Freya" Emma said with a sigh.

"That's OK. How are you doing? Feeling ready to become a married woman?" Freya wanted to know.

"Yes I do feel ready actually. I'm nervous but only because I want everything to go smoothly. I have no doubts about Yiannis. I love him more than anyone could love anybody" Emma informed her.

"You are going to make me puke" Freya answered.

"The dress looks lovely on you" Emma remarked as she looked at Freya who was wearing the off the shoulder chocolate brown bridesmaid dress Agatha had made.

"Chocolate is definitely me, there is little doubt about that" Freya agreed.

"So, today's the day" Emma stated, with a smile at her reflection in the mirror.

"Yes today is the day I lose a girlfriend but gain a handsome Greek chap who can cook a mean meatball" Freya responded.

"You haven't lost me, I will always be here for you, giving you advice when you don't want it, forcing my opinions on you" Emma replied.

"Giving me somewhere to stay when I have done a bunk" Freya added.

"Sticking my nose in where it's not wanted" Emma carried on.

"Oh I don't think you've ever been guilty of doing that" Freya responded.

"Yes, well, all I want is the best for you" Emma told her.

"I know..........but why are we talking about me? Today is your day and you are the star of the show so I think as soon as your mum gets back we should shoehorn you and the bump into the frock" Freya spoke.

"Don't say that you will make me paranoid" Emma remarked.

"Here we are! Something blue! Very naughty of you Freya!" Sue announced as she burst back into the room waving a blue garter in the air.

"Oh no! I might have known you would get a garter" Emma remarked with a laugh.

"Well I had to make sure you had something a little risqué to remind you of when you were a singleton and chased all the boys" Freya told her.

"I never chased all the boys Mum, don't listen to her" Emma exclaimed as she took the garter and pulled it up her leg.

"When I married your father I had two garters, one on each leg. One was 'something old' because it had belonged to my mother and the other was 'something borrowed' because I acquired it from the stripper on my hen night. You don't want to know which part of his anatomy he was wearing it on either" Sue spoke with a loud guffaw of laughter.

"It's conjuring up some delightful images for me" Freya responded with a smile.

"My Gran had a garter" Emma stated with a surprised look on her face.

"Your grandmother was a dancer in her day, now if there was ever anyone who chased the boys it was definitely her" Sue informed the two.

"I've heard enough. I want to remember Gran warm and cosy, dressed in her favourite cardigan and making me cakes" Emma spoke, standing up and going over to her dress which was hanging on the front of the wardrobe.

"How all grans should be. Let's leave her with that comforting thought on her wedding day shall we Sue?" Freya suggested, going to help Emma with her dress.

"Your grandmother humped half the local barracks before she met your grandfather" Sue answered, seeming almost unaware of their presence.

"I think she's had too much Bucks Fizz" Emma remarked, stepping into her dress.

"She's just nervous because her little girl is getting married. Here, let me hold that and you put your shoulders in like that, OK, now turn around and I will do it up" Freya said as Emma manoeuvred herself into the dress.

"I hope Yiannis is OK" Emma said as Freya began to do up the bodice at the back of the dress.

"He will be absolutely fine, besides what does a man have to do on his big day apart from stick a suit on and run a comb through his hair? Yiannis is wearing a suit isn't he?

I suddenly had visions of him wearing Greek National costume" Freya spoke.

"No he's wearing a suit with a chocolate cravat" Emma informed.

"And who is the best man? Worth copping off with?" Freya wanted to know.

"It's Leandros" Emma answered.

"Probably not" the two women said in unison and laughed with each other.

"Oh well, never mind, no distractions from the buffet which is fine by me. Right then, let me look at you" Freya said as she stepped around the dress to face Emma.

Sue let out a yelp and put her hands to her mouth, tears spilling from her eyes as she saw her daughter's appearance.

"What's the matter? What's wrong?" Emma questioned, turning to look at herself in the mirror.

"Nothing's wrong, you look so beautiful it's driven your mother to tears. You look amazing" Freya told her proudly.

"And not too pregnant?" Emma asked, smoothing the dress down over her stomach.

"If people didn't already know then no one would guess from looking at you, apart from the cleavage, which is surely an advantage" Freya stated.

"How do I look Mum?" Emma asked, swishing the skirt of the dress around and looking at Sue.

"Beautiful. Like a princess" Sue managed to speak through her tears and she blew her nose loudly.

"Right, mother and bride, let me take some photographs. I know I'm not the official camera person today but I want some for the album. Sue, come and pull up Emma's dress and show off that garter of hers" Freya instructed with a smile, as she put Claude around her neck and prepared to take a shot.

Richard, Emma's father, arrived at the apartments only seconds before Yiannis, Leandros, the priest and Mr and Mrs Petroholis turned up. It was Greek tradition for a flag bearer to lead the groom and his family from the groom's home to the bride, to officiate their engagement. This was so that the father of the bride could agree to the marriage.

Richard was red faced, looking uncomfortable in his suit and complaining about Sue's fussing.

"Your mother says my cravat is crooked" Richard said to Emma as they watched the party arrive behind the wedding flag.

"Dad you look lovely, very handsome and it's not crooked honestly" Emma spoke with a smile.

"Anyone would think you were the nervous groom Richard" Freya remarked, handing Emma her bouquet.

"Hmm, not sure I could go through that day again" Richard replied.

"No? Not even for the prize of deflowering a woman wearing two garters?" Freya asked, making Emma laugh.

At exactly twelve o clock Emma, Freya and Richard arrived outside the church of Our Lady of Kassiopi. There were lots of well wishers from the village there to greet them, most of who had been invited to the blessing on the beach and afterwards to the reception. A huge marquee had been set up right across the road by the harbour and all traffic had been completely banned from entering that part of the village for the day.

After more photographs had been taken outside the church, Emma, Freya and Richard moved into the lobby and waited for the priest.

"OK?" Freya asked Emma with a smile.

"Yiannis' here" Emma said, catching sight of her husband to be, at the front of the church.

"Yes he is, but seeing as he was being led here by Leandros, the flag bearer and the priest, there was nowhere to run" Freya responded.

"No" Emma replied with a deep breath.

"Don't be nervous, this is your special day, the one you have been waiting for for a long time, enjoy every second Em. Besides it's me that has to get this switching of the crowns thing right" Freya reminded her.

"You'll be fine"

"I promise even if I get it wrong I won't make a scene" Freya assured her.

"Right…. I'm ready now" Emma told her.

The first part of the service involved the bride and groom having a crown placed on their heads by the priest and Leandros, as the *Boron Koumbara*, and Freya, as the *Koumera*, switching the crowns between Emma and Yiannis three times. Freya felt immediately better once this part of the service was over.

The ceremony was entirely in Greek and Freya had no idea what was being said. The church was beautiful though and she only wished they permitted photography inside, as some of the icons actually dated back to the fifteenth century.

As Emma and Yiannis began their walk around the ceremonial table, Freya took a look around the church at the people attending.

There were a few of Emma's work colleagues she recognised and some of Emma's family. There seemed to be dozens of children on the groom's side of the church, which Freya could only assume were relations of the Petroholis'. There were also a few villagers including Zorba from the Greek dancing bar and Samos from the kebab shop.

Then, right at the very back of the church, almost completely out of view, Freya saw someone that seemed familiar. The back of the church was gloomy and he was wearing a dark suit. His head was bent down as if reading something. She pushed her glasses further up her nose and focused harder. Then, as the priest began singing a hymn to the martyrs, the man raised his head. Freya caught her breath in her throat and hastily turned back to face the front. She was sure she had seen Nicholas.

Freya felt her face flush and her heart quicken. She felt sick. What was he doing here? Was it really him or was she seeing things? The back of the church was poorly lit now the main door had been shut. She didn't dare look back again.

The priest began chanting, Freya could only assume in prayer, and then Emma and Yiannis were sharing communion. Wine. Wine was what Freya needed right now. She supposed it would be frowned upon if she invited herself to join in with the communion and snatched Emma's cup from her.

She had to look back. She had to know if it was him, but she didn't want to catch his eye. It would be difficult, she was at the front of the church, stood behind the bride and all eyes were on them. But she needed to know, before she had to walk down the aisle towards him.

Inhaling deeply and bracing herself, Freya turned her head around and looked to the very back of the church again. There was no one there. The person she had thought was Nicholas had gone. Freya scanned the other rows of people for the man in the dark suit but there was no one matching that description now.

Freya turned back to the front and let out her breath just as Emma and Yiannis began exchanging rings.

The whole ceremony took an hour and at the end, after the bride and groom had been spoon fed honey and walnuts, the whole congregation were given honey and walnut sweets by Mrs Petroholis.

They had photographs taken outside the church and were soon on their way to the beach for the blessing by Reverend Roberts.

"Yiannis, have I said congratulations?" Freya asked the groom as they walked down to the beach, people waving and calling out to them.

"You have said this twice" Yiannis answered.

"Well I'm making sure that you are actually married, because you know what my Greek is like, for all I know we could have just sat through Harvest Festival" Freya remarked.

"I am learning your humour Freya, Emma has been helping me" Yiannis replied, with a smile.

"Oh Freya! Oh no! I've left something at the church! God I'm an idiot, I've left my bouquet" Emma announced, waving about a pair of empty hands.

"Look, don't panic! I'll get it for you, you carry on your way and I'll rush back and get it, I'll be two minutes" Freya told her.

"Well don't be long or we'll have to start without you and this is the service in English, the one you will understand" Emma reminded her.

"I wouldn't miss it for the world, I'll be right back" Freya announced as she trotted back up the road towards the church.

Emma watched her go out of sight and took hold of Yiannis' hand.

"How was my acting?" Emma asked her husband.

"I think Nick has been teaching you and you are too good at lying for a new married woman, I will have to keep eyes on you" Yiannis responded, squeezing her hand.

"Mum, pass me my bouquet will you?" Emma called to Sue who was ahead of her.

The church was deserted when Freya got there and having searched every square inch of the building she still hadn't found Emma's flowers. The only other place to look was the altar which Freya felt a little uncomfortable searching around, incase the cross toppled onto her or she broke something. She was just about to make herself look there when she heard the door of the church shut.

She turned around at the noise and saw Nicholas standing at the back of the church, having closed the door. He had been the man in church. He was wearing a dark suit, with a cream shirt, open at the neck. He was tanned and his hair was darker than Freya remembered it, but he looked every bit as handsome.

Seconds passed by and neither of them said anything. Freya's heart was in her mouth and she was suddenly trembling inside, scared to death, like a rabbit caught in the headlights.

"I'm looking for Emma's bouquet" Freya spoke suddenly.

She hardly recognised her own voice when it came out it was such an unusual pitch. It had wavered weakly and she immediately had to clear her throat.

"I know" Nicholas replied as he began to walk towards the front of the church and Freya.

"Have you seen it?" Freya wanted to know, pretending to search around places she knew she had already looked.

"Last time I saw it her mom was carrying it down the road for her" Nicholas informed her.

"She set me up" Freya stated, standing still and realising the search really was fruitless.

"You didn't give her much choice. She told me she had tried but you were adamant you weren't going to speak to me" Nicholas continued.

"So she sent me on a wild goose chase and planned for you to be here. Well, some friend she is" Freya responded angrily.

"She is a devoted friend Freya, you know that. She's a loyal friend who has stuck up for you your whole life and told lie after lie on your behalf to protect you. But everyone has their breaking point and she decided she was done with hiding the truth" Nicholas spoke, standing right in front of Freya.

"What are you talking about?" Freya asked, looking at him.

"She told me about your father, the phone call on the night of the dinner in Athens. She told me what he said and why you ended things" Nicholas informed Freya.

Freya pursed her lips and shook her head, not knowing what to do. She moved to go past him but he grabbed her arm and made her stop.

"No! We are going to talk about this, we have to talk about this" Nicholas insisted, holding on to her.

"In case you haven't realised, I am a bridesmaid and there is a service going on at the beach that I am meant to be part of" Freya stated.

"That's an excuse and you know it. Emma doesn't need you there, she sent you here to get her flowers remember" Nicholas spoke, still holding her arm.

"I haven't got anything to say Nick, please don't do this, it isn't fair. If Emma's told you what my father said then you know everything and there's nothing left to discuss" Freya insisted.

"There's the rest of our lives to discuss as far as I'm concerned" Nicholas spoke seriously.

Freya didn't respond. She didn't know what to say. He still had hold of her arm and the strength of his hold, the feeling of his fingers on her bare skin was torturing her.

"What did you think I would do when I got back to America Freya? Forget all about you? Pretend you and I never happened? Perhaps drown my sorrows and lose myself in the next female that came along?" Nicholas wanted to know.

"I don't know, I didn't think about it, I..." Freya started.

"No, you're right, you didn't think about it and you didn't think about me. All you thought about was yourself and what was right for you. Never mind talking to me about it or asking my opinion, you made your mind up and you ran for the hills. And what was with the interview in the magazine denying those stories about your father, saying what a great relationship you have? That really sucked, after all you went through, all the heartache all of us went through, you, me, Emma, Emma's baby" Nicholas carried on.

"It was all about you and Emma, my father said...." Freya began.

"Your father said he was going to ruin my career or, if that wasn't enough for him he was going to have me killed. I know, Emma told me, but guess what? His threats do not scare me" Nicholas informed her.

"He didn't just threaten you, he threatened Emma too and Nick he meant it. He's not right in the head, he could do that and get away with it, I know he could" Freya told him, tears forming in her eyes.

"He is a manipulator Freya, nothing more. He has been manipulating you your whole life and he will carry on doing it as long as you let him. When you had the magazine print that article apologising to him, you gave in to him" Nicholas spoke seriously.

"I had to. I didn't want him to hurt you or Emma, the people that matter to me most" Freya admitted, tears rolling down her face now.

"Well he couldn't have hurt me any more than you did when you said goodbye" Nicholas told her.

He took hold of her hand and squeezed it tightly.

"I didn't know what to do, I was frightened and if I'm honest it wasn't just him, it was everything, the being in the limelight again, the constant scrutiny, people pointing the finger and judging" Freya began, as she continued to cry.

"You should have talked to me" Nicholas responded.

"Well, it doesn't matter now, you know it all and that's the end of it" Freya answered, wiping at her eyes and trying to compose herself.

"The only thing it's the end of is your father interfering in your life. It stops here and now" Nicholas stated firmly.

"What do you mean?" Freya inquired.

"I'm not leaving this island without you Freya. I didn't come all this way on an economy flight to go home empty handed" Nicholas said and he put his hand into the pocket of his jacket.

"You never came here economy class" Freya remarked.

"It was the only seat available. Here" Nicholas said and he handed Freya a small wooden box.

"What is it?" Freya asked him.

"Open it" Nicholas urged.

Freya opened the lid of the box and her mouth automatically fell open before she could stop it. Her eyes glazed over as she saw the ring inside. It was a platinum band with a cross shape attached to it encrusted with diamonds and aquamarine. It was the ring from the jewellery shop in Kassiopi, her ring.

"I don't know what to say, it's the most beautiful thing I've ever seen" Freya spoke unable to take her eyes off the jewellery.

"Freya, you are the most beautiful thing I've ever seen and I can't lose you. I was going to ask you to marry me but I don't want to do anything to make you uncomfortable or make you feel like you need to run. But if you accept that ring, to me that means forever" Nicholas told her.

Freya looked up from the ring box and met his gaze. She could see his blue eyes were filled with tears and the hand that was holding hers was trembling.

"I love you" he told her, squeezing her hand tightly.

"I love you too" Freya admitted, her voice full of emotion.

He grabbed hold of her and pulled her into his arms, holding her close to him and almost squeezing the air from her lungs as he hugged her. Freya rested her head on his shoulder and closed her eyes as she savoured the way he felt. The weeks of longing for him hit her like a thunderbolt and she remembered how good it felt to hold him.

He kissed her, deeply, not letting her go and she held his face in her hands, not wanting him to stop. When they parted they couldn't keep their eyes from each other.

"I don't feel uncomfortable and I'm not going to run" Freya stated, looking at Nicholas and then at the ring.

"No?" Nicholas checked.

"No" Freya repeated.

"Freya, will you marry me?" Nicholas asked her, taking the ring from the box.

"Yes" Freya answered and she held out her left hand.

Nicholas slipped the ring on her finger and held her hand, looking at the band in place.

"Then I believe we have a wedding to get to" he remarked with a smile.

When they arrived at the beach the service was over and everyone had moved to the marquee to begin the party. It was a little while before Freya was able to speak to Emma due to a long line of Yiannis' cousins waiting their turn to kiss the bride.

"Found your bouquet then did you?" Freya spoke, fixing her friend with a glare.

"Do you know, my mum had it all along! I'm sorry I sent you to the church for nothing" Emma said gingerly.

"I ought to be really mad with you for lots of reasons" Freya stated.

"But?" Emma asked.

"I'm getting married" Freya announced and she held out her hand for Emma to see.

Emma screamed out loud, causing Mrs Petroholis, who was stood behind her, to drop a plate full of food on the floor. She grabbed Freya and pulled her into a bear hug as they jumped up and down excitedly.

"You told him about the ring didn't you?" Freya said when they had stopped jumping and she was again admiring her hand.

"Yes I did. He was the one who needed to know about the ring, the only one who's needed to know about the ring" Emma told her.

"Thank you Emma, for everything" Freya said smiling.

"Don't be silly, what are friends for? By the way, your fiancé gave us a great wedding gift, I was bursting to tell you this morning but obviously I couldn't. He's letting us live in Villa Kamia until our house is built" Emma informed her.

"My fiancé" Freya said, looking over to where Nicholas was chatting with Samos.

"You deserve this Freya, it's time you started believing that" Emma told her.

"And it's time you started slicing up that four tier wedding cake of yours because I'm starving" Freya announced.

Printed in the United Kingdom
by Lightning Source UK Ltd.
135281UK00001B/298-315/P